Still House Pond

# STILL HOUSE POND

### Jan Watson

*Tyndale House Publishers, Inc., Carol Stream, Illinois*

Visit Tyndale's exciting Web site at www.tyndale.com.

Visit Jan Watson's Web site at www.janwatson.net.

TYNDALE and Tyndale's quill logo are registered trademarks of Tyndale House Publishers, Inc.

*Still House Pond*

Designed by Jessie McGrath

Edited by Lorie Popp

Published in association with the literary agency of Mark Sweeney & Associates, at 28540 Altessa Way, Suite 201, Bonita Springs, Florida 34135.

Scripture quotations are taken from the *Holy Bible*, King James Version.

This novel is a work of fiction. Names, characters, places, and incidents either are the product of the author's imagination or are used fictitiously. Any resemblance to actual events, locales, organizations, or persons living or dead is entirely coincidental and beyond the intent of either the author or the publisher.

**Library of Congress Cataloging-in-Publication Data**

Watson, Jan.
  Still House Pond / Jan Watson.
    p. cm.
  ISBN 978-1-4143-2386-2 (pbk.)
  1. Women—Kentucky—Fiction.  2. Kentucky—History—1865—Fiction.
3. Domestic fiction.  I. Title.

PS3623.A8724S75 2010
813'.6—dc22                                                                2010004141

Printed in the United States of America

16  15  14  13  12  11  10
 7   6   5   4   3   2   1

*For David Andrew Watson.*
*And for the staff, past and present, of the Communities*
*at Oakwood in Somerset, Kentucky.*

# Acknowledgments

For my readers: "It is hard to believe long together that anything is 'worthwhile,' unless . . . what is infinitely precious to us is precious alike to another mind." George Eliot

Thank you for buying my books, checking out my books, reading my books, and sharing my books. Thank you for your kind words to me and for your prayers. You are each a cherished gift from the Lord, and I appreciate you.

I loved writing the story of *Still House Pond*. My hope is that you will enjoy reading it.

# 1

1896

The squeaky screen door slapped shut. Lilly Gray Corbett couldn't wait to start the day. Her skin tingled in late spring's early morning chill. She could practically taste adventure waiting, urgent as an icicle against her tongue.

"Lilly," her mother reminded from behind the screen, "please don't slam the door. You'll wake the baby."

"Oh, bother," Lilly mumbled. Her mother collected babies like other women collected biscuit tins or china tea-cups. "Sorry. I'm going to see the kits."

Mama stepped out the door. "Don't get too close. You don't want to scare the mother."

Lilly rolled her eyes. "I know everything about foxes. Aunt Remy taught me."

"I'm sure she did," Mama said. "Come here a minute."

"What?"

"Lilly . . ."

"It's just that I'm in a hurry," Lilly said as she walked into her mother's outstretched arms and accepted a kiss to the top of her head. "I didn't get to see them all day yesterday."

"I know," Mama said. "It was busy here, wasn't it? I sure do appreciate your help with the new baby."

"He's so little. How long will he be on the oven door?"

"Just a couple more hours. We don't want him shivering to keep warm and burning up what little fat he has." Mama fiddled with the white silk bow that caught Lilly's dark hair in a cascade partway down her back. "He took half his bottle early this morning, so that's good."

"Why doesn't his mother nurse him?" Lilly asked.

"She's trying, but Mrs. Sizemore is puny still. Remember last year when we had to feed that calf from a bucket? Well, this is kind of the same."

"Can I feed him next?"

"Sure, in about an hour."

Lilly shrugged out of her mother's embrace. "I'll be back in time."

"Oh, Lilly," Mama said, "would you take Adie's breakfast to her?"

Lilly let her shoulders fall. She rolled her eyes, though Mama couldn't see. That was probably a good thing. "Okay."

Mama stepped into the kitchen and came back out with a warm plate of food on an invalid tray. "You know the rules."

"Yes, ma'am," Lilly said. "You don't need to tell me every time."

"Don't be sassy. You're not too big for me to turn over my knee."

*Like she would,* Lilly thought as she walked down the steps carefully balancing the biscuits at the edge of the plate. If Mama ever spanked her, she didn't remember. Even her brother, Jack, didn't get more than a pat on the fanny, and he surely needed it.

It was out of her way to the one-room cabin where Adie stayed. She hoped the door was closed so she didn't have to take the food back to the house. She didn't exactly understand what was wrong with Adie, but it had something to do with germs. None of the children were allowed to breathe the same air Adie did. Manda, Mama's hired girl, wasn't allowed to go in there either, although she was nearly grown-up. It sure was hard to figure Mama's thinking. Sometimes Lilly worried when Mama and Aunt Remy went to care for Adie. She wondered if they would get sick.

The tiny cabin looked forlorn sitting way back under the pines. The door was closed tight. Goody! Lilly set the plate on a table by the door, then knocked. Adie knew what she was supposed to do. She wouldn't come out until Lilly was gone.

Lilly hopped down the stepping stone and hurried toward

the barnyard. She had plenty of time before the baby needed his bottle, time to check on the foxes and spring some traps. Good thing her mother had not caught on to the trap-springing part. Lilly didn't think she would approve. She would say it was too dangerous.

Unlatching the door to the shed beside the barn, Lilly retrieved a piece of toweling and the walking stick she kept there along with various other things like dented pie tins, wooden boxes, and a couple of wire animal pens Daddy John had made for her projects. The boxes and pens were empty for the moment.

The shed sat on a dry-stacked rock foundation. The mother fox had discovered a hole in the underpinning at the back of the small building and chose to deliver her kits under there. They were almost a week old now. Aunt Remy said the mother would be moving them soon. Lilly would have to remind Daddy not to replace the rocks in case the mother fox wanted to use the hole again.

Lilly spread the towel on the ground and straightened the corners. Satisfied, she removed an egg from her pocket before she lay down on the towel. Squinting against the gloom, she looked underneath the shed. The kits slept huddled together in a bundle of reddish fluff. She could make out two pointed noses and one long tail. She wished she could hold them. Wonder where the mother was? A flash of red at the corner of her eye gave the answer to that.

With slow and easy movements, she stood and folded her towel. She'd have to leave the egg in the grass rather than putting it in the hole as she had intended. The mother fox might abandon her babies if she felt threatened. That would be too sad. Lilly's tongue formed the series of soft clicks Aunt Remy had taught her to use around animals. It sent a soothing message.

Down at the creek she looked for turtles and tadpoles. The water was swift and muddy this morning, so she didn't have any luck. It would clear up soon. Right now it still carried silt and other debris from the bad storm on Sunday. The water sang a pretty song though and kept her company as she tromped upstream to search for snares. It was hard to believe Daddy John had once trapped animals and even harder to imagine her mother had helped him. Now someone else left traps along the creek on their property. She'd send him packing if she ever found out who it was.

There! A short chain partially covered by dead leaves was staked to the ground—deadly steel teeth lay in wait for some hapless creature searching for a cool drink of water. Scouting around, she found a stout stick and poked it into the mouth. The trap's vicious jaws snapped like a wild thing and set her heart to thumping. She wanted in the worst way to take the sprung trap and fling it down a sinkhole, but Daddy John said it was stealing to take someone else's property no matter what your reasoning. She heaved a big stone at it instead, relishing the scraping crunch of rock against metal. She wouldn't tell Daddy about that. Nobody needed to know every single thing she did.

Shading her eyes, she checked the rise in the sun. It looked like she'd been gone right at an hour. She'd better hurry if she wanted to feed the baby.

Yesterday was the first time she'd seen a baby so new it still had cheesy, sticky stuff all over it. Mama called that *vernix*. Lilly got to help with the bath. The baby was long and skinny with a pointed head, but it seemed his mother liked him anyway.

When he was clean and oiled, Mama put a belly binder on him before wrapping him snug as a bug in a warmed receiving blanket. Mrs. Sizemore was all weak smiles when Mama handed him over, despite the fact she had been screaming just a short time before. Lilly had heard all the commotion from the porch, where she was entertaining her brother and sisters. Usually Mama went to other people's houses to catch babies, but Mrs. Sizemore had something called complications. She had been living in the sickroom in the back of the house for days. Mama told Aunt Remy it was touch and go. Lilly wasn't worried though. Her mama could make anything better. And what she couldn't fix, Aunt Remy could.

Last summer Lilly had found a beautiful orange and black butterfly lying by the side of the road. His wings didn't flutter when she blew on them, but when she knelt for a closer look, his antennae twitched. She carried him home carefully cupped in her palm. Mama soaked a piece of cotton gauze in sugar water and set it in the window. She perched the butterfly on top. Lilly sat on the window seat reading a book about insects and their habitats while she waited. In a couple of hours the monarch was spreading his wings, looking ever so happy. Lilly set him free in the flower garden beside the porch.

Swishing the tall grasses and weeds with her walking stick, she warned snakes of her approach. Daddy John had carved the stick for her eleventh birthday last November. It was white sycamore and just her size. A dry rattle from near a rotted stump gave a warning back to her. She took the long way around and called, "Sorry, Mr. Snake. Sorry to disturb your morning." She scripted the air with her stick as if writing the new word she'd just learned. "*Avouch*," she said. "I *avouch* I won't bother you again today."

When she got back to the house, she stared at her dress in dismay. Sticktights covered the hem and smattered the ankles of her dark hose. "Mama," she yelled.

Instead of her mother, her sister Mazy popped out the door, closely followed by her spitting image, Molly. "Mama's feedin' the baby."

"We helping," Molly chimed in. The twins were three, and they talked up a storm. Lilly could decipher their chatter better than anyone.

"Bother," Lilly said, pushing around her sisters and heading through the door to her mother. "You said I could feed him."

"Sorry. He was hungry. Want to finish?"

Lilly flounced toward the room she shared with her sisters. "No! Everything's ruined now." She closed the door, but she didn't slam it like she wanted to. Mrs. Sizemore might be resting. She plopped down on the side of her bed and looked out the window. Jack was sitting alone in the tree swing, flailing his short legs to no avail. Maybe she'd go give him a push.

Mama nudged the door open with her elbow. "You want to burp him?"

"Look," Lilly said as tears flowed. "Just look at my dress tail."

"Didn't I warn you about wearing your church clothes for every day?" Mama asked.

Lilly tucked her chin. "Yes, ma'am, but I couldn't resist."

"Take it off and I'll pick sticker weeds while you burp Jumbo here."

Lilly laughed as she pulled her dress over her head. "He's too skinny to be a Jumbo."

Mama put the baby in Lilly's arms with his head on Lilly's shoulder. She made a patting motion on the baby's back.

Lilly patted. "Is this too hard?"

A funny sound came from the baby. His rounded chin bounced on Lilly's shoulder.

Mazy and Molly giggled. "Brrrurp," they said in unison.

"Sounds just right." Mama bent over the skirt of the weed-covered dress. "Forevermore, Lilly, where did you go, anyway?"

Uh-oh, Mama was getting curious. "Why is Jack outside all by his lonesome?" she asked.

"Jack?" Mama swiveled toward the window. She raised the sash. "Son, what are you doing out there?"

Jack flung himself around and around, twisting the swing's ropes ever tighter. The ropes released, twirling Jack like a tornado.

"He's going to fall off and crack like an egg," Lilly said.

"Like Hunky Dunky?" Mazy asked.

"Yes," Lilly said, "just like Humpty Dumpty."

"I need to remind your daddy to lengthen the ropes," Mama said. "That swing's too high for Jack."

"The swing's not too high." Lilly thumped the baby's back. "Jack's too short."

"Don't be telling him that. For a four-year-old he's got a big attitude." Mama shook the dress out the open window. "There, good as new. Stick out your feet."

Mama pulled at least a million stickers from Lilly's hose.

"Why do you imagine God made sticktights?" Lilly asked.

"Probably to remind girls of places they have no business being. You'd best pull your hose off and wash your feet and legs. You'll itch to death if these nettles scraped your skin."

"Bath?" Mazy jumped up and down, her silky blonde hair flying. "We go swimming?"

Jack climbed over the windowsill and tumbled headfirst to the floor. "I'm drunk."

"John William Pelfrey," Mama said in her sternest voice, "do you want me to wash your mouth out with soap?"

"Soap?" Molly said. "Blow bubbles?"

Mama laid Lilly's pretty dress across the bed, shut the window, uprighted Jack, and took Jumbo from Lilly. "Forevermore," she said.

It was like a party at the supper table. Manda had cooked Lilly's favorite chicken and dumplings. Plus, Reverend Jasper and his wife and family had stopped by, as well as three of the Sheltons. Mama insisted they all stay for the meal. Daddy brought in chairs from the porch. That made fifteen, but the little kids didn't need chairs. They could sit on laps and eat off other people's plates. She probably shouldn't count Aunt Remy either because she kept leaving the table to check on Mrs. Sizemore and Jumbo.

The last time Aunt Remy jumped up, Manda covered her plate with a tea towel. Mama would have reprimanded Lilly if she had left the table without being excused, but nobody ever fussed at Aunt Remy. Besides, she was an adult even if she was child-size. Lilly would be glad when she was a grown-up and could do as she pleased.

After supper, all the kids played Mother, may I? in the front yard while the adults settled on the porch to talk. Jay Shelton got to be mother because he was company, and company came first. He drew broom straws with Kate Jasper and won. Lilly could tell Kate was miffed, but she was always upset over something. Lilly thought it was because Kate was the baby of the family.

It would have been more fun if Manda played with them, but she was sharing a bench with Gurney Jasper. Funny, Manda had nearly scooted over the side of the bench. Maybe she didn't like Gurney being so close. So it was Lilly, Kate, Jay and his little brother, Wilton, and Jack who were playing, and Molly and Mazy who were getting in the way. That's why she needed Manda.

"Take two giant steps," Jay called. "Take five baby steps." Finally he sang, "Take ten scissor steps." Lilly's favorite.

"Mother, may I?" she sang back.

"Yes, you may," Jay said.

Lilly maneuvered a quick cross-step but got tangled up with Mazy.

Kate, who was Lilly's age and her best friend, easily passed everyone else.

"Go back," Jay demanded. "You forgot to say 'Mother, may I?'"

Kate stomped back to where they'd started while Lilly happily crossed the finish line. Now she got to be mother and call out the orders. She did her call outs all in baby steps so the little ones would have a chance. "Yay for Jack," she yelled when he was first. He had a big grin on his face.

Over Jack's head, she saw Aunt Remy open the door and motion for Mama. She hurried into the house followed closely by Brother Jasper, who thumbed through the pages of his big black Bible as he went. Mrs. Jasper knelt beside her chair and folded her hands in prayer.

Manda came out in the yard to get Jack and the twins. "It's time to wash your feet for bed," she told them in her I-mean-business voice.

Lilly went to sit on the porch steps with Kate, Jay, and Wilton.

"What's wrong?" Kate whispered.

Lilly thought she knew, but she didn't answer. She didn't want to talk about it.

# 2

COPPER PELFREY PACED the porch floor. It was five o'clock in the morning. The rooster wasn't even awake yet.

Remy handed her a cup of strong black coffee.

"I've never come that close to losing a patient."

Remy poured some of her own coffee into a saucer and blew across the top. "It was right scary, I'll warrant."

"It makes me sad that Tillie had no family with her."

"I reckon she needed you and me worse than she needed anybody else last night."

Copper wrapped both hands around her cup. The warmth seeped through the ironstone mug, warming her hands. "Still, a woman needs her husband at a time like that."

"And what good would Abe Sizemore have been, shiftless thing that he is?"

Setting her cup on the porch rail, Copper stretched backward, working the kink out of the small of her back. "Why don't you go get some rest?"

"I'll catch me a nap on the cot in the sickroom after while," Remy said. "I'm going to the shed first to see about Foxy."

The rooster heralded the break of dawn as Copper watched her friend's halting progress until the fog that hung across the yard in thick gray curtains swallowed Remy up. Copper's thoughts turned to a simpler time when she was young and Remy was whole. They had been the best of friends when Copper lived with her daddy and stepmother up Troublesome Creek.

Remy was a wild thing, out on her own at twelve, while Copper at fifteen was cosseted in the arms of her family. They'd met in a cave of all places, and Copper had been determined to save Remy from her lonesome state. But Remy refused to be saved.

Copper retrieved her coffee and took a sip. It was nearly cold; she'd let it sit too long. Remy was her first lesson in what it meant to be truly independent. A lesson Copper sorely needed when her first husband, Lilly's father, died and she was left alone to try to make a go of the farm passed down from her daddy. Now Remy lived close as kin on Copper and John's property, free to come and go as she pleased. Thankfully, she chose to be near Copper and her family most of the time. *Good thing,* Copper thought. *What would I do without Remy?*

She dashed the bitter coffee dregs out into the yard. She'd have a hot cup with breakfast, but for now she needed to get to the barn. Bertha waited.

Before she could step off the porch, strong arms encircled her from behind. John nuzzled her neck. "Why don't I do the milking this morning?" he asked.

Leaning back into his warmth, she felt the tension of the night drain away. He was her rock. "Let's just stay here instead. Bertha can wait a minute." She turned in his arms and stood on tiptoe for a morning kiss.

"Don't tempt me," he said.

She laughed. "No chance of that. You know the twins will be up with the rooster."

"Yeah." He sighed. "And you're itching to get to the barn. I think you love that cow more than me."

"You're a very close second," she teased. "Besides, Bertha's easier to get along with."

John sat on the step and pulled on his boots. "What should a man expect but disrespect from a woman who'd name her twin daughters after cows?"

She made her way around him and down the steps. "Speaking of which, I'd better get a wiggle on. The girls will want warm milk with their breakfast. Where are you off to this morning?"

He looked up from lacing his boots. "Nowhere right now. I'm waiting to watch the wiggle."

"John Pelfrey, anybody could be listening."

He gave her his slow, easy smile, the one that crinkled his

green eyes at the corners, the one that was hers alone. "Let them listen."

"You're not leaving before you eat, are you?"

"I thought I'd go get Abe Sizemore early on before he has a chance to shirk his responsibility another day." His bootlace snapped midlace. Patiently he pulled it out and rethreaded it, tying a knot instead of a bow. "Fool man needs to see his wife and baby."

Copper pushed curling tendrils of thick red hair under her work bonnet. "That's true enough, but shouldn't you wait until Abe's ready to come?"

"When do you reckon that might be? His head's as empty as a Simlon gourd. If I don't go fetch him, he's likely to forget he has a wife." John examined the short piece of leather string, then stuck it in his pocket. "Waste not, want not."

He joined her on the walk to the stable. "Seriously though, Tillie Sizemore could have died last night."

Copper shuddered. "Don't remind me."

"I always thought once a woman made it through childbirth, you didn't have to worry anymore," John said. "What went wrong last night?"

"She started flooding. You know how sickly she is. That's why I brought her here instead of delivering her at home. Something told me she needed close watching."

"Will she be all right?" he asked while opening the stable door and standing aside for Copper to enter first.

"Well, she'll be eating beef liver for a while, but I think she'll be fine."

"What's that do?"

"Puts some iron back in her blood. Don't you remember how anemic I got with the twins? I ate so much liver and onions, I didn't think I would ever eat them again."

He paused just inside the door as she scooped feed from a wooden bin into a bucket. "I remember how scared I was for you. It makes me think Molly and Mazy should be our last."

The grain hit the bucket with a pleasant whoosh. It smelled sweet and summery. Copper loved the ritual of feeding and milking Bertha every morning and evening. It was good to have an animal to tend to. "You don't mean that, I hope. I want a dozen babies or thirteen like your mother. Remember how happy she always was and how welcoming?"

"I do," he replied. "Still, it was hard on her."

Bertha bawled impatiently.

Copper kissed John on the cheek. "You fret too much. Go fetch Abe. He can have breakfast with us."

It was a good thing Manda had fried extra bacon and eggs because Abe Sizemore ate like a man coming off a fast.

After breakfast, Copper took him to the invalid room. His grin spread ear to ear when he saw his baby son for the first time. "Ah, Tillie, you done good."

Sweet Tillie beamed and lifted her wan hand to her husband's whiskered cheek. "How are you making out without me?"

"It is hard being on my lonesome. I've near starved without

your cooking." Standing, he turned to Copper. "Can I carry them home now? I brought the wagon."

Copper had seen many men like Abe Sizemore in her years of baby catching. He was good as gold but lazy as lead. "I was going to ask you about that. What do you think about Tillie staying here a couple more days?" She chose her words carefully. With men like Abe it was best to let them think they came up with their own answers.

"Well, I thank ye kindly, but we couldn't put you out no more'n we've already done."

Tillie flinched like she'd been struck, but she reached for the dress that was neatly folded on a chair beside the bed. The baby fretted in his cradle.

"Tillie," Copper said, "why don't you nurse the baby first? Abe and I will take a little walk."

"Now, Abe," she said as he followed her outdoors like a puppy at her heels, "I know I can trust you to do what's best for Tillie."

"Sure thing," he said as they paused beneath the apple tree in the side yard.

"All right then. First make sure she doesn't do anything but feed the baby for two weeks. Okay? No cooking, washing, cleaning, ironing, or anything that might tire her in the least. Have you ever changed a nappy? I must show you that before you go. Oh, and you'll want to freshen the bed linens every day."

Abe nodded, but he was beginning to look as pale as his wife.

"You'll get the hang of it easy enough," Copper said. "Just soak the linens in cold water overnight. That will take any stains out." Starting back, she stopped midstride as if she had forgotten something. "Make sure you cook nutritious foods."

"I ain't sure what that means," he replied.

"Food that is good for your wife and son," she said kindly. The man was trying. "Tillie is still eating for two."

"Are you certain Tillie's ready to come home?" he asked. "Seemed like she looked a little peaked."

"I trust your judgment on that. I can see where you'd want to get them home. But if you'd like, she can stay a few more days." Copper made a puzzled face. "You could come by for visits—maybe around suppertime? Tillie will be upset if she doesn't see you every day. We don't want that, do we?"

He dropped his head and scuffed the toe of his worn boot in the dirt of the yard. "Tillie means the world to me. I sure do thank ye."

Remembering John's unkind words about Abe, Copper studied him. The young man's head did kindly favor a gourd—a gourd with ears. She touched his shoulder. "You're more than welcome."

"Hey, Abe," John called from the barn. A grubbing hoe rested on his shoulder. "Want to earn a few bucks?"

Abe rubbed his palms on the front of his britches. "Sure thing. I reckon I could help you out."

Copper hid a smile behind her hand and watched as John showed Abe to the lot beside the barn. John had been clearing it of brush and scrub trees. He aimed to start a pear orchard there. John might act tough, but he had a kind heart. Abe would earn his supper and a few bucks besides.

Something glinted at her feet. She bent to retrieve the tea strainer. Why was it in the yard? And there was her favorite pie tin, the one that had belonged to John's mother. "John William Pelfrey!"

Jack struggled through the kitchen door. His arms bowed with a pot, a yellowware bowl, and her glass rolling pin. "Hey, you found my pie pan."

With a firm hand she guided her son back through the door. "Just why are you taking the kitchen outdoors?"

Red curls tumbled in his eyes as he shook his head. "Just call me Jack, please. My long name sounds like you're on a tear."

"Be mindful of your words." She ran her hand through her son's tangled locks. John was always after her to cut it, but she couldn't resist those bright red tresses. "I'm not mad, just perplexed."

"I was setting up shop. Me and Molly and Mazy are making mud pies today. We're going down to that big flat rock by the creek."

"That sounds like fun," she said, "but you can't take our kitchen tools. Maybe Lilly will help you find some other things if you ask her nicely."

"I'm turning into a prune," Lilly said, lifting her hands out of the pan where she was washing the breakfast dishes.

"Let me see," Jack clamored, dumping his load on the table.

"Do I have to wash those?" Lilly whined. "The water's cold already."

Copper lifted the kettle from the stove and poured more hot water into the granite dishpan. "Just this pie tin and the tea strainer." She handed Jack a towel. "Help your sister."

"Then can we make mud pies?" Jack asked, polishing the tines of a fork.

"I was going to take a walk," Lilly said, "by myself."

"You can do that after," Copper replied. "The girls can't go to the creek alone."

Jack puffed up like a bullfrog. "I can watch the twins."

"Peep, peep," came from under the table.

Copper pulled back the red- and white-checked cloth.

The girls were underneath. As soon as they saw their mother, giggles broke out. "We be doodles." Mazy leaped out, followed by Molly. "Peep, peep."

"You look more like frogs than chicks," Lilly said.

Soon the twins and Jack were jumping all over the kitchen. Frog croaks mixed with doodle peeps.

"Has anyone seen Manda?" Copper asked.

Suddenly Lilly Gray was concentrating on the tea strainer. Twirling away from the dishpan, she held the utensil up to the window light and polished it vigorously with the cotton towel Jack had discarded. Something was up. Copper toyed with questioning Lilly further, but Manda was a good girl, and even good girls needed to have a secret now and then.

She'd sure had her share. When she was fifteen, she'd planned to run away from home and live in a cave just to spite her stepmother. *Poor Mam,* Copper thought. *I don't know how she survived raising me.*

"Lilly, if you'll take the twins and Jack down to the creek to play, I'll finish the dishes." She knew Lilly hated washing the heavy cast-iron skillet, where bits of egg clung as stubborn as oak leaves in autumn.

Relief flooded Lilly's face as she hung her apron on a peg behind the door. "Thank you. I'll watch them close."

"Find your shoes, Jack," Copper reminded.

"But the grass is green! You said I didn't hafta wear shoes when the grass turned green."

"Get your shoes on or we're not going," Lilly said.

Jack scooted under the table and came back with both shoes. It amazed Copper how quickly he would mind his big sister, never putting up an argument like he did with her.

John said she spoiled their son. Maybe so.

Her heart swelled with pride as she watched her children cross the yard. Lilly held the twins' hands. Her hair bow bounced as she walked. She liked a freshly ironed ribbon every morning, usually choosing white because she thought it complimented the swath of platinum that emanated from her perfect widow's peak and shot through her shiny black hair like quicksilver. When Lilly was a newborn, women would comment on that unexpected vein of silver saying she was marked by the death of her father. But Copper knew where it came from. Lilly's aunt Alice had that same wayward streak.

Sometimes Copper searched her daughter's face looking for some resemblance to herself, but Lilly was a miniature

Alice Corbett Upchurch—same hair, porcelain complexion, arched eyebrows, and expressive eyes. Looks were not the problem, for Alice was very beautiful. It was her exacting manner Copper had to guard against Lilly adopting.

Reaching behind a stack of platters on the bottom shelf of the corner cupboard, she withdrew the letter that had come last week. Lilly would be incensed if she knew her mother was keeping it from her. But in truth, she'd only meant to keep it for an opportune time. Then Tillie's unexpected complications took over her household and the letter had slipped her mind.

Alice's precise cursive in her signature navy blue ink adorned her signature pale gray stationery, intruding into Copper's signature sunny mood. She tapped the edge of the envelope against her chin. Her stomach knotted. She was not ready to share her daughter in such a big way with her former sister-in-law. Though her request was broached in kindness, Copper was not deceived. She felt like a fish on the line—one little nibble and she'd be reeled to shore by the barbed hook of Alice's allure.

Ever since Simon died, Copper had felt Alice biding her time like an eight-day clock—ever ticking off the minutes of the past—hurrying her along to the future. She couldn't blame Alice for wanting more of Lilly. She was her niece after all, and Alice had adored Simon. Copper had adored him too. He was an easy man to love.

Copper stepped outside. A string of clouds the color of gunpowder scuttled across the sky. Grief crept into her heart, marring her spirits in much the same way the clouds blemished the bright June day. It would be summer before they knew it.

Clinching her fists against her sides, she said, "Not now. I don't have time for this."

She allowed only a short storm of memory. There was work to be done. She needed to take her doctor's bag to the little house and assess Adie, Jumbo should be weighed, the milk needed separating, and she dearly wanted time to scratch around in the garden with her hoe.

When she raised her hand to wipe her eyes, she saw Alice's missive crumpled in her fist. Pressing the stationery added to her list of chores, she went back into the house and retrieved the sadiron from the pantry. She set it on a burner to heat just a smidgen. She didn't want the letter to go up in smoke, did she? Copper smiled as she folded a towel in quarters and laid it on the kitchen table, making a protective surface. As she carefully ran the iron over the expensive stationery, she pictured the paper bursting into flame. The perfect answer to her problem. Oh, sometimes her thoughts were naughty. Alice would be appalled.

Copper put the iron aside to cool, folded the letter, and stuck it back in the cupboard. Time enough to think on that later.

# 3

MANDA WHITT WAS climbing steadily up the side of Spare Mountain. It was a harder task in her new shoes than she had thought it would be, and now a blister threatened on her right heel. She supposed a trek in her clogging shoes had not been a good idea. But she wanted to break them in before the dance on Saturday night.

She could have picked an easier hike, but she had a special place where she liked to sit and dream, and it was such a pretty day. Her dress for the dance was already pressed and hanging in the chiffonier at home. She could just imagine its skirt flaring out as she twirled around the dance floor. This was no place to practice twirling, however. The narrow trail she climbed was bordered by rugged trees and thick brush on one side and a hundred-foot drop down a sheer sandstone wall on the other. Fall over that and you wouldn't even get a chance to bounce.

Just around the bend was the familiar jutting cliff where she loved to sit and read from the *Woman's Home Companion* magazine Miz Copper received in the post each month. Of course, Miz Copper wouldn't mind if she read at the kitchen table or on the porch, but there were so many distractions in the Pelfrey house.

And then there was Miss Remy always studying her. If Miss Remy caught her with a book in hand, she was sure to find more wash to do or a floor to sweep. Manda's fingertips were still sore from one of Miss Remy's found jobs that had Manda stuffing all the pillow ticks with fresh feathers. Pushing a needle through that thick ticking was hard even with a thimble, and each seam had to be sewn twice over. Miss Remy put that old saw "Idle hands are the devil's workshop" to test. Manda tried to stay out of her way as much as possible.

Miz Copper took pity sometimes, though. She would breeze by and see Manda bent over some job. "Go do something fun for a while," she'd say. Or she might take time to help Manda peel potatoes or wash a window. It gave them a chance to talk. Manda loved that.

Manda rounded a curve in the cow path and dusted leaves and twigs from the wide ledge that provided a fine seat on the safe side of the cliff. From where she sat, she could look across the narrow trail to the top of Devil's Eyebrow, so named for what it put you in mind of if you stood at the foot of Spare Mountain and looked upward. The overhang was bare save for a few scraggly cedars seeking nourishment in the scant film of soil atop the solid rock. A breeze always wafted across the stone plate as if a giant hand brandished a pasteboard fan across its surface.

Manda untied her bonnet strings and set the bonnet on the ledge beside her. With a contented sigh she twisted the top off a jug she'd stopped at Sweetwater Creek to fill on her way up the mountain. She was thirsty as a lizard in a dry creek bed, and the cold, pure water sure hit the spot.

With her thirst slaked, she took a magazine from the linen bag she carried over her shoulder and quickly found her place. Oh, what had happened to the willful Rose Feathergay since last month's serial chapter ended? Rose had fled her home after a dreadful argument with her mother over Rose's broken engagement to Laurence Shallow, the town's most eligible bachelor.

Cracking the spine of the magazine, Manda read breathlessly as Rose, heiress to the Feathergay estate, granddaughter of a governor, wheeled a bicycle through the bustling streets of Boston.

A bicycle! Manda couldn't get her mind around that. She couldn't figure how Rose kept it going fast as the wind. And what did she do with her skirts? What kept them from catching in the spokes and tipping the beautiful, misunderstood Rose headfirst over the handlebars? Perhaps she wore a split skirt like Miz Copper did when she rode Chessie. Manda thumbed back through the magazine to the pattern section, but she didn't find any pictures of riding habits. Still puzzled, she returned to the story, underlining each typed word with one finger.

In a flush of anger, the headstrong Rose cycled through the city and was soon out of town, bumping along on an unfamiliar road. She would not be forced into marriage just to please her parents, Rose vowed, while dashing hot tears from her porcelain cheeks. She would not. As if in punctuation to her mood, the skies darkened threateningly and the road turned desolate.

Manda shivered. She hoped it didn't rain and ruin Rose's straw hat. Rose had grabbed the newly fashionable boater when she fled out the door of her father's three-story mansion.

The wind picked up, whipping like a gale. She should turn back. It was not too late to make amends, though her mother would have to accept that Rose was an enlightened woman. She would live her own life and not bow to the dictates of old-fashioned society. Rose turned her conveyance and pedaled hard against the wind. Rain stung her eyes as a sudden gust jerked her hat and sailed it into the trees that lined the uneven roadway. She could barely see, and pedaling became more and more difficult. Suddenly the bike careened into a bank. Rose could hear the hiss of the punctured tire even over the howling wind. She was stranded miles and miles from civilization.

Manda glanced about. She could hardly believe it was still sunny here on the side of the mountain, for she could fairly feel the raindrops that wet Rose's heart-shaped face. Whatever would happen next?

The daring Rose had thought to carry a patching kit and a tire pump in her handlebar basket, and now she proceeded to change her own tire.

As luck would have it, a handsome young man appeared from the forest with the straw boater clutched in his workingman's hands. "Can I help you with that, miss?"

Rose looked him over from his wide shoulders and narrow waist to his tightly laced logging boots. She liked what she saw. As her eyes met his, sparks flew. Easily, Rose handed over the patching kit. What began as a punctured tire on a rough road paved the way for a new adventure as the thoroughly modern Rose Feathergay met the old impasse of love.

Manda closed the magazine. Her shoulders slumped. Why couldn't she find romance like the fetching Rose Feathergay?

Gurney Jasper was her sort-of boyfriend, she supposed. He was meeting her at the dance, after all, and everybody teased her about him. But he wasn't one bit stirring. Gurney didn't move quick enough to strike sparks.

Manda ran through the couples she knew. Her brother Dimmert and his wife, Cara, were happy together, but they were dull as dishwater. Now her sister Dance and her husband, Ace, had sparks. Oh my, did they—always exchanging heated barbs, acting like they could set each other afire but not in a good way. That left Miz Copper and Mr. John. They were so sweet together Manda could see sparks sometimes, but actually they weren't very exciting.

Manda put the periodical in her linen poke and rose from her seat. Stepping across the path, she walked to the rim of Devil's Eyebrow. In the valley far below, she spied a wisp of smoke rising lazily from the chimney of Dimmert's toy-size cabin. Yonder was the house that belonged to Dance. Funny, as Manda looked down on land that held her bountiful family, she felt as alone as a church house on Monday morning. Here she was eighteen years old and not even promised, much less married.

It was more than a year now since she had left her father and stepmother's place in Virginia to come to Kentucky to live with her brother. She was sure her pa didn't miss her one bit. He probably hadn't noticed she was gone. And Manda sure didn't miss her stepmother. When Pa married Nora, Manda had been excited and pleased. Her own ma had been dead for a long time, and Manda longed for a mother's touch.

Why, she'd even changed her name to please Pa's new wife. All the Whitt kids had names that started with *D* except Ezra. Hers was Dory. Nora made fun of it. She called her Porky Dory. So Manda used her middle name. It hadn't made a difference. Nora had children of her own and was not given to motherly ways. Manda was little more than a Cinderella before the ball in her stepmother's house.

It wasn't that she minded working for Miz Copper—most of the time, anyway. Manda liked to stay busy, and she liked earning her own keep. But she wanted a house of her own, a real home full of sunshine and laughter like what she remembered of her grandmother's house. Miz Copper's was like that too. And busy—my goodness, the work never stopped. Manda lived at the Pelfreys' during the week, helping with the cooking and cleaning, and went to her brother's house for the weekends.

Manda felt a flicker of guilt. She probably should have told Miz Copper she was going up mountain. And she probably shouldn't have told Lilly instead. Sometimes Manda just needed some space.

Just beyond easy reach was a tiny white blossom springing up in a fissure. Manda thought the fragile bloom very brave to pick such a barren place to live. Maybe she could pluck it for her album. She steadied herself with a handful of cedar and leaned out as far as she dared, then bent to pick the flower. It took her a moment to realize the branch that steadied her was slowly tearing away from the trunk of the tree. The soles of her slippers slid like sled runners as she tried to scramble backward across the overhang. Her body careened toward thin air and certain death until an unseen hand grabbed her arm and knocked her off her feet. The sharp, clean scent of crushed cedar brought her to her senses. She was down, but she was alive.

"What are you doing up here, girl?" Gurney Jasper asked as he hunkered down at her side.

"I was just taking a walk," she said, "taking in the air."

"You come in a hair of taking a little too much air." He helped her disentangle from the cedar. "They don't call this place Devil's Eyebrow for nothing."

She'd never felt so foolish. "I need to sit down," she said, her voice all aquiver, her arms and legs shaking like the palsy.

Gurney took her arm and guided her to the relative safety of the narrow trail. After taking off his light jacket, he spread it on the ledge rock and indicated for her to sit. "Do you want a swallow?" he asked, twisting the top from a canteen.

Water spilled out her mouth and trickled down her chin as she took a long draught. "Thank you. I'd be singing with the angels if you hadn't come along."

Gurney shoved his hands in his pockets and looked away.

"Say," she said, "what are you doing up here?"

He hung his head as a flush crept up his neck.

"Gurney Jasper, were you following me?"

"Well . . . not exactly."

"You were spying on me," she said, feeling the heat rise

in her face to match his. "Oh, that makes me mad enough to spit."

Gurney took a lethal-looking slingshot from his back pocket, seated a small stone in the pouch, and pulled it back. "See that blacksnake sunning himself in the crook of yon sycamore?"

She peered at the tree. Sure enough, a blacksnake was coiled tight as a spring in the fork of a big limb. "So?"

*Zing,* she heard as Gurney released the pouch, then *whop-whop-whop* as the snake struck one limb after another in his rapid plunge to the ground.

"I come up to practice with my sling—then I saw you, I'll admit. I was curious is all."

"Looks like you could have chosen another place to practice," she replied, picking sticky cedar from the cuffs of her sleeves.

"Since when do you own this mountain, Miss High-and-Mighty?" Gurney snatched up another stone and let it fly over the cliff.

"I'm sorry. Here you've saved my life, and I've trounced on your feelings."

"Sticks and stones." He started to walk away. "Your words don't hurt me none."

Manda worked off her shoes. "Wait up," she called. The packed dirt of the trail felt smooth and cool on the bottoms of her feet. "I'll walk with you."

Quick-stepping to keep pace, she followed his broad shoulders down the steep and winding path. "I'm fixing dried apple pies for the dance," she appeased, sorry for her hurtful words.

He stopped and she nearly smacked into him. "Really?" he said. "That's my favorite."

*The way to a man's heart,* Manda thought. She wondered if Rose Feathergay knew how to cook.

# 4

COPPER KNOCKED AT the cabin door. "Adie? Open up. It's me."

Slowly the door creaked open. Adie stood behind it, barefoot and hugely pregnant. Generally Copper hated the word *pity*. It conjured up an air of superiority to her mind, but pity was what she felt for Adie Still. The woman was skinny as a string bean, all elbows and knees and bulging belly. Her hair was tied in a looping knot that hung halfway down her back, and she wore a wool sweater although it was a pleasantly warm day.

"So how are you getting along today?" Copper said,

embarrassed by her own muffled, cheerful tone behind her cotton mask. "Are you feeling well?"

"I been racked by chills off and on." Adie slumped down in a straight-backed chair at a small table. "Last night it was the fever, and now I can't seem to get warm."

Copper pulled a stethoscope from her doctor's bag. Pressing the bell to Adie's narrow chest, she listened. "Your heart sounds good," she said before she put the bell to Adie's back. "Breathe deep through your nose. Again," she said before she had to stop for Adie's torturous hacking cough. "Any blood today?"

"Not so much—little streaks."

"Say *aah*." When Adie complied, Copper was glad to see her tongue looked less scalded, but tiny ulcers peppered the back of her throat. This disease was so odd. Yesterday Adie was abed so weak she couldn't blow her own nose, but today she was sitting up and talking.

Remy thought Adie's general bad health made her a poor candidate to survive this illness, but Copper felt they could fatten her up and give her a good chance if she didn't pox. Thank the good Lord she had had Lilly vaccinated when they were all in Philadelphia visiting her parents. What a hard decision that had been. She would have the other children done when they were old enough. Women of child-bearing age couldn't receive the vaccine, but she protected herself with the mask and gown.

"Have you been drinking your beef tea?"

Adie ran her fingers up and down her neck. "Some. It pains me to swallow. I et a pinch of biscuit this morning."

"Maybe I shouldn't have sent the biscuit if it hurts you to swallow."

"It tasted good soaked in the broth, gave me a change from that milk toast."

Copper moved the stethoscope to the mound of Adie's belly and listened intently. She laughed when a tiny kick rewarded her efforts. "He's a strong one."

"You reckon it's a boy?" Adie asked. "That'd please Isa aright smart. He don't want no girls."

Behind her mask, Copper chewed her bottom lip. *Give me the right words, Lord,* she prayed. "Adie, about Isa, will he be able to care for you and the baby properly when you go home?"

Adie rested her hand on her belly. "He's got his old mommy a-living there with us. I reckon she can help care for this'n. She's been good with the rest."

"I hope he doesn't still blame me for you being here," Copper said. "It was the only solution I could come up with that day the nurse from the board of health brought the law to your place."

"Isa don't like the government a-telling him what to do with his own property," Adie said, slowly lacing the long tail of her hair through her fingers. "He figures you're part and parcel of them."

*Property.* The word Adie applied to herself stuck in Copper's craw. "The law couldn't ignore the fact that you have a contagious disease. It would have been nigh impossible for you to keep in quarantine at home." *Careful,* Copper reminded herself. One wrong word and Adie would walk right out the door.

"What was that quare woman doing in town anyways?" Adie took a raggedy breath and struggled to continue. "Why am I any of her business?"

"From what I've gathered, the nurse has been staying out at the settlement school with a missions group. She's teaching hygiene and disease prevention to anyone who comes to the meetings they've set up. I guess she just happened to be in town the day you collapsed or else someone sent for her."

"I was just tired. I wanted . . . to set a spell. Ain't no law against it, far as I know."

"She thought you were coming down with smallpox. You can't fault her for acting so quickly, and honestly, if you'd stayed home, your children might have come down with this scarlatina. I know you wouldn't want that."

"Oh, I miss them kids. I ain't gone a day without a baby in my arms since I was sixteen."

"I can only imagine," Copper replied.

Wrapping her arms around her trunk, Adie rocked back and forth. "If I was to leave for a little bit—just long enough to see my young'uns, would you sic the law on me?"

Copper longed to put her arms around the slight woman, but she daren't. She had a family of her own to protect, and she was doing the best she could for Adie. "I have faith you wouldn't put me in that position. Listen, what if John went to talk to Isa? Isa could come for a visit. You could see each other through the window glass."

Adie's eyes were red with fever. A fine rash bloomed on her cheeks. She shrugged and shook her head. "He won't come here." Her body seemed to collapse into itself. She turned her face toward the window. "I feel so unnecessary."

Copper studied her patient. Adie needed something to keep her spirits up. She patted Adie's knee. "I'm going to bring you some sassafras tea to cut your fever and some yarn and needles to cut your boredom. This wee one will need a gown and a hat. And how about some socks for your husband and the boys?"

A flicker of interest lit up Adie's dull eyes. "I'd dearly love to put my hands to work."

Copper stood. "I'm sorry. I should have thought of it before."

Inside the washhouse, Copper stripped off the duster that covered her day dress, removed her bonnet, and hung both on the same nail. The mask she stuck in the duster pocket to be used again the next day. After pouring water from a bucket into the granite pan she kept handy on an old washstand, she scrubbed her hands and arms to the elbows with lye soap. The clean, strong smell of lye tickled her nose and caused her to sneeze.

From the direction of the creek she could hear childish laughter. The sound lightened her heart, and she paused to thank the Lord for her blessings, specifically her husband and her children. Smiling, she thought of John. He didn't mind a whit that she had been married before and that she brought a child to their union. From where she stood at the washhouse door, she could see the proof of his love for her. He had built their home himself, and it was more than the usual cabin. It was open and spacious with room for their family and the occasional patient. Even the burbling creek was a sign of his love. He had started building in a different location only to move everything when she decided she could not be happy without the sound of Troublesome Creek out her kitchen door.

John had not been pleased when she brought poor Adie home with her a few days ago, and he continued to worry about her safety. But what was she to do? It wasn't Adie's fault that she had scarlatina and that she was due to deliver a baby within the month. Copper couldn't just ignore her, so she had sworn to the law that she would keep Mrs. Still in quarantine at least until the baby came.

Copper carried the pan several feet behind the wash-house, then dumped the contents in a pit John had dug for her. She returned the pan to the washstand. She wouldn't need to clean up again if she put Adie's tea outside her door. Hefting a bucket of disinfectant, she carried it to the place where she had dumped the wastewater and other refuse from the sickroom and the invalid house. With an old dipper she sprinkled the solution all around. The bucket used to dissolve the solution of zinc and common salt in water was almost empty. She'd need to mix more disinfectant soon. Lastly, she changed her shoes and set the dirty pair on the windowsill to catch some sun.

JAN WATSON

When she got back to the house, she was pleasantly surprised to see Tillie sitting on the porch with Jumbo.

Tillie flashed a big smile. "Look how well we're doing," she said, pulling the blanket back from the baby's face. "Miss Remy said it would do us a world of good to get some air."

"Wonderful," Copper replied, studying the infant's face. With her thumb she retracted his lower eyelid. "Looks like Jumbo's got a bit of yellow jaundice. Let's move your chair so you're sitting in the sun. Sunshine will clear this right up."

Tillie thanked her profusely—so different from Adie.

"It is my pleasure to see you doing well." Copper chucked Jumbo lightly under the chin. "Would you like a cup of sassafras? I'm just going in to make a pot."

The cookstove was almost cold. Jamming a long-handled prong into a cast-iron burner plate, Copper lifted it and was rewarded by the sight of live coals. A chunk of wood from the wood box soon had the fire going again. What had gotten into Manda? She knew to keep one burner going under the teakettle. Not to mention the ironing board was still in the pantry, and it was nearly ten o'clock. Manda should have been half-done with Tuesday's task by now. Maybe she should have a talk with the young woman, but she hated to say anything. It wasn't like Manda didn't work hard when she worked. She just seemed to have her head in the clouds lately.

Copper drew the back of her hand across her forehead. Goodness, she was tired. There was so much to do. If she didn't keep on top of things, her household would fall apart. While in the pantry fetching the sassafras root, she got the

41

ironing board from behind the door and brought it out too. After the kettle boiled, she would put the iron to heat.

Copper warmed the inside of a teapot with hot water, then emptied it into the slop bucket. The sassafras shavings made the prettiest light red tea when it steeped, and the aroma was heavenly—best treatment for the ague she knew of. She added a skein of yarn and two knitting needles to Adie's tray.

"I see you got too many irons in the fire as usual," Remy said as she came into the kitchen with a wad of linen clutched to her chest.

Copper laughed. "I was going to press a couple of things while the tea steeped."

"Waste of time if you ask me," Remy said. "Why iron things that are just going to wrinkle again as soon as you sit down? Besides, ain't that Manda's job?"

"I learned ironing from my mam. It's soothing to stand in one place for a while."

Remy hefted the tea tray. "I'll take this and a cup for Tillie. I'm going out anyway—got to leave these sheets in the washhouse. I took the opportunity to strip the sickroom bed whilst Tillie gets some air." She looked aggrieved. "Somebody forgot them yesterday, the same somebody who forgot the ironing today."

Copper upended the sadiron and spit on the bottom. The spit sizzled and popped. "Don't you want a cup of tea first?" she asked as she pressed the collar of John's Sunday shirt.

"Maybe when I get back." Remy elbowed her way out the

door. "I still got to mop the floor in there and wipe down the woodwork."

Copper kept her mug on the end of the ironing board. The flowery aroma of the sassafras mingled with the starchy smell released from the laundry by the hot iron. Copper inhaled deeply, smelling work and reward at the same time. She suppressed the urge to give aid as Remy backed out the screen door with the tea tray on one hip and the bundle of wash on the other.

Remy was allergic to help, and it was a pure blessing when she could move about without the aid of her crutch. Warm weather greased her arthritic hip, giving her freedom from the usual pain. Remy never complained about her troubles, though she surely had reason. Years ago, before she was saved, Remy used to raid henhouses and cellars for sustenance. One day she picked the wrong henhouse, and an old lady came at her with a shotgun. Remy lost a lot that day and came within a hair's breadth of dying, but the shooting brought her back into Copper's life and into the arms of the Lord. "'All things work together for good,'" Copper said.

"Are you talking to me?" Tillie called from the porch.

Copper laughed as she positioned a shirtsleeve for ironing. "I'm just citing Scripture." Taking the opportunity she had been praying for, Copper put the iron back on the burner and stepped outside with her Bible and a mug of tea. "Do you know that verse?"

"Can't say that I do," Tillie murmured.

Copper pulled a chair alongside the young mother and

opened her Bible to Romans 8:28 and read, "'All things work together for good to them that love God, to them who are called according to his purpose.' Isn't that a wonderful promise?"

"Do you reckon that means me too? I don't go to church or nothing."

Copper covered one of Tillie's hands with her own. "Do you love the Lord?"

"Oh yes, ma'am—with all my heart. My mommy taught me about Jesus."

"It sounds to me like God meant you, then. It says 'to them that love God.' The Word of God never fails." Copper stood and laid her Bible on the chair seat. "Let's get you back in the shade. I believe the baby has had enough sun."

Tillie looked contemplative as she arranged the blanket around the baby. "How long do ye reckon before I could take Abe Jr. to church? I'd like to think I raised my son to have that promise for his own self."

Copper felt a tingle walk her spine, which always happened when she sensed the Holy Spirit moving. She couldn't wait to tell John what had just happened. "I'd say wait about three months to take the baby out. By then he'll have good protection against sickness, and you'll be stronger too. In the meantime, Brother Jasper could visit you and Abe at home if you would like."

Tillie sipped from the teacup that Remy had brought out earlier. "I would like that. I heard him praying for me the night I flooded so bad. The room got so dark I thought I could see the stars. I was swirling down a dark river; then I heard Brother Jasper calling me back to my baby." Her eyes spurted tears. "I was so scared. I thought I was about to die."

"Lord love your heart. That was a frightening time for all of us."

The screen door creaked. Copper had been so intent on Tillie that Manda was nearly inside the house before she noticed the girl had come up on the porch. Manda was carrying her shoes, and she ducked when she caught Copper looking.

Just as Copper opened her mouth in question, the children straggled across the yard. Jack was covered in mud, and the twins' dress tails were wet. Lilly Gray was mad. Copper could tell by the set of her fists on her nearly nonexistent hips.

"Mama," Lilly said, "your children do not mind very well."

"Obviously." Copper herded Jack to the end of the porch and stripped off his pants and shirt. She'd have to scrape the mud off his clothes with a butter knife. *Oh, well, boys will be boys.* "Stand still," she said while watching a horse and rider draw up in the yard.

"Miz Pelfrey," a neighbor called from horseback, "can you come? It's Mary's time."

# 5

MARY RANDALL WAS made for birthing babies, Copper decided as she held a squirming newborn upside down and smacked her round bottom. The infant squalled in protest, quickly turning from blue to pink. "Mary, she's a beauty. Have you picked out a name?"

"Prude, I'm thinking," Mary said as Copper secured the umbilical string in two places, then cut between the ties.

Copper bit her tongue. *What a name to settle on a baby,* she thought. With one more push, Mary delivered the afterbirth. All of a piece, Copper saw. Tillie Sizemore's had come out tattered. A retained piece of placenta was why she'd nearly bled to death. A million and one things could go wrong at a birthing, but this one was perfect—except for the baby's name. Folks often lived up to their forename, so what would become of little Prude?

Copper wrapped the wee one in a warmed receiving blanket and placed her on Mary's chest. "Are you naming her for someone special?"

"My ma, God rest her soul. Everybody called her Prude." Mary unwrapped the swaddling and counted ten tiny fingers and ten tiny toes. "I sure wish she was here to see her namesake."

"Did your mother have a middle name?" Copper asked while she helped the baby to suckle.

Mary grimaced when the baby clamped on. "Merry. With two *r*'s, like 'happy.' Prudence Merry was her Christian name."

With one fingertip Copper broke the suction from the baby's mouth and repositioned her. "Does that feel better?"

"Much." Mary settled back against the pillows Copper had stacked there.

"Merry's sure a pretty name. You could switch your mom's name around. Merry Prudence has a good ring to it. Don't you think?"

Mary fondled her infant's head. "She is pretty, ain't she? Look at her ears—so perfect. Let's see what she wants to be called. Prude?"

The baby nursed in bursts of sucks but never lost hold.

"She's good at this," Copper said, smiling at the ease with which the feeding was going. That was not always the case.

It took some infants hours to catch on, but then Mary was a natural. Copper had oft noticed that the calmer the mother, the quicker the baby latched. She herself had loved nursing, though the twins had presented a bit of a challenge. She'd learned to hold them backward, tucked around her waist like sacks of potatoes. It seemed like all she did the first year of their life was feed them. Watching Mary made her yearn to have another baby. She'd have to talk to John. The girls were three, after all. But he seemed set against it, and she would never go against his wishes.

The baby mewed like a kitten. Her head lolled away from the breast.

"Merry?" her mother said.

As if in response, the baby's eyes popped open. She stared at her mother's face.

Mary stroked the baby's palm and smiled as the small hand curled around her finger. "Looks like she's picked what she likes best."

Copper retrieved a certificate, a pen, and a capped pot of ink from her delivery kit. "It's Merry Prudence Randall then, is it?" When Mary nodded, Copper began to fill out the form, noting place, date, hour, day of the week, and the weight and length. She always took her time with this part of the delivery process for this was an important document and would most likely be cherished in the family Bible along with, hopefully, a record of baptism and someday a certificate of marriage.

Dipping the nib of the pen in the pot, she said, "I need your maiden name and your husband's given name."

"I was an Allen," Mary said, shifting the baby to her other side, "and believe it or not, my husband's given name is Big Boy."

"Really? I figured that to be a nickname," Copper replied.

"Everyone does, but Big Boy is the name his father gave him. Too bad you weren't at that delivery. He might have had a proper first name."

"You've got me there," Copper said, scribing a cursive *B*. "It's just that names are so important. I once delivered a baby whose father insisted on naming him Nimrod Axel. That bothers me to this day."

After pressing a piece of blotting paper over the document, Copper set it aside to dry before she put her seal on it. "Speaking of Big Boy, I'd best go fetch him so he can meet his daughter. Last time I checked, he was walking a circle in the barn. He said he was too nervous to wait in the kitchen."

Mary clasped Copper's hand. "Thank you ever so much. I would never have made it without you."

Big Boy was indeed right where she had left him, but now he was polishing tack. "You're going to wear that leather out," she said.

Big Boy dropped the harness. "Is Mary all right?"

"Mary is fine, and your daughter is beautiful."

Big Boy caught her in a bear hug and whirled her around the barn. "A girl. Are you sure?"

Copper laughed. He was the nicest man. He reminded her of her father. "I'm sure. Go see for yourself."

Big Boy dashed a tear from his eye. "I never thought to see this day. I feel like the luckiest man alive."

Copper followed him across the yard, tarrying outside to give the parents some privacy with their newborn. Those moments alone were precious, and she felt it strengthened the couple's union.

Exhaustion overtook her, and she paused to rest under the large leaves and low-hanging beans of a catalpa tree. Her shoulders and lower back ached from the day's hard work. They didn't call it labor for nothing. But even as her muscles protested, her spirit soared. What sweet glory to guide a new life into the world. Nothing else gave her such satisfaction.

Looking toward the distance, she watched twilight sashay down the face of the mountains. The vivid greens of the forest turned to shadowy gray and muted khaki. This day would soon be over. She wondered how her children were and what they'd had for supper. She felt a heart pang knowing she wouldn't be there to tuck them into bed. John would, though. She could count on him.

As if her thoughts had conjured him up, there John rode across the yard. "Hey, sweetheart," he said before he even dismounted. "How goes it?"

"A baby girl," she replied, "six pounds, eight ounces."

"And Mary?"

"She did great. Everything went smooth as clockwork."

John handed over a basket before he tethered the horse. "Manda sent supper."

"Smells good. I'll get it on the table."

John took the basket back and set it on the ground. "First things first," he said, tilting her chin. His kiss was light and easy as befitted the place, but it claimed her still.

"That's almost as good as the fried chicken I know is in this basket."

"Almost?" he said, with a smack to her fanny. "Since when do I vie with fried chicken?"

She scampered ahead of him through the door. "The last time I ate was breakfast. I'm starved."

"So am I. But not for chicken."

Way after dark, John took his leave. Copper kissed him good-bye under the catalpa.

"I don't see why you have to stay," he said, holding her close. "You said Mary was doing well."

She shook her head as it rested on his broad chest. Her forehead scraped across the pocket of his rough overalls. "We've talked about this before. Please don't make me feel guilty."

He lifted her up as if she had no more substance than a will-o'-the-wisp. "It's just I hate being home without you."

"I know, honey. I know." She leaned into him as the infant's cry called to her from the lit cabin.

She traced the curve of his neck, feeling his strong pulse against her fingertips. His heart beat in perfect harmony with hers—like an orchestra of two. She often thought if his heart stilled, hers would surely follow suit. It was only when she was in the midst of her work that discord threatened their union. It was simple enough to figure out. He wanted her home—always within easy reach. You'd think he would have adjusted to her ways by now. She had to his, but if John was as close as a waltz, she was a square dance keeping a little distance.

"I wonder," he said in a low, gruff voice, "if you would take down your hair for me."

It surprised her that he would ask for something so intimate outside the walls of their bedroom, but her fingers sought the pins and combs and her hair fell free. A rush like a thousand butterfly wings filled her chest when he ran his big hands through her tumbled locks.

"Gracious," she said, breathless. "Maybe you'd best take your leave now."

The baby's cry grew louder—more insistent.

"Your hair is like the hottest flame," he said. "It draws me."

With her hands on his chest, she pushed him away. "John, really I need to go in."

"All right," he said, stealing one last kiss. "But you come home tomorrow."

Copper was stacking kindling under the washtub just as dawn broke. She had slept like a cat last night in fits and starts, once falling asleep in a chair with baby Merry on her chest. It was always like this when she was away from her own bed and the comfort of John's arms. Plus, there was so much to do and so little time in which to do it. She'd already fired up the cookstove, boiled coffee, and made biscuits. It was early to do a wash, but she wanted to get the soiled birthing linens washed and on the line before Mary's sister came to take over.

When bubbles roiled across the surface of the water, Copper dumped in the sheets and toweling she'd let soak overnight. It was good to be outside so early in the morning while the mist swirled around her feet like the skirts of dancing girls and the sweet breath of the mountains restored her strength. As she stirred the laundry with a wooden paddle, her thoughts strayed to the time she had lived in the city with Simon. Obviously she had loved him enough to be there, but it was a hard place. Everyone lived cheek to jowl like hogs in a pen, and whenever you stepped out of doors, you saw your neighbor and your neighbor saw you. She wondered if anyone who lived in such tight places ever took a truly deep breath.

She'd been seventeen when Simon swept her off her feet and carried her far away to live in the big city. It was an adjustment for sure, but she found her place and learned so much. She might not be birthing babies now if it hadn't been for the teachings of her doctor husband. Thoughts of Simon turned to thoughts of his sister, Alice, and the letter Copper carried deep inside her pocket.

Things had not been good with Alice. No matter how hard Copper tried, she had never been the frilly socialite Alice craved for her only brother. The corners of Copper's mouth twitched and a laugh escaped as she thought of the day, years ago in Lexington, when Alice, along with the upright president of the hospital auxiliary, came calling and found Copper barefoot in the garden. Alice was nearly apoplectic. There were many times Copper unkindly wished she were.

As Copper rubbed a stubborn stain up and down the washboard, she wondered why she still needed to please Alice—especially since she was quite sure that was never going to happen. Of course there were ties that bound tight as apron strings; at first it was their shared love of Simon, and now it was his daughter, Lilly Gray.

Lost in thought, she'd scrubbed too hard and scraped her knuckle raw against the ribbed board. *This is what happens when I don't pay attention,* she chided herself as she wrung out the piece of wash and dunked it in the rinse water.

Sucking on the injured knuckle, she took out the letter with her other hand. It was barely light enough to read, but unfortunately there was no mistaking Alice's request—no, demand! She wanted Lilly, just Lilly, for the month of July. Round-trip train tickets were enclosed. Alice had thought of everything. All Copper had to do was get Lilly to the depot.

The desire to hold the missive to the flame that flickered under the washtub was so strong, Copper had to step back. Last year, she had accompanied Lilly on her yearly visit, along with the twins and Jack. Alice put up a good front with the other children although she had eyes only for Lilly Gray. Then Copper had given in to Alice's pleading and Lilly's whining and allowed Lilly to stay a week beyond Copper's visit. Like the first tentative pull of a moth's wing against a spider's web, Copper could see now how expertly her sister-in-law had woven her manipulative trap. Alice could rightly reason that Lilly would be perfectly safe to travel without her mother. After all, Copper had allowed it before.

Lilly would love the trip. So what was really so upsetting? Copper tried to think it through as she hung dripping laundry on the line.

For one thing there was the time. A month was way too long for Lilly to be gone from her family. Copper would have to negotiate with Alice over that. And it bothered her that Alice thought she would so easily acquiesce to her demands—like a dog flopping on its back and showing its belly. Copper snapped a bedsheet so hard, it flew from her hands and landed in the dirt.

*Give me patience, Lord,* she prayed as she put the sheet back in the burbling wash water. She would have prayed for understanding, but she wasn't quite ready for that. There was no use in praying for something she wasn't ready to receive, and she was in no way ready to empathize with Alice Corbett Upchurch.

By midmorning, when Mary's sister arrived with *ooh*s and *aah*s for her brand-new niece, Copper was ready to go home.

Big Boy saddled her chestnut mare and led the horse from the stable. He stroked the horse's long nose. "She's a beauty."

"Yes, she is," Copper agreed, putting a foot in the stirrup and accepting Big Boy's hand up. "I'm glad to have her."

"Say, do you ever hear from Darcy Thomas?"

Copper was not surprised at the question, for she had purchased the mare from Darcy, who happened to be her hired girl's sister. Darcy's husband had assaulted Darcy's brother-in-law Ace Shelton and nearly killed him. Although Ace had recovered, Darcy's husband was still in a federal prison. Darcy had moved from Troublesome Creek with her infant son to be near her husband. It was a complicated situation, and folks still talked about it.

By all accounts Darcy was doing well, though. The dressmaker's shop she owned in the city was a thriving business. She made all of Copper's family's attire except for John's heavy overalls. Those she ordered by the half dozen from the Sears Book of Bargains catalog.

"We got a note from Darcy just last week. She sent it in a package of dresses I ordered for the girls." Copper took the reins Big Boy unwound from the hitching post. "It sounds like things are going well for her."

"I'm glad," Big Boy said. "It weren't her fault—what her husband did. I always wondered why she didn't stay here with her family while he served his time."

"There's no figuring love," Copper said.

Little Merry Prudence set up a wail that could be heard all the way to the stable.

"Speaking of which," Big Boy said with a chuckle.

Copper waved as she rode away.

"Thanks again," Big Boy called after her. "Mary and I sure do appreciate you."

Copper let Chessie amble along. Although she was anxious to get home, she enjoyed the slow pace. It seemed the only quiet time she had was on horseback while returning from her midwifery duties. She used the time wisely in silent contemplation and prayer.

Chessie seemed to like their quiet time also. She was such a sweet and docile horse even if skittish at times. Copper leaned forward and patted Chessie's muscular neck. The horse gave a little whinny of satisfaction before something pinged off her left flank. Chessie's ears perked, and she raised her front hoofs in alarm.

Copper pulled the reins in tightly and looked behind them on the packed trail. It was just a pinecone, large and well-formed, left over from last fall. It had startled Chessie, but she was not hurt. Copper studied the woods. There were many pines lining the road.

This would be a good place to bring the children later in the year to gather pine knots for the fireplace and for Christmas decorations. Lilly would especially like that. She gathered pretty things all year to decorate their tree with.

Chessie picked up to a trot. It seemed that neither of them could wait to get home.

# 6

LILLY SKIPPED DOWN the lane to the creek. She was so happy, she hopscotched without a hopscotch board. But if there had been one, she thought, she would have won. She bet she could even beat Kate Jasper right now. And that was never easy, for Kate had longer legs than Lilly. That was a definite advantage when you played a hopping game.

Maybe she would see Kate tomorrow night at the school-house dance. Mama was letting her go with Manda and her family. Lilly thought it would be fun. Wow, two fun things to think about—a dance and a visit with Aunt Alice for the whole month of July!

Lilly had butterflies in her stomach just thinking about

the trip. She would go on the train—she loved trains, with all the screeching of brakes and whistling of whistles and belching of smoke. And then Aunt Alice said that a circus was coming to Lexington. They had missed the circus last year.

Lilly wondered if Aunt Alice would have chocolate ice cream again. She licked her lips. She would like to meet the man who invented ice cream and the one who invented shaved ice too. Purple was her favorite color of shaved ice.

It would pay to be extra grown-up for the next couple of weeks so Mama and Daddy wouldn't have any reason not to let her take a train trip by herself. Last night after supper when she was given Aunt Alice's invitation, she could tell her mother didn't really want to let her go to Lexington alone. Good grief. You'd think she was still a little kid. She held out her arms, threw back her head, and twirled around in excitement. When she stopped, the world kept spinning.

When her eyes settled, she saw a turtle trundling up the bank of the creek. He made slow but steady progress until a thick piece of driftwood blocked the way. Lilly watched to see how the turtle would solve his predicament. With his clawed front feet, the turtle tried to climb the refuse.

"Go around," she said. "It will only take a little longer."

But the turtle didn't listen and fell backward in slow motion. The poor thing waved his stubby legs, rocking his shell, trying to right himself.

Lilly laughed. It reminded her of Jack flailing about on the rope swing.

When Lilly got close, the turtle's head and feet disappeared lickety-split inside his domicile. It was the only fast thing a turtle could do. Carefully, she turned the creature over and lifted him by his middle. Stepping over the piece of driftwood, she carried the turtle up the bank and set him down facing away from the creek. She didn't know his destination, but now he had a head start.

She wondered why animals were always wandering. There he had the perfect home with food and running water close at hand, but he wanted to be someplace else. It was like that with other creatures too, she had noticed. Sometimes on the way to town she would see a skunk or a possum lying dead by the side of the road. Why didn't they stay on the safe side of the track? She would have to ask Daddy John.

Maybe traveling was an adventure for them like going to Lexington to visit Aunt Alice was for her. If so, she could understand, but there was no chocolate ice cream reward for turtles and skunks at the end of their journey.

As she walked along, Lilly watched for pretties to add to her treasure box. She had every color of feather you could think of: blue from bluebirds and blue jays, red from cardinals, rusty orange from a robin's chest, soft gray from doves, brown from mockingbirds and wrens, gold from finches, and yellow from wild canaries. She kept them pressed in a heavy book. Maybe she would take the book to the city with her. If she asked, Aunt Alice would have her dressmaker sew Lilly a dress in each feather color. She thought about it. Would that make her spoiled? Mama always worried about Aunt Alice spoiling her, like she was a jar of tomatoes going bad. Maybe she'd just ask for ribbons in each color. She'd leave out the brown feather though. Brown did not go well with her hair.

Giving a wide berth, Lilly passed by the stump where the rattlesnake lived. Thankfully, he did not come out to greet her with his whirring tail today.

Farther up the creek she searched for traps. She didn't find a single one. And the one she had busted was gone too. There was nothing left but a hole in the ground where the stake had been. Lilly puffed out her chest in pride. Someone was getting her message. Kneeling, Lilly smoothed the disturbed ground and covered it with decaying leaves. Because of her, no other animal would die on this spot.

Two chattering chipmunks chased each other around the trunk of a tree. High overhead a squirrel snapped his tail in warning.

Lilly walked on until she came to a low fieldstone wall. Her side of the wall was deep in the shadow of trees, so she stepped over and sat with her back against the warm rock, admiring the meadow full of wildflowers spread out before her. She wrapped her arms around her knees and closed her eyes to sharpen her hearing. Something scratched for food. A towhee, she decided. And that slow, deliberate pad of hooves was surely a doe. Holding her breath, she opened her eyes the least bit and peered at the backside of a huge buck. Suddenly the meadow was alive with deer. She had never seen so many. She wished Aunt Remy were sitting beside her. This was a sight meant to be shared.

She could hear the soft snort of the buck's breath as he

munched sweet grass and the tumble of clear water rushing over creek rock. A foreign but unmistakable sound intruded on the peaceful scene—the sharp, metallic cock of a gun.

What she was about to do was wrong—wrong and dangerous. Daddy John had explained to her about chickens and pigs and squirrels and deer and how God gave us meat to nourish our bodies, but she couldn't sit by and watch. She jumped up and waved her arms. "Run! Run for your lives!"

At the sound of her voice, the meadow that had been so peaceful was full of thumping and thrashing as the deer bolted. Lilly's heart thumped in tune.

A tall boy about her age stepped out from behind a walnut tree. He was barefoot and carried his gun in the crook of his arm with the barrel aimed at the ground. The hindquarters of two freshly killed rabbits protruded from a leather pouch fastened to his belt.

"You're not supposed to hunt here," Lilly said. "This is private property."

"You've crossed over." The boy pointed to the rock fence with the barrel of his gun. "Yon side's Pelfreys'. This side's Stills'. Best you mind your whereabouts."

The threat made Lilly uneasy. She scrambled over to the shadowy side of the fence. "I'm sorry."

A fat beagle ran up behind the boy, sniffing at his heels. The boy kicked backward, catching the dog under its chin. The beagle yelped and backed up.

"That was mean," Lilly said, reaching across the top of the wall and snapping her fingers toward the dog.

"I never hurt her none. I barely touched her. Besides a hunting dog's got to be tough." The boy stared at her. "You're over the line again." With the barrel of the gun, he moved her arm aside.

"You're being silly now," she said.

"Are you one of them Pelfreys?"

"I'm Lilly Gray Corbett. What's your name?"

"Tern Still."

"How come I've never met you before? Don't you go to school?"

Tern raked a shock of black hair out of his eyes. "I get my learning at the school of hard knocks."

"Hmm," Lilly said. "Hard Knocks. That's a funny name for a place. Did you ever hear of Monkey's Eyebrow?"

"Are you poking fun at me?" Tern asked.

Lilly broke a piece of the biscuit snack she had in her pocket and pitched it over the fence. The dog gobbled it up and looked for more. "She's awful hungry to be so fat."

"She ain't fat. She's expecting puppies."

Puppies! Lilly's heart turned over. "Oh, then you must feed her extra."

"Ha," Tern sniggered. "Fat chance. If she don't hunt, she don't eat."

Lilly's temper flared. She shook her finger at him. "Listen, I know a bunch about babies. If you don't feed the mother right, the babies won't be born healthy."

The boy looked at Lilly. His eyes were the the oddest pale blue, like icicles in moonlight.

"It don't matter none," he said. "She'll whelp curs. We won't be keeping them."

"Are they all promised already?" Lilly asked. "Maybe my mother would let me have one."

A sharp whistle caused Tern to jerk his head around. "I've got to go," he said.

Lilly held out the rest of the biscuit. "Would you take this for her?"

Tern's hand was warm when it brushed hers.

"Good-bye," she called as he walked away. "It was nice meeting you."

He didn't answer.

*He isn't very polite,* Lilly thought. *They must not teach manners at Hard Knocks School.* Actually, she didn't learn much about deportment at her school either, but her mother knew about such things, and Aunt Alice was a stickler. Lilly was to have private lessons on table manners while she was at Aunt Alice's house. Aunt Alice had said so in her letter. Lilly couldn't wait.

Tern and his dog were almost out of sight. The beagle was nosing the boy's cupped hand. Lilly could tell she was eating the biscuit. That made her heart feel good, but she was disappointed that Tern had not offered to give her a puppy. She was all but certain her mother would have said yes to it, and if she didn't, Lilly would have gone to Daddy John. She could talk him into anything.

# 7

MANDA SAT ON her bed and buckled her shoes. Her hike up Spare Mountain had had the desired effect on the two-piece wooden soles. They were nicely scuffed. She gathered her skirts in both hands and practiced a few clogging steps.

"You're pretty as a picture," her sister-in-law Cara said, holding a brush aloft. "Sit here at the dresser and let me do your hair."

"Yours looks good," Manda said. "I like it piled on top of your head like that."

Cara tucked a flyaway strand of plain brown hair behind her ear. "I'd give anything for a head of hair like yours, so thick and shiny." She expertly braided one thick plait, starting at the crown of Manda's head. "And such a pretty gold color. Hand me that comb." Cara stepped back and tilted her head, looking Manda over. "Perfect. You won't be able to shake that loose no matter how much you dance."

Manda held a silver-backed hand mirror behind her head and peered into the dresser's looking glass. "I just hope there's somebody to dance with."

"Isn't Gurney going?"

Manda put the mirror on the dresser. "I meant somebody different. Somebody exciting."

"So Gurney Jasper's not giving you a thrill?" Cara teased.

Manda opened the dresser drawer and took out a small pot of rouge. She tapped the powder with her forefinger, then rubbed the apples of her cheeks. "Gurney's boring as yesterday's news. He's so predictable. Want some?" she asked, holding out the rouge.

"Predictable can be good." Cara leaned in behind her, patted color with the tips of two fingers, and glanced at her own reflection. "Gracious, I look like a clown."

"Let me." Manda wiped half the color from Cara's cheeks with a piece of cotton wool before she mixed a bit of rouge with petroleum jelly and applied it to Cara's lips. "There, now you've got a touch of color."

"How do you know how to do this?" Cara asked. "I can never get it right. So I usually don't bother."

"I read all of Miz Copper's magazines. They have a wealth of knowledge."

"You sound so worldly."

Manda picked up the hand mirror and did her lips, then blotted them. "Don't you ever long for something else? somewhere else? maybe even somebody else?"

"Manda!"

Manda turned on the dresser bench to face Cara. "Oh, don't get exercised. I know you're true to Dimmert. But don't you ever get tired of the same old, same old?"

"Scoot," Cara said, sliding onto the bench and sitting shoulder to shoulder with Manda. "The love of a good man is a gift from heaven. You should give Gurney a chance."

"I want sparks. Shouldn't there be sparks?"

Cara laughed. "Has Gurney stolen a kiss yet?"

Manda rolled her eyes. "Well, no, and he'd better not, either."

"Then how do you know there won't be sparks? He just might surprise you." Cara twirled a strand of hair around her finger. "I didn't especially warm up to Dimm until that first kiss. His passion for me led to my passion for him."

"You're ruining your hair," Manda said, smoothing a bit of pomade into Cara's wispy locks. "Did you ever kiss anybody but Dimmert?"

"No." Cara stood and smoothed her skirts. "And I've never wanted to."

"So you think I should let Gurney kiss me tonight?" Manda asked with a last look in the mirror and a last pat to her hair.

"Kisses shouldn't be planned for. You have to let them come naturally."

"I don't know about that. If Gurney had any get-up about him, I believe he would have already tried."

Cara smiled and shook her head. "Manda, Manda. Be careful lest you get rain up your nose."

Manda answered with more clogging steps. "Let's go. I'd rather dance than eat fried chicken on Sunday."

"Speaking of which," Cara said, "don't forget your box supper."

<hr />

The thump of dance music met them a mile away. Lilly clapped and snuggled closer to Manda. They were sitting on the back of the wagon with their legs dangling over the edge. Every time the wagon hit a bump, Lilly squealed.

Cara looked back at them from her place on the wagon's bench between Dimmert and her little niece Merky. "You hold her tight, Manda."

Manda gave Lilly a little shove. "I was thinking of flinging her out onto the roadside."

Lilly giggled. "You're ever so much fun. I'm so glad Mama let me come."

"Just you remember to stay close to me or Cara. Don't go wandering off by yourself."

"Mama's already given me that speech," Lilly said. "I'll be watching Merky anyway."

"That will keep you out of trouble for sure," Manda said. "Merky's a live wire."

The wagon hit a hole in the roadbed. Lilly bounced. Manda's encircling arm kept her safely seated.

"You know, Manda, I'm good with children."

Manda chuckled. Lilly was such a serious child. "You are that."

As soon as they got inside the schoolhouse, Manda let the crowd swallow her up. Lilly would be fine with the rest of the Whitt family. Dance and Ace and their passel of kids had come also. She wouldn't spend much time with them. She and Dance were never close. Dance was way older than Manda, and she never seemed to warm up to Manda. Truthfully, all Manda really liked about her sister was her name. Why couldn't she have been named Dance instead of Dory?

The crowd was thick on the dance floor and lined two or three deep along the walls. Box suppers and dances always brought people from all over. It was a good way to meet new folks. Manda's feet twitched to the music as she elbowed over to the maids' table with her decorated pasteboard box chock-full of fried chicken, potato salad, and dried apple pie. The table was dubbed the young maids' table to keep from hurting feelings. Only eligible women participated in the box auction— young maids verging on being old maids like Manda. Wives and mothers brought food for their families. But maybe if the right person bid on her box tonight, this would be her last year at the spinsters' table. Manda was ever hopeful.

The auctioneer stood behind the table, picking his teeth with a broom straw and lifting one box lid after another. "What you got there, Miss Manda?" he asked. As soon as she put her supper on the table, he pried the corner up. "Well, well, fried chicken and still warm." The broom straw bobbed in the corner of his mouth. "I just might have to save this one for last and bid on it myself."

Manda cringed. Joe Little must be forty years old, and he was bald to boot. Not to mention he was a widower with eight kids. Manda didn't aim to take on that job. From the corner of her eye, she saw a boy sidle up to a second table, where delicious-looking cakes waited for the cakewalk. She watched as the boy ran his finger around the bottom of a caramel-iced confection. When he saw Manda watching, he popped his finger into his mouth and walked away.

"Better mind the cakes, Mr. Little," she said.

A tap on her shoulder and she was waltzed away by Gurney. "You sure look nice, Manda," he said.

*Nice?* she thought. Sisters looked *nice*. Mothers looked *nice*. Even grandmothers looked *nice*. Manda wanted to be beautiful—or at the very least pretty. She held her body stiffly in Gurney's arms. He didn't seem to notice.

Dimmert and Cara danced by. Cara raised her eyebrows. Manda shook her head in answer. No, no sparks yet.

"What?" Gurney asked. "Did I do something wrong?"

"Not a thing," Manda snapped.

"I can't wait until the auction," he said. "My belly's rumbling for your dried apple pie."

The song ended, and one of the musicians stepped forward, teasing a fast tune from his fiddle. Gurney turned to face the crowd and started clogging, heel-toe, heel-toe, emphasizing

the downbeat of the music. Soon other folks fell in until a line
stretched clear across the room. Some danced with eyes closed,
and some slapped their knees in perfect time, energized by the
percussive rhythm.

Manda's feet started up a little jig. It was hard to ignore
the music. Gurney smiled and ran a set around her, his knees
bent, his arms folded behind his back. Swishing her skirts,
she matched him fancy step for fancy step. The other cloggers
fell out until it was just she and Gurney facing each other,
performing the time-honored dance to whoops and whistles
from the crowd.

The fiddler rocked the bow, burning up the strings.
Gurney leaned in as if to steal a kiss. She leaned back. The
crowd roared with laughter. Manda loved it. She could dance
all night.

It was over Gurney's shoulder she first noticed the musician.
He was a middling sort of guy—middling height, middling
weight, and brown hair, nothing special except for his eyes,
which were locked on her. She looked away and then looked
back. He never broke his stare. Flustered, she lost a step.

Laughing, Gurney caught her hand. Wild applause broke
out. Manda and Gurney bowed like actors on a stage.

The mood of the crowd shifted abruptly when the middling man took up a small, slender, three-stringed music box
and strummed it like a guitar. The other pickers stood silently
behind him. Nobody danced to the strains of "Pretty Polly."
Most just stood in place and swayed in time to the middling
man's high, lonesome voice. He sang of a girl murdered by

her faithless boyfriend, an innocent girl who now lay silent in her grave with only the wild wind for comfort.

Gurney chanced to slide an arm around her shoulders. She wished he wouldn't.

The middling man closed his eyes as if his song were a prayer. His voice was pure as an angel's. When he finished, nobody clapped or hooted or hollered. Many women dabbed at their eyes, and several men cleared their throats. Manda was mesmerized. She didn't notice when Gurney took his arm away.

The auctioneer broke the spell when he called for the auctioning of the maids' boxes.

The musicians leaned their instruments against the wall. Two men stepped off the stage and headed for the door. The middling man rolled a cigarette.

Lilly and Jay, Dance's eldest son, appeared at Manda's side. They were going to eat with her and whoever bid the most for her box supper.

The children clutched at her, pulling her toward the maids' table. Manda looked over her shoulder and saw the middling man strike a match on the sole of his shoe to light his smoke. He squinted with his first puff. Was he still looking at her? Her hands trembled inside the children's clasp. What if he bought her box? Her heart skipped a beat.

"Aunt Manda," Jay said, "look, the auctioneer's holding up your parcel. Reckon who will buy it?"

"Everybody knows Gurney Jasper will," Lilly said. "He's Manda's beau. Right, Manda?"

Manda didn't answer.

When the auctioneer called for bids on her supper, nary a soul bid against Gurney. After he claimed his prize, Gurney selected one of the school desks pushed up against the back wall and spread the supper across its top. Lilly and Jay took a chicken leg each. Gurney smiled so big that mustard-style potato salad spilled from the corner of his mouth. Manda handed him one of the red- and white-checked napkins she'd ironed this morning. He wiped his mouth on one corner.

"This here will put a man in hog heaven," Gurney said.

Manda split a biscuit for the children. "I'm glad you like it."

"What's not to like? Say, you ain't et a bite."

Manda's emotions churned like the butter she spread on the biscuit. She couldn't wait for the music to resume. All she wanted was to watch the middling man again.

When they had finished supper, Cara came over and claimed the children. "Gurney asked permission from Dimmert to see you home," she whispered in Manda's ear. "Don't worry about Lilly. I'll take care of her. You have some fun."

So she was supposed to jump at the chance to ride home with Gurney? It was just taken for granted? Says who? Then again, Dimmert and Cara were likely to leave earlier than Gurney. If she let him take her home, she could stay until the very end of the dance like the other young folks would do. This could work in her favor. "Thanks," she said.

"Sounds like they're starting the cakewalk," Cara said with a tinge of excitement. "I hope my chocolate cake brings a lot of money. I think the school board's buying maps of the world for the students with the proceeds." She squeezed Manda's shoulder. "See you later."

Manda always enjoyed cakewalks. It was lots of fun watching.

Gurney nudged her. "See that cake at the end of the table? The widow Sparrow always brings one."

"It looks like a fruitcake," Manda said.

"It is a Christmas cake—leftover that is. One year my pa bid on it out of kindness. We used it for a doorstop."

Manda laughed. "You did not."

Gurney held his right hand aloft. "Upon my honor."

After several rounds of heavy bidding on all manner of confections, Mrs. Sparrow's doorstop cake was the only one remaining. Manda was interested to see what would happen. Who would take pity on the poor widow this time?

Joe Little looked at the cake. He looked at Mrs. Sparrow. "I believe I'll buy this one myself," he said, bringing his gavel down with a smack.

*Soon Mrs. Sparrow will be baking cakes for a passel of young'uns,* Manda surmised. *Better her than me.*

The fun picked up as the evening progressed. By nine o'clock most of the families with children had gone and many of the old folks as well. Manda danced every dance. She had no idea there were so many unattached men around. It would be better if Gurney would stop cutting in, but he wasn't a man to take a hint. She didn't mind too much though, for Gurney was easy to maneuver toward the stage, which was

JAN WATSON

where she really wanted to be. If it was true you could talk with your eyes, then she was talking, and by all accounts the middling man was listening.

An hour later, the last dance—a slow, sweet waltz—was announced. Gurney pulled her into a tight embrace. She didn't protest but laid her head on his shoulder and let him be her guide. She had never been this close to a grown man before. An odd sense of power, her power over him, startled her and she pulled back a bit. Was this strange feeling the "feminine wiles" she read about in the ladies' magazines? If so, she needed to be careful lest she entice Gurney. She'd read about that too—enticing. It could get you into trouble and ruin your reputation quick as a cat's sneeze.

Besides, she didn't want to waste those wiles. The magazine didn't say how long they lasted, and she might want to try them out again sometime—say on the middling man.

# 8

COPPER FELT GUILTY as she rode Chessie across the forest floor. The little girls had pitched a fit when she left, and it was wash day. But instead of scrubbing grass stains from the knees of Jack's trousers or starching the girls' Sunday dresses, she was off on a lark. Well, maybe not a lark, but she was out of the house. When she left, Manda was separating whites from darks while Remy was building a fire under the wash-tub. Lilly was charged with keeping her brother and sisters out from underfoot, a task she was very good at. It made Copper wonder if Lilly might be a schoolteacher one day.

Chessie paused at the edge of a pond. She was a cautious mare and wouldn't venture into the water unless Copper strongly urged her to. Copper dismounted. The still water reflected the blue sky and a few white buttermilk clouds. It was wide, but it didn't seem deep. Water could fool the eye, however. They could go around, but stands of silver tulip tree saplings banked the pool, and besides, Chessie needed to learn to deal with the fear of losing her footing.

It hadn't happened yet, but there was sure to come a day when both horse and rider would need to cross a swollen body of water to get to a patient up some holler or another. This area was notorious for violent flooding, especially in the spring and in the winter when snowmelt turned quietly meandering creeks into lethal rivers. Copper should know—many years ago her own mother had drowned in one such flood.

She picked up a good-size rock and lobbed it to the center of the pool. It hit bottom with a plunk and a smallish splash. A frog with legs like bouncing springs jumped from the water's edge, startling both her and Chessie. Crouching down, Copper watched skimmer bugs skate across the surface of the water. It was amazing how creation worked. This newly formed pool was already a home for some of God's most fascinating creatures.

Copper stood and took a crudely drawn map from her pocket and studied it. If she kept following Goose Creek for about two miles, veered left at the big rock, then right at the bent sycamore, she'd wind up at the Mortons'. At least that was what Mr. Morton's X marks the spot indicated. Maybe she should pray there was only one big rock on this trail. She hefted herself into the saddle, then urged Chessie on.

Mr. Morton had called John aside in the churchyard yesterday to ask his permission for Copper to call on his wife. Mr. Morton didn't attend their church, but he knew where to find John on a Sunday morning. Copper was a little aggravated that he hadn't asked for her directly. John didn't tell her what she could or couldn't do. The man was respectful, though, tipping his hat when John introduced them and answering her questions thoughtfully.

Evidently, Mrs. Morton had lost three babies in the past. Mr. Morton told Copper he had heard from kin about the lady who caught babies on Troublesome Creek and so had come in search of her. It was a smart move on his part and unusual. Most folks still waited until labor was well under way to seek help.

Copper prided herself on making some inroads into that old-fashioned way of doing things. Generally it was another woman who told her of a sister or a daughter or a friend who was newly in the family way. Copper would take the information and start preconfinement visits. People were learning they could trust her, except for the Stills. She could stand in the middle of the week and see both ways to Sunday on that one.

The Stills had a right to be upset. The law, under the direction of a traveling nurse with the state board of health located in Bowling Green, had forced Adie Still to leave her family, after all. But as Copper saw it, the Stills' anger was futile and misdirected. It was not her fault, nor the law's, that Adie had an active, contagious disease. It was nobody's fault that the traveling nurse, backed up by the sheriff, did not believe Adie could be properly quarantined from her family unless she left that family. Adie's husband, Isa, had a reputation and it was not a good one. The only neighbor he had not feuded with over property lines or straying livestock was John.

Naively, Copper had thought she could help the whole family by providing a safe place for Adie until the baby was born. She had imagined herself taking care of Adie and her household until Adie had her baby and regained her strength. So she volunteered the little house and her services, but the Stills were not appreciative. Clannish people, Copper mused. Though they had lived on Troublesome Creek as long as she could remember, she had rarely seen them.

One day in late April when she was shopping at the dry goods store in town, she'd spotted Adie through the store's plate-glass window. Her husband walked ahead of her, a long-handled pistol in a holster on his hip, a row of silver-tipped bullets on the belt. The oldest boy walked shoulder to shoulder with his father. The barrel of the boy's shotgun pointed toward the ground. Adie, with a sack of sugar on her shoulder and a five-pound bucket of lard in her hand, struggled to keep up. A string of stairstep children followed her like ducks. Adie was obviously expectant. She was carrying the baby high, and it stuck out round as a pumpkin on her thin frame. To Copper's practiced eye, the woman looked ill. Of course she had to visit the Still house—and she didn't wait for an invitation.

John had warned her not to get involved with their reclusive neighbors. "The only way to get along with a Still is to stay away from a Still."

"How could I not offer my help to Adie?" Copper had demanded of him.

"No good will come of it," he had responded angrily.

Maybe John was right, but she truly had no choice. Midwifery was her ministry, and she could not pick and choose to whom she would minister. She had discovered her calling while living in Lexington with her first husband. Life in the city was stifling to Copper. Playing the socialite wife of an up-and-coming doctor bored her to tears. She had a beautiful home with servants at her beck and call, lovely gowns, and too many fancy hats and pairs of gloves to count, but she was terribly unhappy. In the midst of such plenty she yearned for more.

Her unhappiness had spilled over into her relationship with Simon. She wanted him to bring her back to the mountains. It seemed to her she'd left herself behind when they married. She'd become like a shell lying useless on the beach—pretty on the outside but empty within.

Thankfully, her husband had seen to the root of her problem and began to involve her in his medical practice. Looking back, Copper could see the finger of God directing her paths. What seemed such a hardship at the time was ultimately what enabled her to minister to the women of Troublesome Creek and beyond. Women like Adie Still. God was so good.

Copper's mind had wandered so that Chessie had to nicker to bring her back. Goodness, they'd almost passed the big rock. The boulder loomed over the trail, casting horse and rider into heavy shadow. She reached out and patted its cool gray surface as she rode by. Alert now, she watched for the next point of interest and guided Chessie to the right just past the bent sycamore.

She soon arrived at the Mortons' simple abode. A drift of smoke from the cabin's chimney told her there was life inside. "Hello," she called out. "Is anyone to home?"

Two women—one young, one middle-aged—looked out around the doorframe.

Copper waved. "Hey, Mrs. Morton. I'm Copper Pelfrey."

She could see her welcome on their faces even before they stepped out onto the porch and invited her in. *Two peas in a pod,* Copper thought, eyeing the women's short statures and ample figures. The ladies had to be mother and daughter.

"Come in. Come in," the younger woman said. "I'm Emerald and this is my mother, Ruby. We're ever so glad to see you."

"I'm glad to be here. I met Mr. Morton on Sunday, and he asked me to come."

Ruby pulled out a chair and indicated for Copper to have a seat at the kitchen table. "You two sit whilst I check my cake."

"Smells wonderful," Copper said.

Ruby cracked the oven door and looked in. "It's a pork cake—my specialty." She laid the oven door down and pulled a pan onto its surface, prodding the center of the batter with a long splinter. "Five more minutes—give or take." The cake went back in the oven, and she closed the door.

"I've never had pork cake," Copper said. "What's in it?"

Ruby wrapped a dishrag around the handle of a coffeepot and poured coffee into waiting mugs. "The main ingredient is a goodly slab of fat salt pork, about a pound. Now you got to chop it real fine and soak it in strong, boiling hot coffee before you add your soda, brown sugar, flour, cinnamon, nutmeg . . . What am I forgetting, Emerald? They's something else."

"The raisins, Mommy. You forgot to say raisins."

"Oh, my aching back," Ruby said. "My head won't hold on to nothing anymore. It's like a sieve." She offered Copper a cream pitcher. "Four cups of stoned raisins or currants. Then you got to dredge the fruit in a little flour, you understand. Dredge them or they'll settle to the bottom."

Copper sipped her cream- and sugar-laced drink. She hadn't liked coffee until she started delivering babies at all hours of the night. Now she appreciated the jolt of energy a cup gave her.

Ruby bustled about, refilling the cups, hustling to the pantry for more sugar, skimming thick yellow cream from a jug of milk.

Maybe Emerald looked like a younger version of her mother, but their temperaments did not seem to match. She didn't lift a finger to help her mother.

"I feel a draft," Emerald said.

Ruby darted out of the room and came back with a knit shawl, which she draped around her daughter's shoulders. "Here," she said, pulling up a low stool, "rest your feet." Back at the stove, Ruby removed the cake from the oven, set the pan on a shelf, and lifted the coffeepot.

Copper laid her hand across her cup. "Thank you, but no more for me."

"Would you druther have tea? Or I could fetch a bucket of fresh water. Why don't I do that?" Ruby took a granite bucket from the top of the food safe. "I'll be right back."

"I'm sorry to put your mother to so much trouble," Copper said.

"Oh, she don't mind. Mommy's bound and determined this baby's going to draw air," Emerald said, patting her belly. "Between her and my husband, they won't let me do a thing. I don't know if that's good or not. I ain't sure what the right thing to do is."

"Maybe I can help," Copper said, "if you want me to."

Tears spurted from Emerald's lustrous green eyes. It was easy to see where she'd gotten her name. "I'd surely appreciate it. I don't know if I can stand to go through another disappointment. I just about lost my mind after burying the third one."

Copper murmured understanding.

Emerald looked up shyly from downcast eyes. Her eyelashes were thick and long. "Sometimes I think it would be better if we put all that to rest. But you know how it is— I don't want to lose my man, either."

Copper understood. It was a point of contention in many a marriage. "Tell me about your other confinements and about your labors."

Through tears Emerald shared her history. She was twenty-one and had delivered three stillborn babes in three years. With Copper's prodding, she was able to relay some specifics: the babies, two girls and a boy, were all full-term with good weights, and there were no outward signs of disease or disability. The only unusual aspect of her deliveries was that her babies were in such a hurry to be born that their feet came first.

*Ah,* Copper thought, *footling breech. That explains it.* "Did you have an attendant?"

"With the last one I did," Emerald said.

"Did she try to turn the baby in the womb? make it come out headfirst?"

"I was too busy to rightly take notice."

"Have you figured your due date?" Copper asked.

"Would you mind to get the calendar?" Emerald pointed to the wall by the door, where a calendar hung from a nail. "I've kept track of my monthlies there."

Copper fetched it.

Emerald turned the pages back. "Looks like I was last ill on January 10."

"So if we count back three months from January 10 . . ." Copper took a small notebook and a pencil from her doctor's kit and made a notation. "We get October 10. Add seven days and looks like your date of confinement is October 17. What a nice month to have a baby."

Ruby hustled into the house with a full bucket of water and set it on the table. "Whew," she said, wiping her forehead with the back of one hand, "I'm out of breath. The least thing wears me out anymore."

Emerald started to rise, but her mother laid a hand on her shoulder.

"Mommy, I wish you'd let me help."

"You'll have plenty to do once you get me a grandbaby." From behind her daughter's chair, Ruby kneaded Emerald's shoulders. "You ain't losing this one if I have any say in the matter."

Emerald reached up and clasped her mother's hands. The simple displays of affection between mother and daughter nearly brought Copper to tears.

Ruby poured goblets of cold water and sliced the still-warm cake. A sudden breeze blew the scent of rain in through the open kitchen door. "Oh, my aching back. I'd best get the laundry off the line."

"Poor Mommy," Emerald said as she and Copper watched Ruby scurry outside, the woven laundry basket against her hip. "I don't know how she keeps a-going like she does."

Copper tasted the cake. It was not to her liking. "It might be best if I put you on my list of rounds. What do you think?"

"Oh, would you? Everybody says you're the best."

"I'll do what I can," Copper replied, mashing a bit of cake with her fork. "Would you be willing to stay at my house when your time draws near?"

"I'll do anything. You can hang me upside down by my toes if need be," Emerald said, her eyes sparkling. "You give me hope."

Copper waited until the light rain dissipated before she started home. She used the time to explain to both women what she thought might have been the cause of Emerald's losses. Emerald seemed relieved, as if just knowing what happened lessened her fear. Copper also left a simple laxative for Emerald comprised of senna, cream of tartar, sulfur, and ginger for easing her piles and to keep her from straining, possibly bringing on an early labor.

Ruby protested when Copper said Emerald should return to light housekeeping, but Copper prevailed. It was a rare illness that justified inactivity. "Just don't do any chores that require you to reach overhead, like hanging clothes on the line," she told Emerald. "You don't want to cause the cord to wrap around the baby's neck."

Copper was at ease as she rode Chessie home. She had delivered breech babies before and was confident she could help Emerald. Chessie didn't even pause when they came to the pool of standing water. Copper figured the mare was anxious to get home, where she would get an extra rasher of sweet timothy hay. She reined in Chessie only once when an unfamiliar dog waddled across their path. It looked like she'd be dropping a litter soon. Copper wondered who she belonged to.

Copper unfolded her handkerchief and let the piece of

pork cake she had secreted there fall to the ground. The dog scarfed it up and wagged her tail for more.

Copper pointed back up the trail. "There's a whole cake back there. You're welcome to it."

The dog cocked her head as if trying to understand. Something in the animal's manner reminded Copper of her old hound Paw-paw. My, she missed that dog. Maybe they should think of getting the children a pet. Lilly had waged a campaign to get one for months. She'd talk to John about it.

The beagle followed Chessie for a short time, then trotted away in response to a sudden piercing whistle.

*Good,* Copper thought. The dog wasn't lost and following her home. She wouldn't mind the children having one pet, but they didn't need a brood of pups.

# 9

SATURDAY! FINALLY! MANDA never thought the day would come. She'd suffered Monday: wash day; Tuesday: ironing; Wednesday: cleaning—including the kitchen and sickroom windows—ugh; Thursday: mending; Friday: baking light bread, pies, and a cake. And now it was glorious Saturday. It was her free day, and she was on her way to town with Dimmert. In her pocket was a scrap of dress material, and she was set on finding the right buttons to match it at Coomb's Dry Goods.

Wednesday's post had brought a letter addressed just to her from Darcy, who lived in Eddyville, Kentucky. She couldn't remember ever getting a piece of mail addressed singly to her. It made her feel special. The letter was wonderful enough, but the little bit of material enfolded in its pages made it even better. Darcy would make a dress for her after Manda mailed back a pattern and buttons. Manda was delighted.

Of all the Whitt sisters, and there were many, Darcy was the one who had made it, as far as Manda was concerned. Darcy was a dressmaker and owned her own shop. She had a house at the edge of town—a solid brick house with flower boxes at the windows. She had two full-time employees at the dress shop and a woman who came to her home to care for her little son, clean her house, and cook her supper. Manda could not imagine the freedom of such a life: no scrubbing floors on hands and knees, no endless tending of stoves, no hauling buckets of water, no coddling other women's children.

"Sure was good you hearing from Darcy," Dimmert said, flicking the horse's reins and startling her out of her reverie.

"Yes," Manda said. "I brought the letter with me. Do you want me to read it aloud?"

"Maybe just the high points," Dimmert said.

Manda took the missive from her linen poke and slid it from the envelope. Since Dimmert couldn't read, she was happy to share it with him.

"The first part talks about the baby, how he is walking well now and has most all his teeth. Then she says the shop is doing good; 'business is booming' is exactly how she puts it."

"Booming," Dimmert said. "That does sound good."

"She bought a new living room suite. It's overstuffed."

Manda looked at Dimmert. "What do you think that means—overstuffed?"

"Sounds like me after one of Cara's Sunday dinners. I reckon it means it hurts to sit on it."

Manda shared a laugh with her brother. "Can't you just see a big old sofa popping its buttons all over the room?"

Dimmert whooped. "You're going to make me drive off the road, Sis."

A load of wagon wheels shifted in the bed of the wagon, clicking and clacking when the wagon hit a hole in the road.

"You're supposed to go around the chunk holes."

"Your fault," he said, wiping his eyes on the sleeve of his shirt. "You got me laughing so hard I can't see to drive."

"Want me to take the reins?" she said hopefully.

"Nah. How would that look? My sister driving this load of wheels into town? Why, folks would think you made them instead of me."

"So? What if they did?"

"Don't get too full of yourself. We don't want you being overstuffed."

That set them to laughing again.

They were nearly to town before Dimmert sobered and asked, "Does Darcy say anything about her husband?"

Manda slid page one behind page two. She ran her finger down the filmy onionskin stationery. "It's right near the end." She hated to put words to the nightmare that attached itself to Darcy's dream like a tick on a dog. "Darcy writes that Henry is doing as best he can. He has lost weight. The prison food does not agree with him. And he has blisters on top of blisters from swinging a sledgehammer day after day."

"Are we supposed to feel sorrow for him?" Dimmert asked. "He has got to make restitution one way or another for what he done. Breaking big rocks into little rocks is a start."

Manda folded the fancy paper and stuck it back in the envelope. "Darcy isn't fishing for sympathy. She says, 'Don't say anything about my Henry unless someone asks.' You asked, Dimm."

"Well, Darcy is family, and I do feel pity for her and her baby. But as for her husband—nary a whit."

Manda put the letter away and leaned back against the wagon seat. It was warm from the sun. "I didn't live here when the accident happened. So all I know is what I've gathered from listening to others. Ace and Dance don't talk about it."

"*Accident* is putting it kindly. I guess that's how Darcy chooses to see it; otherwise she couldn't live with herself."

A buggy driven much too fast overtook them and whizzed by on the right side. Manda dodged a rock that was churned up by the buggy's wheels. It hit the seat and bounced back to the road.

Dimmert threw out his arm as if he could protect her in hindsight. "You okay?"

Manda shivered. *That's just how quick your life could take a turn for the worse.* "So what do you think happened that day at the sweetwater run? I've never heard you talk about it."

"I guess I shouldn't judge Darcy's husband. I wasn't there when it happened either," Dimm said in his slow and thoughtful way. "But I don't think Henry Thomas cleaving Ace Shelton's head with a tomahawk was ary fluke of nature."

"Having an opinion is not the same as judging someone, is it?"

"That's one for the preacher to answer," Dimmert said.

Manda turned on the bench until she could see her brother. "I'd really like to know what you think."

Dimmert's face turned pensive. "I had a little dealing with the lawyer Henry Thomas when I had my brush with the law. I think Henry was hatching his plans even then. He was lusting for Whitt land, and he aimed to get it any way he could."

"How do you mean?"

Dimm pulled over to the side of the road. Laying the reins across his knee, he counted off his fingers as he talked. "Number one: get me sent to prison. Like he did by not taking proper care of my case, so's he could trick Cara out of my land. Number two: marry Darcy Mae and steal her inheritance from our dying mammaw. Number three: slip up to the sweetwater run like a sheep-killing dog and *accidentally* bash Dance's husband's head in. Dance would be no match for a slick Willie like Henry. He'd've got her acreage by hook or by crook once Ace was out of the picture." He whisked his hands together with a loud slap. "Wham, bam—line up the lambs."

Startled by the loud noise, Manda jumped. "Don't seem like the land handed down by our ancestors is valuable enough to drive a man to all that evil."

Dimmert gave her a long, studying look. "There ain't nothing but the land." From where they sat, they could stare off into the distance at layer upon layer of fog-shrouded mountains. "God ain't making any more of this as far as I know." He flicked the reins and they were on the road again. "Where you heading to this morning?"

"Drop me off at the dry goods store. I'm looking at patterns and also picking up some items from Cara's list."

"Done," Dimmert said, pulling in front of Coomb's store. "You want to walk down to the livery stable after your shopping? I hope to sell all these wheels by morning's end."

Manda hopped down from the wagon. "Sounds good."

"Leave your parcels here and we'll pick them up on the way back," Dimm said as he drove off, leaving Manda to her pleasure.

Mr. Coomb was out front polishing the store's plate-glass window. *Coomb's Dry Goods and Apothecary* was etched across the glass in flowing black script. Underneath in small print was *If we don't have it, you don't need it.*

"Morning," Manda said as she crossed behind him.

Mr. Coomb laid his cloth aside and hurried to the door, which he opened with a flourish. "Good morning, Miss Whitt. Beautiful day."

"That it is," Manda murmured and stepped inside. She loved the feeling of plenty emanating from the store shelves and cases. Slowly she wandered up and down the aisles, stopping now and then to finger a bolt of cloth or to drool over a display of confections behind the glassed-in candy case. She could picture Darcy doing this daily. What must it be like to have such freedom? Dimmert's feelings aside, Manda would trade every mountain on Troublesome Creek to live in a proper city. She was sure she would never tire of shopping.

"Could I help you find something?" a store clerk asked.

"Oh," Manda said with a sigh, "I'm just taking it all in."

"We got some new patterns from New York City just this week," the salesclerk said, steering Manda toward the notions display and a rack of patterns. "These are up-to-the-minute," she said discreetly as if she were telling Manda a secret meant for her ears alone. "I hear a modified bustle is the latest necessity."

Like Manda didn't know all about braided wire bustles and Empire corsets and Hygeia bust forms. She probably studied more fashion magazines in one month's time than this clerk had ever seen. Manda took Cara's mundane list from her pocket and handed it to the clerk. "Could you get these things for me? I'll be picking out buttons for a new frock."

*Frock*—that sounded like something Rose Feathergay would wear.

"Certainly," the young woman said, pulling out a long drawer containing cards of snaps and buttons and fabric frogs. "Let me know if I can assist."

Manda was glad when the saleswoman bustled away leaving her to enjoy the sudden wealth at her fingertips: pearl buttons and jet buttons and nickel-size blue buttons shaped like daisies among dozens of other fasteners. Manda took two cards of buttons from the drawer and held them up to the light. The pearl buttons were pretty and the least expensive, but the daisies . . . oh my. Ten cents for a card of eight—that was much more than she had expected to pay, but she simply had to have them.

A wire rack of Standard Designer patterns squeaked when she turned it. She really should have picked the pattern before selecting the buttons. Now she would have to find a dress to fit the notions instead of the other way round.

She selected one envelope from the dozens of offerings. The pattern was of a ladies' blouse waist over a five-gored bell skirt. The blouse was closed with hooks and eyes but needed six buttons for embellishment. Perfect. The pattern cost twenty cents and was cut in eight sizes from thirty-two to forty inches bust measure. According to the instructions on the back of the envelope, Darcy would need four and three-eighths yards of material for a dress Manda's size. Darcy had not said how much dress goods she had, but Manda supposed it would not be a problem.

"Have you decided?" The pesky clerk popped up again, ruining Manda's concentration.

"Almost," she said.

The bell over the door tinkled. The clerk hurried off.

Manda lingered over a display case of women's products including Milk Weed Cream, Mennen's borated talcum, and Madame Rowley's Face Glove. *What a creepy contraption,* Manda thought. Madame Rowley's toilet mask was held in place with a series of elastic bands. The printing on the box stated the face glove, if worn three times a week, was guaranteed by eminent physicians and scientists to remove wrinkles and brown spots on the face without the injurious effects of cosmetics. Manda studied her reflection in a counter mirror. Maybe she should think about it.

There were so many powders and potions, it was hard to decide on one. Her eyes lit on the one thing she really needed, a self-heating hair curler. It would be worth every penny of the one-dollar ticket.

"Could I show you something?" the clerk asked, walking behind the case and sliding the heavy glass door open. "Maybe some Correll's Goat Milk Soap? I personally use the crème oatmeal toilet bar—guaranteed to lighten the complexion."

"Might I see the curling iron?" Manda calculated the price of the curler along with her buttons and the pattern. She should have just enough.

"This is nice." The clerk set the shiny curling rod on top of the case. "You can get it in the silver for just two dollars."

"I thought the tag said one dollar."

"Oh, that's if you buy the nickel finish. I'm sure you'd want the silver." The woman put a pretty leatherette case with a velvet lining alongside the curling iron. "The case is only one dollar more."

Three dollars? The silver was nice, though. Manda sighed. Maybe next time. She handed her pattern and packet of buttons to the clerk. "I'll just take these for now." Manda patted her upper lip with her index finger as she stared down into the case. "And give me one bar of the oatmeal soap."

Manda felt light as air when she stepped out the door onto the wooden sidewalk. She'd left Cara's order for later pickup but she carried hers, swinging the paper bag against her skirts. If no one had been watching, she would have skipped, but the town was bustling with folks doing their weekly shopping.

In front of the barbershop, she saw a couple of ladies she knew from church and stopped to chat, which led to showing off her purchases.

"My," one of the ladies exclaimed, "I don't know when I've seen a prettier button."

"What are you looking for today?" Manda asked.

"Just stocking the pantry," one said. "Nothing near as nice as what you bought."

"A new broom," the other said. "Mine's near worn to a nub."

"I saw some in the window of the hardware store," Manda said. "See you all tomorrow?"

"Certainly," one of the women said. "See you in church."

The livery station where Dimmert was selling his wares was on the outskirts of town. She walked on. Just across the street in front of the hotel, a crowd was forming. A little boy danced a jig as a familiar voice filled the air—soaring and dipping like a bird on the wing. She paused to listen. "Come All Ye Fair and Tender Ladies," surely one of her favorites. How often did she and her sisters sing that tender tune of young love and dire warning? In a flash the song carried her right back to her childhood before the death of her mother turned things wrong.

Mommy hadn't been one to cuddle and spoil her children. She had been a woman of few words and could go days without uttering an unnecessary one. But on hot summer nights after a supper of lard on biscuits or soup beans from the bottom of the pot, Mommy's fine voice would soften the edges of their hunger. She would start a song, and soon the girls would join in harmonizing and singing parts. They had loved "Barbara Allen" and "Pretty Polly," "Mary of the Wild Moors" and "The Wayfaring Stranger."

And "Tender Ladies," of course. Mommy had sung those words like a promise: "Love is handsome. Love is charming. Love is beauty while it's new. Love grows old. Love grows colder and fades away like morning dew."

Mommy had had her reasons to be a little jaded by love's sweet promise, Manda suspected.

Manda crossed the street. It was the middling man. Manda knew it before the crowd dispersed, pitching change in a felt hat at his feet. She watched as he tucked a fiddle in a black case before pocketing the coins. Her heart trilled. Any moment now he might notice her and say hello. Instead, he slicked back his hair, stuck the wide-brimmed hat on his head, and quick as a wink disappeared around the side of the building.

Manda couldn't believe it. She'd lost her chance.

Heart speeding up, she brushed past the bench where he had been sitting and glanced down the alleyway between the hotel and the grocery store next door. Two men and a dog with a long, skinny tail stood halfway down the alley, just past an overflowing trash bin. After a moment's bickering, money and liquor changed hands. *White mule,* Manda thought, seeing what looked clear as springwater in the quart jar the middling man held. Nobody'd pay money for water. The other man elbowed the middling man, and he looked up the alley, catching her watching. Her heart thumped, beating painfully against her rib cage.

She ducked around the corner and nearly ran across the street. She kept glancing over her shoulder as she hurried along the slatted wooden sidewalk, but nobody followed. Her heart didn't settle until she neared the livery station, where she could see several men selling wares from the beds of wagons: ax handles and one-eyed hoes and gallon jars of molasses. She'd just spotted Dimmert and started his way when she felt a presence close as a shadow behind her.

"Where you going in such a hurry, good-looking?" the middling man said, stepping around to block her path. "I been watching you watching me."

Manda didn't know whether to run or pass out. Maybe run and then pass out. It was his eyes that stopped her from doing either. Lightning seemed to leap from them and send teasing sparks up and down her arms. "I-I um . . ."

"What's your name, little lady?"

Manda would have gladly told him, but at that moment she didn't rightly know.

With one finger he traced the line of her jaw. "I bet it's right pretty. A pretty girl's bound to have a pretty name." His breath smelled like liquor, too bright and perilous.

Manda went weak in the knees. She closed her eyes and reached out a hand to steady herself against a lamppost. When she opened them, he was gone.

She was home and eating supper before she realized that somewhere along the way she had taken leave of her shopping. Somehow it no longer seemed important. All that mattered was the kindling heat along the set of her jaw where the middling man had left his mark. Over and over her hand traced what his had mapped. She had never felt so beautiful.

# 10

SOMETIMES LILLY DIDN'T know why she picked Kate Jasper for her best friend. Kate never wanted to do anything but play with Mazy and Molly. Right now she was trying to braid Molly's wispy hair while Mazy waited her turn. Lilly got more than enough of that every day.

"Don't you want to go catch crawdads?" Lilly asked.

"No." Kate sighed. "I've told you a thousand times. Besides, they're vile."

"They are not. You just think that because they build their houses out of mud."

"Stands to reason if they live in mud houses, they have to be dirty. We could go down to the creek, though. We could play house on the big, flat rock. I'll be the mother and you can be the father. Mazy and Molly can be our babies."

Lilly plopped down on the porch steps with her back to her friend. She rested her elbows on her knees. She wanted to walk along the creek in the worst way. She'd been looking forward to showing Kate the rock wall where she had first seen the beagle, not to mention Tern Still. A couple of times after supper she'd gone to the wall with scraps for the dog, who was always hungry, but she'd not seen Tern again.

"We played house last time. It's my turn to pick what we do."

"Pick all you want," Kate said, "but I'm not touching any disgusting crawdads."

"Lilly," her mother called from the kitchen, "could you come here a minute?"

Lilly rolled her eyes, but she got up. "What?" she said when she got inside.

"You're not treating your guest very nicely," Mama said, cupping Lilly's chin in her hand. "I'm very disappointed in you."

"But, Mama—"

"No buts. You go out there and apologize to Kate."

Lilly could feel tears damming up behind her eyes. "Why can't I—?"

Mama's hand tightened on Lilly's chin. "Right. This. Minute."

When Lilly turned, she could see her friend's round, freckled face pushed up against the screen. "I'm sorry, Kate," she said before she even opened the door. "We'll play house if you want."

"Can we take Molly and Mazy?" Kate asked.

"Sure. They can be the babies and you can be the mother." Lilly remembered to close the screen door gently. "I'll be the father off catching crawdads for supper."

Kate jumped up and down. "Oh, good. Molly can be the baby girl, and Mazy can be the boy."

Lilly hoisted Molly to her hip.

Kate took Mazy's hand. "We'll need a cook pot," she chattered, "and a fishing pole. What'll you use for bait?"

"I know just the thing," Lilly said. "We'll stop by the corncrib for an ear, and we can get a pot from the shed. This will be fun."

Kate stuck out her tongue. "Told you."

Lilly blew a raspberry against Molly's neck. Molly laughed.

The day had turned out sticky and hot, but it was cool there on the flat rock overhung by the plate-size leaves of a sycamore tree.

Kate settled down, arranging the stash of old kitchenware Lilly kept handy for making mud pies. "Find a piece of shale," she bossed Lilly, "and mark off the rooms."

Finding the shale was easy enough, but marking the rooms was another matter. "This rock isn't big enough for rooms. It's only big enough for a kitchen."

Kate stood in the middle of the rock and looked around. "Well, let's pretend it is. Mark it off exact—we need a kitchen, a parlor, and two bedrooms."

Lilly scraped a line straight down the middle of the rock with the thin, sharp shale, then dissected the line. There, four rooms. "Nobody has a parlor on Troublesome Creek."

"My granny does."

"Your granny doesn't live on Troublesome."

"You know what your problem is? You don't have any mind's eye."

"I do too have a mind's eye."

"Do not," Kate replied, pointing to a corner of the kitchen. "Mark a *P* here. We have to have a pantry."

Lilly wanted to toss the piece of shale into the creek, but she scribed a big *P* instead. Despite herself, she always got caught up in Kate's games.

"Now, husband," Kate said, "our children are hungry. We must think of dinner."

"Do our children have names?"

"I think Amelia for Molly and August for Mazy. Those are my favorite names."

"Do I get a say?" Lilly asked.

"No, silly, you're the husband." Kate made like she was tying an apron around her neck. Reaching up, she pulled four leaves from a low-hanging sycamore branch. She put them neatly on the rock as if she set a table. "Children," she said to August and Amelia, "you need to busy yourself in the other room. Mommy is cooking dinner."

Lilly stood there for a minute wondering how Kate would keep Molly and Mazy from tearing up the plates, but that wasn't her problem. She was going fishing. With the heel of one hand, she shelled a few kernels of corn and then went looking for a crawdad hole. She found a fine, two-story mud stack near the creek bank, but she couldn't bring herself to tear it down. Surely she could find one that the raccoons had already torn the top off of. Raccoons loved crawdads.

Just a few steps away she found what she was looking for. She crouched and looked down the tower. Two beady black eyes stared back at her. Sensing a threat, the crawdad waved his claws and twitched his antennae. Lilly dropped a piece of corn into the hole. If a crawdad could look surprised, this one did. Lilly didn't know if crawdads actually ate corn, but she knew it piqued their curiosity.

"Manna from heaven." Lilly stuck another kernel near the top of the hole. Then she sat, positioning herself so she could keep an eye on her sisters, and waited. It took a lot of patience to catch a crawdad. She might not have a good imagination, but she had an abundance of patience. Kate was the baby of her family, so she probably didn't have any. It took babies to teach you endurance. Sticky, crying, spitting-up, smelly babies. She liked being around them, though.

Aha! Mr. Crawdad's antennae poked into daylight. Lilly pounced. She pinched him right behind his head and lifted him out. "Oh, you're a fine one."

"Look, honey," she said to her wife. "I caught a fat fish for our supper."

"Wonderful, husband," Kate said. "Tear his head off and I'll cook him."

"Kate Jasper, I will not tear this crawdad's head off."

"Well, I can't bear to put him in the skillet with those eyes staring at me," Kate said.

"I know—let's pretend I take his head off."

"Good idea. Now wash up for supper. I've fixed potatoes your favorite way."

Lilly went and put the crawdad back down his hole, dropping a few more kernels in his nest to thank him for his trouble. Back at the rock, she made hand-washing motions. Mazy and Molly were napping, curled up on the rock, tucked together like kittens.

"Oh, look, wife," Lilly said. "Our babies are asleep."

"I know," Kate said. "It's my favorite time of the day."

"Prithee hand me the pot and I will fetch some water."

"Speak English, Lilly."

"*Prithee* is English. It's a word I'm learning. It's old-fashioned, but I like the sound it makes, kind of like a bird's call. *Prithee* means—"

Kate cut her off. "Sounds like something my granny would say."

"Yeah, while sitting in her parlor."

Kate stirred pretend food in the skillet. She shook the spoon in Lilly's face. "Stop poking fun at me."

"I'm hungry," Lilly said. "We should have brought some real food."

"Me too," Kate said. "Eating air doesn't keep my belly from grumbling."

"Manda made spice cake this morning. I'll go get some. You keep a close eye on Molly and Mazy."

"You mean August and Amelia?"

"Whoever. Just don't let them fall in the creek."

Lilly brought back four pieces of cake wrapped in a dish towel and a pint jar of sweet milk. She tickled her sleeping sisters' cheeks with a blade of grass. "Wake up, sleepyheads. I brought you a treat."

Kate was nearly finished with her cake when she cried out, "My tooth hurts."

"Let me see."

Kate opened her mouth wide for Lilly. "Ow, that makes it worse."

Lilly picked up the towel and the milk jar. "Let's all go tell Mama."

"Oh, sweetie," Mama said when she saw the tears in Kate's eyes, "I'm sorry you're hurting. I've got something to soothe the pain."

"I just want to go home." Kate sobbed.

Mama tapped her foot against the floor. She was studying what to do. "Remy and Manda are both gone, so I can't take you right now."

"I can take her," Lilly said. "I can ride her home on Chessie."

"Why, of course you can," Mama said. "Go put a bridle on Chessie while I doctor Kate."

Lilly's heart leaped. She often rode Chessie, but she'd never been allowed to take her out of the barnyard. She scooted out the door before Mama could change her mind.

When Lilly rode bareback to the porch, Kate was standing

there with a red bandanna looped around her chin. It was tied in a knot on top of her head.

Mama hefted Kate up behind. "Lay your cheek against Lilly's back. That will help to keep the flannel warm."

Mama handed Lilly a tiny brown bottle. "Put this in your pocket and give it to Mrs. Jasper. Tell her to use the dropper sparingly and to keep a warm flannel on Kate's cheek. The bandanna will keep it in place." Mama patted Kate's knee. "Does it feel better?"

Lilly could feel the nod of Kate's head against her shoulder. Kate smelled like cloves.

"Be careful, Lilly. Hold tight to the reins and come straight home."

Lilly kept Chessie going slow, slow, slow. She was afraid Kate would bounce right off onto the forest floor. It was not a far piece to the Jaspers'—just through the woods and around the bend and straight on past the church where Kate's father preached. Brother Jasper had baptized Lilly and fourteen other people in the river last fall. That was a powerful thing, Lilly thought—washing folks white as snow. She loved knowing she belonged to Jesus now.

She felt a smidgen of shame to be so happy riding Chessie when her friend was feeling poorly, holding on to her for dear life. But she was doing a good deed. It relieved her guilt to think about it that way. Poor Kate. Lilly would never be cross with her again.

Mrs. Jasper was in the garden when they rode up. She dropped her hoe and hurried to Chessie's side. "Whatever is the matter, baby?" she said to Kate as she lifted her down.

"She has a toothache. Mama sent some soothing medicine. She said be spare with the drops and keep a warm flannel on Kate's cheek."

Mrs. Jasper thanked Lilly and asked her to come in, but Lilly had to get back. "I hope you feel better soon, Kate."

Later that day after her bedtime, Lilly went to the kitchen for a drink. Through the screen door, she could see her mother and Daddy John sitting on the top porch step with their heads together. That gave her such a warm and safe feeling. She didn't mean to eavesdrop, but it was hard not to listen when you heard your own name in someone else's conversation. Mama told Daddy about Lilly taking Kate home.

"I suddenly realized how capable she is," Mama said.

"And smart as a whip," Daddy said.

"Our little girl is growing up."

"Maybe we could put a rock on her head," Daddy teased.

Lilly had to clamp her mouth shut to keep from giggling. She wanted to hear the rest of the conversation.

"It makes me sad. I can't bear to think about her going to Alice's in July, much less leaving home for good someday. I'm really thinking of not letting her go. I just don't feel at ease about her traveling alone."

Lilly almost dropped her water cup. She thought her trip to Lexington was settled.

Daddy put his arm around Mama's shoulders. "She'll be

all right. It's not like she has to change trains. It's a straight shot. You mustn't hold her back."

"I guess," Mama said. "Mrs. Jasper said she would see her safely on the right train. She and Kate will be taking the same coach to the depot and then board a different train for a visit with her mother. Their train will leave after Lilly's."

"Sounds like a plan. Lilly will love the adventure. And you know Alice will be right there waiting for her." Daddy gave Mama a hug. "Now let's get to bed. Morning comes early."

Lilly left her cup on the table and hurried back to her room. She was so excited thinking of her trip, she thought she wouldn't be able to sleep. But the harmony of the twins' breathing soon lulled her, and she drifted off to dream of trains and chocolate ice cream and circus wagons.

# 11

ON TIPTOE, MANDA flicked a feather duster over the top of a bookcase. It was Wednesday—again. It seemed to her like it was always Wednesday, her least favorite day of the week. God should have put Saturday smack in the middle instead of another dreadful cleaning day. Manda's shoulders tightened. She could hear Miss Remy coming down the hall from the invalid room. She could tell it was her from the way she dragged one foot when she didn't use her crutch. That sound put Manda's teeth on edge, irritating as a mockingbird's trill after midnight.

Manda stepped up a rung on the four-step utility ladder and let the duster fly. Her eyes stung from the grit and her nose twitched. She sneezed so hard the ladder tipped over. She plopped on her fanny right at Miss Remy's feet.

"Give me that there foo-frau." Remy reached for the duster. "Taint the way to do a decent job."

Despite the hitch in her giddyup, Remy stalked to the door. Each room of the Pelfreys' house had a door opening onto a wraparound porch. Remy fairly flung this one open. Manda watched her beat the feather duster against a post. A little blast of dust sailed out into the yard. Back inside, she closed the door behind her.

"Fotch me down them purties," she said, indicating the chocolate set Miz Copper kept atop the bookcase, safe from little hands.

Manda climbed the ladder and carefully handed down each cup and saucer and the tall pitcher with attached lid of the chocolate service. Remy set each piece on a side table. Manda stood and waited.

"Well, get down," Remy said. "Go fetch a clean rag and the furniture polish, if ye even know where they be."

Manda knew exactly where the polish was kept, and she knew where the rags were. Wasn't she the one who washed, dried, and folded them each Monday? She'd just hoped to make the dusting go faster today. That's all. What was the harm?

Back on the ladder, she tipped the bottle of polish and poured a smallish amount of oily, red liquid onto her cloth.

Below her, Remy flicked feathers over the delicate rose-patterned chocolate pot. "See, this here's for breakables.

116

You cain't get a shine on furniture withouten you use some elbow grease."

"That chocolate set sure is pretty, but I've never seen it used."

"Purty carried this all the way from Lexington and never broke a piece." Remy handed up a saucer, then a cup. "It belonged to Lilly Gray's grandmother Corbett. It's to be passed down to her. She's her grandmother's namesake."

The thought of owning something that once belonged to her grandmother fanned a little heartache. Dance took ownership of all their mammaw Whitt's things when Mammaw passed away. All the dishes and handmade quilts and embroidered pillowcases were locked up in the steamer trunk that Dance kept at the foot of her bed. The trunk had belonged to Mammaw too. Manda didn't care so much about those things, but she loved the miniature coal-oil lamp and chimney that Mammaw lit in the kitchen window each night. She said it was a light against the dark in case her grandchildren lost their way. The one time Manda got brave enough to ask Dimmert about what gave Dance the right, he said they were just things. He said Mammaw meant a lot to Dance. That didn't make Manda feel any better. Someday when she had a kitchen window of her own, she would ask Dance if she could have the little lamp.

The top shelf of the bookcase gleamed when Manda positioned the pretties just as they had been. *Such a waste of time. Nobody can even see up there,* she thought as she stepped down a rung to reach the first row of books. She dusted each cover, polished each shelf, and put the books back in alphabetical order. She wasn't sure Miss Remy could read well enough to know if they were out of place, but she wasn't taking any chances.

Remy flitted in and out of the room like she was in charge of the bookcase and Manda might miss a spot.

"Can I ask you something?" Manda said when Remy stood staring at her.

"If ye can see fit to talk and work at the same time," Remy said.

Manda sloshed a jag more polish on her rag. Sometimes Miss Remy was ill as a red hornet. "Why do you call Miz Copper Purty?"

Remy didn't answer right off, as if she had to turn the question over in her mind a few times first. But when she did, the answer caught Manda by surprise. "Because she is, I reckon." Remy walked to the door and reached for the knob before she stopped and turned back. "I ain't never knowed a truer person than Purty. She don't try to take on airs, don't try to polish nothing. That's what makes her purty—inside and out."

Manda stood on the bottom rung of the ladder for the longest time after Remy left. The dust rag hung limply from her hand. That was the first real conversation they'd ever had. Maybe Manda needed to ask more questions.

After the bookcase was finished, Manda began to clean the wood floor with Murphy Oil Soap. Midjob she stopped and sat back on her heels to admire her progress. The dark wood floor gleamed where the sun shone in from the floor-to-ceiling windows. Mr. John had torn down an old barn and laid the floor with the deeply grained siding. She liked how he had combined the old with the new. The many-paned windows were like nothing she had ever seen. There were no curtains, so it was like inviting the outside in. The room had a big fireplace, but it also had a Warm Morning stove so they didn't have to depend on the fireplace for heat in the dead of winter. This was the only place Manda had ever lived where it was warm all the time.

Copper looked in from the kitchen doorway. "That floor never looked so good. I don't know what I'd do without your help."

Manda felt her face flush with pleasure. "Thank you." She bent to her task again, dipping the floor rag in the bucket and wringing it out until it was nearly dry. She wiped back and forth in steady strokes so the wood wouldn't streak.

"Hold on a second," Copper said. She left and returned with a piece of ratty toweling, which she folded and handed to Manda. "Tuck this under your knees. It will ease them and take the strain off your lower back."

That was so like Miz Copper, Manda thought. She was always thinking of others. "It sure is quiet since Tillie and the baby left."

"Poor Abe thought he was going to starve to death without Tillie standing at his stove, but she was more than ready to go home. I need to check on her tomorrow."

"I'm glad not to be cooking for Abe no more," Manda said. "For a man too skinny to make a shadow, he sure could pack it away."

"He could that." Copper laughed. "When you're finished with the floor, why don't you take a breather? The new *Woman's Home Companion* came in the mail yesterday. I put it aside for you."

Manda looked up from hands and knees. "What about dinner?"

"Well, John's gone, so we don't need to cook at noon. I'll feed the kids biscuits and apple butter. We'll have rabbit for supper. I dressed two this morning after I milked. They're in the springhouse in the meat keeper."

"What do you want to go with it?"

"How about smashed potatoes and a wilted salad? We've got more lettuce than I know what to do with—hence the rabbits. They can't get enough of my garden."

"Will Mr. John be back?"

"Yes, he's just over to Dimmert's. They're building a new wagon. Ours is giving down."

"Sounds good to me."

Miz Copper got a gleam in her eye. "You know what would be fun? We could fix a picnic supper and carry it over to the Whitts'."

Manda followed her gaze to the clock on the mantel.

"It's eleven now, so we have plenty of time. If you start frying the rabbit about two o'clock, we can finish up and be over there before Cara starts her supper."

Miz Copper's enthusiasm was contagious. She had the best ideas.

"I left the magazine in the basket by the corner cupboard.

I'll just go check on the children; then I think I'll bake a pie. Dimmert always loved my pies."

Manda split two biscuits and spread them thickly with apple butter. Miz Copper never minded how much she ate. She always acted like there was plenty enough to go around with some left over. Unlike her stepmother. Nora knew the exact number of eggs in the basket and the level of milk in the jug. At Nora's table, if Manda dared to reach for seconds, Nora would fix her with a stare. Manda had probably gained ten pounds since she started working for the Pelfreys. She wrapped the buttered biscuits in waxed paper and stuck them in her linen poke along with the new periodical and a jar for springwater.

Manda felt free as a bird as she hiked up Spare Mountain. She had plenty of time to go to her favorite spot and read. About halfway there, she detoured from the narrow cow path to cross a meadow to the spring. Years ago Ace had discovered the spring and dubbed it sweetwater run. It had the sweetest, coldest water you ever tasted. She wasn't supposed to know this, but Ace used to make corn liquor with that water. Of course that was before Ace was saved. Thinking of Ace made her feel sorrowful. She couldn't help but feel pity for the way he seized up sometimes. He'd be perfectly fine one minute, then lock up like a pair of rusty pliers before falling flat out on the ground.

She knelt by the rocky aperture where the clear mountain water bubbled out in a steady stream and half filled the fruit jar. After taking a long draught from the lip of the jar, she twisted the zinc lid in place. She wasn't going to waste her precious time thinking about sad things. Anyhow, Ace never let his circumstance get in his way. He traveled hither and yon on that old mule Pancake, visiting the sick, sitting up at all-night wakes, and such. The old mule was really Dimmert's, but he had loaned it to his brother-in-law so Ace would have safe transportation. If Ace happened to fall from the saddle, Pancake would stop dead in his tracks and wait. Ace would recover directly and climb back on, dusting his hat, like nothing out of the ordinary had happened. Manda had seen it twice. Once on the way to town with Miz Copper and once heading to church with Dimm and Cara. Miz Copper told her the best thing to do was stay with Ace and make sure he didn't swallow his tongue. Manda didn't know if she could do that or not, but she guessed she would try.

Dimmert and Cara were over to the Sheltons' most every day, helping. One of the Sheltons' kids—Merky—lived with them. She had lived with Cara after her father was hurt and now she was partial to Cara. Dance was good to let her stay. Maybe she did have a spark of kindness. Cara said Dance was much stronger since Ace got mostly well. Manda was glad of that. Even though she aggravated Manda, Dance was her sister.

Manda sat on a fallen tree limb and took another drink of water. She wished she knew what Darcy was doing today. It was sure to be something industrious, something worthwhile. Right before she got her job with the Pelfreys, she had visited her sister in the city. She should have stayed. Darcy had asked her to. As soon as the time was right, she would go back. She needed to stay out of Coomb's Dry Goods, though, or she'd wind up spending the money she had saved for a train ticket. She was determined to follow Darcy's example and be independent just like the dashing Rose Feathergay.

Maybe she'd just sit here and read. An auburn-haired beauty in a low-cut gown graced the cover of *Woman's Home Companion*. Her complexion was flawless. Manda wondered if she used oatmeal toilet soap. She would have herself, but she'd lost the soap along with her pattern and her buttons. That was sure a waste of hard-earned money.

Manda flipped through the pages looking for a serial to read. She missed Rose and her exciting life. A sharp sting in the tender crease of her inner arm caused her to cry out in pain. She unbuttoned her bodice and freed one arm, turning the sleeve inside out. A sweat bee was caught in the sleeve. His tiny body thrummed with anger. Manda didn't know if he could sting again or not. She flicked the bee away. A red welt formed where the stinger went in.

How could it hurt so badly when the sweat bee was so tiny? Holding her blouse together, she went back to the spring and laid her arm under the steady, icy flow. The water felt so good, she bathed her face and neck, letting the water trickle down her chest. Comforted, she picked up the hem of her skirt to dry her face. A daddy longlegs meandered up her skirt as if he were surveying a plot of land. She plucked him off by one of his appendages, being careful not to touch the second-longest pair, and watched to see in which direction he would point with his longest leg. It was a known fact that a daddy longlegs held in such a way would indicate where to find the cows. Not that she needed to go get the cows, or cow as the case may be . . .

The spider twitched and dropped back onto her skirt, leaving one leg pinched between her fingers. She shook her skirts and the daddy longlegs ambled away, bobbing up and down on the seven limbs he had left. The one that was missing would grow back. Even though daddy longlegs didn't bite, Manda was not happy to be in this buggy place. Buttoning her blouse, she went back to the fallen limb to gather her things. She still could make it to the ledge and read for a few more minutes.

As she reached for the magazine, an eerie feeling came over her. Her spine prickled. She looked off into the forest that bordered the small meadow but saw nothing untoward. A gust of wind set the top of the trees to dancing, and a dark cloud scuttled across the sun. Chilled, she grabbed the linen poke and dropped the water jug in, uncaring if it crushed her biscuits. Halfway across the meadow, she remembered the *Woman's Home Companion*. She would have to go back—the magazine didn't belong to her.

She decided she was being silly. Probably a bear was searching for berries in the woods or maybe a wampus cat was stalking a rabbit or some other prey. Neither would be hunting her. What would Rose Feathergay do in such a situation? Why, she'd make some noise and march right back.

Manda decided to whistle. It wasn't smart to come upon a bear without giving fair warning. She puckered up her lips like she was eating green persimmons, but she managed only a trifling note. You couldn't scare a fodder mouse with that. What she needed was something to starch her backbone. A song from church came to mind. Swinging her arms, she stalked back toward the spring singing loud enough to make Rose Feathergay proud. "'I love the Lord; He heard my cries, and pitied every groan; long as I live, when troubles rise, I'll hasten to His throne. I love the Lord: He bowed His ear, and chased my griefs . . .'"

She couldn't rightly remember the rest of the second verse, but that was okay because the fallen limb was just a step away. She'd left the magazine open to a story, but the wind had blown it shut. When she picked it up, a small, round object fell from between the pages and plunked down right in front of her. Hardly believing her own eyes, she picked up a blue daisy-shaped button. Beyond the log, she could see where grass and weeds had been trodden. This was no gift from a bear. Someone had walked out of the woods and left the button while she was bathing her arm in the spring.

More curious than afraid, she put the magazine in her poke and followed the faint path to a black walnut tree. The tree was ancient and huge. Tiny green globes of fruit hung like ornaments from every branch. A gray squirrel, high over her head, chattered and flipped his long tail in anger.

Manda's arm throbbed where she'd thoughtlessly carried her linen bag in the crook of her elbow. Looking down, she covered her mouth and stared, for at her feet lay the butt of a perfectly rolled cigarette. The unmistakable heady scent of tobacco lingered in the air like a whispered secret.

It seemed a long way back to the house. Manda's mind played with possibility. Might it be the middling man had picked up her lost package? Was he playing with her mind and with her heart? The spring had become a popular meeting spot, so it wouldn't be a stretch that he knew about it. Her pulse quickened. Excitement nearly took her breath. Could it be so? Not likely. He surely had a dozen girls from which to choose. He'd have no need to track her comings and goings.

More likely she had disturbed a couple's trysting spot. Maybe the woman had also chosen the pretty buttons to adorn her blouse. Maybe she hadn't stitched the button on quite well enough. But how did it get in her magazine? Could the wind have blown it there? Possibly. So what about the tromped-down grass and the rollie?

Lost in thought, Manda turned the button over and over, liking the way it felt in her fingers. If she had disturbed a courting couple, they had more than likely fled to the shelter of the tree. Then, when Manda went to the spring, they fled—him leaving his unfinished cigarette, her not realizing she had lost a button. It all made perfect sense.

The wind picked up a little. She hoped it didn't blow up a storm and ruin their picnic.

# 12

ADIE'S TIME CAME in the middle of a hailstorm. Remy awakened Copper just after 3 a.m. "Hit's time" was all she had to say. Copper was instantly awake.

Now the two of them hurried across the yard and down the path to the little house while stones the size of marbles pelted them and lightning cracked the night sky.

"Any other time and this would be fun," Remy said. "I love me a good storm."

"Me too," Copper yelled over the tempest, "but I like it best when I'm not in the middle of it."

Copper struggled against the gusting wind, trying to keep John's slicker over their heads. Remy held on to her arm with both hands. She carried her crutch up over her arm like a fancy purse. When they reached the porch, the bouncing hail reverberated like gunshots against the tin roof.

Copper shook rain from the oilcloth slicker and opened the cabin door. A cheery fire greeted her from the potbellied stove in the corner. A lamp burned brightly on the nightstand beside the birthing bed. A stack of linen was neatly folded on a chair. An open kettle of water and a cast-iron teapot heated atop the stove. Remy always set up a sickroom perfectly.

"One or two hours," Remy said, throwing out the answer before Copper even asked how close Adie was. "More likely two."

Copper shrugged into the gown she'd carried to the house, then tied a mask to cover her nose and mouth. It wouldn't have done any good to bring one for Remy. Remy took her chances.

Adie lay on the bed. She looked at Remy. "Did ye bring a knife?"

Remy opened a blade on a pocketknife and slid it under Adie's mattress. "I should have thought of this before."

Adie grimaced. "My husband's old mommy always puts a knife under my bed to cut the pain."

"My ma done the same thing," Remy said, standing back. "Maybe it'll relieve you somewhat."

Copper stood at the table scrubbing her hands. She wished it were that simple to ease the pangs of childbirth. Adie was doing well, though; many would be screaming by this time. But it was her sixth. She knew what to expect.

With first-timers the pain fed on their fear until pain was the biggest thing in the room. It was a rare woman who hadn't been indoctrinated with horror stories about other women's labors.

It wasn't the pain that had Copper fretting for Adie. It was the frailty of her tissue-thin lungs and her toiling heart.

With a kitchen tong, Copper fished a pair of scissors from the kettle and laid them on an ironed cloth beside a pair of antiseptic ligatures. Remy made her ligatures using six strands of sewing thread, eight inches long, knotted together at either end. They worked flawlessly for tying off the navel string.

Adie took a coughing fit. Copper eased her into a sitting position and offered her a sip of cold water. Adie was on fire with fever.

"I wish it was winter." Adie spit out words and phlegm. "I wish I could go to the pond and lay out on the ice."

"I'll need a pan of warm water," Copper told Remy, "and the bottle of alcohol."

Adie's head fell back over Copper's arm like a weary child's as Copper bathed her face and shoulders. "Tell me about the pond. Do you skate on the ice when it freezes over?"

Adie rallied. "The young'uns do. It puts you in mind of a fairyland all sparkly and bright. Betimes I'll chip a piece and let it melt against my tongue."

Copper bathed Adie's arms and dried them with a soft flannel. A pain overtook Adie, and her body shook from its fierceness.

Copper murmured comfort as she wiped her patient's

thin but shapely feet. The scent of rubbing alcohol and freshly ironed linen mingled, giving an air of industry to the room.

Adie turned eyes like live coals on Copper. "Did ye ever eat snow cream?"

"Do you make yours with sugar and vanilla?" Copper asked, nudging Adie onto her left side so she could check her progress.

"Ye should try it with a drib of molasses," Adie said between gritted teeth. "Oh, I wish I could go lay flat out on the frozen pond."

Copper smoothed strands of hair from Adie's forehead. "It won't be long now. Try to rest."

Thunder boomed. Remy peered out the window. "It's a-striking now," she said of the lightning. "I hope Foxy is in out of it."

Copper smiled as she worked. Remy had had a series of adopted foxes, all named Foxy. "She should have stayed under the shed."

"She had to move to protect her young'uns," Remy said. "She's got a lair up under the cliff by the springhouse."

"Well, she didn't go far, did she?" Copper said.

Remy chuckled. "No, I reckon not. She's got too used to the soft life what with Lilly feeding her eggs."

"Wonder who taught Lilly to do that."

"That child's a natural with animals. I never seen the like."

Copper emptied the dirty water into a slop bucket. "She takes after you. I hope it doesn't get her into trouble someday."

Remy tipped the teapot and poured boiling water into the wash pan. She rinsed the pan, filled it halfway, and let it sit. "Lilly will always land on her feet, Purty. Don't you worry about that."

Copper tested Adie's forehead with the back of her hand. "Much cooler and she's dozing."

"That's good, for she ain't nothing but skin and bones with a hank of hair. I'll be right surprised iffen she's got enough gumption left to push."

"This baby will be small, so maybe it won't take more effort than she can give, but I've got forceps in the kettle if need be."

Remy made two cups of tea and added a teaspoon of honey to each. "I should have made coffee."

"This is just right," Copper said, taking a seat at the table. "I'm jittery enough without coffee."

Copper looked across the table at her friend. Remy poured tea into her saucer and blew on it before taking a long slurp. "Remy, you are such a good friend to me. Thank you for your help."

"Where else would I druther be?" Remy asked. "What else would I want to be doing?"

"You know I feel the same way. It's like God led us to this very moment in time." Copper stirred her tea with a bent spoon. She took it out of the cup and laid it aside. John could heat it up and straighten it. "Why do you suppose that is?"

"To bless us, I reckon." Remy left her tea to add a chunk of wood to the potbellied stove. She jabbed deep into the fire with the poker, then latched the stove door. Holding her hands toward the heat, she rubbed them together. "That storm's put a right chill in the air."

"Is your rheumatism acting up?"

"Aye, ain't it always when the weather changes?"

The windowpanes rattled from the wind and the thunder. Copper's cup clanked in the saucer.

Remy went to the window again. "It's sure enough a frog strangler out there. Cain't see a blessed thing."

A knock at the door startled them both. Remy answered it.

"Just checking to see if you needed more wood," John said.

Copper took the slicker from the peg behind the door and stepped out onto the porch. "John, you needn't come out in this."

"You should have told me when you left the bed. I don't like to wake up and find your side empty."

She nuzzled up against him. "I'm sorry, but you were sleeping so good."

He pulled the slicker tightly around her, then wrapped her in his arms. It felt so good to be wrapped up in his love. "That last big bolt took out the cherry tree."

"Oh no. No cherry pie this summer. Did you check on the kids?"

"No need. They're all piled up in our bed."

"Even Lilly?"

"Even Lilly. Jack was first with his cold feet in the small of my back—then here came the girls. Lilly says, 'Somebody scoot over.'" Copper could feel his smile. "I figured this was where you were."

John was so good, so steady. She didn't have to be so strong when she was in his arms. "I'm afraid for Adie," she said against his chest. "If it wasn't storming, I'd send you for her husband."

"I'd be three times a fool to go on that man's property in the middle of the night," John said. "He'd shoot me and throw me in that pond of his before I said hello."

Copper leaned back, but it was too dark to see John's face. "He can't be that bad. He knows Adie was due anytime."

"Do you think he cares? Would she be so beat down if her husband loved her?"

"That's so sad."

The door opened a crack behind them. "We're getting down to business," Remy said, handing John an empty water bucket. "If ye don't mind."

Adie didn't put up a fight once her baby was safely delivered to Copper's waiting hands. "Is it a boy?" she whispered through cracked lips.

"It is. You did a good job. He's a handsome one."

"Lorne Lee. . . . Tell Isa."

Tears streamed down Copper's cheeks. "I'll tell him. Lorne Lee is a good, strong name."

Copper laid the baby boy on Adie's chest and covered them both with the warmed blanket Remy handed her.

The blue gray of Adie's face pinked up for a moment. "I want to touch him."

Copper lifted Adie's hand and laid it on the baby's back. Remy stuck a pillow under Adie's elbow. Adie gasped for breath as she fumbled with the buttons on her flannel gown.

"Let me help," Copper said, positioning the baby to nurse.

He was a strong little fellow despite how he must have struggled in the womb just to stay alive. Copper guessed him at least five pounds.

Copper wanted to crawl right up in the bed beside Adie and wrap her in her arms. Instead she knelt beside the bed and prayed for God to send His mercy and His love. When she finished, she stayed there watching.

Adie's lips lifted in a smile. "Well, would ye lookee who's come?" Her words an effort between wheezes and gasps. "Granny's a-standing by the garden gate. She's a-holding out her hand."

Adie slipped away as dawn broke over the cabin in the woods. Her baby boy lay quiet in her arms. The storm was over.

Copper sat back on her heels. It was a privilege to be with someone as she passed over. But it was hard to rejoice just now. She'd have to get past her guilt and sorrow before she could be happy for Adie. She had wanted so badly to save her. Wearily, she stood and began to remove the soiled bed linens. There was no need to soak them in cold water—everything would be burned.

"She give her all for him," Remy said as she took the baby

boy and carried him to a chair she had pulled up close to the stove. "Don't seem fair." On the floor she had put a footbath full of warm water. She laid the naked infant across her lap, attending first to his eyes, ears, nose, and mouth. Finished with that, she generously applied Vaseline to all the folds and tiny creases where vernix had collected.

Copper watched from the bed, where she ministered to Adie with her own soft flannels and a pan of water, her clean starched sheets and one flat pillow. She and Remy didn't agree on all matters of infant care. Copper would have used olive oil in the folds instead of Vaseline. But that was a small thing. Besides, trying to change Remy's ways was like trying to turn a train.

As Copper bathed the still body of the mother, Remy soaped the squirming baby, then bent over the footbath and rinsed him clean. While Remy wrapped the baby in a warm towel, Copper pulled a clean nightgown over Adie's head and dressed her feet and legs in cotton stockings. As Remy held a square of old linen to the fire for a minute before slipping it over the raw navel stump, Copper closed Adie's eyes with silver coins. After Remy diapered and dressed tiny Lorne Lee, Copper crossed his mother's hands upon her chest. The babe slept unaware, safe and warm in Remy's care.

Copper felt a hundred years old as she lit a fire behind the quarantine cabin. Every fiber of her being ached from work and worry. She wanted to get everything cleaned up before the children rose.

She struck a sulphur match and held the flare to the corner of a sheet. Smoke billowed up. The ground was so wet it might take a while. How could she possibly explain to Lilly what had happened during the night? She didn't want to frighten her, but it was never right to tiptoe around the truth. It would help that Lilly had never come to know Adie and that she wouldn't see the baby. Remy would keep him in the cabin until Isa Still came.

There—a spark took hold. She fed more linen to the flame. The rooster crowed. At a distance, she saw a light come on in her kitchen. John stepped out the door and sat on the steps as he always did to put on his shoes. He would do the milking. The children would sleep late after being disturbed in the night by the storm. When they waked, they would feast on bacon and eggs and blackberry jam on Manda's baking powder biscuits. They would drink warm milk brought in straight from the cow. What would Adie's children be eating this morning?

A knot formed in Copper's throat. With a long stick she thrust a feather pillow into the fire. In seconds it burst open. Hundreds of flicks of burning feathers shot into the damp air and quickly flamed out. Charred bits of gray ash swirled around Copper's head and shoulders as if it were snowing sorrow.

She needed to hurry and get the linens taken care of. Hurry and wash up—add her clothes and Remy's to the bonfire. Hurry to straighten the sick house. Hurry to boil some sugar water before Remy commenced feeding the infant water in which bread had been soaked. Hurry so the baby wouldn't get the grippe from Remy's gruel. Hurry to make some onion tea in case it already had.

She wiped her forehead with the back of her hand. It came away streaked with ash. She was bone-weary but glad of it. The weariness brought a certain kind of peace. It took energy to grieve. That would come later.

# 13

LILLY HAD FIRM instructions from Mama. "Entertain your brother and sisters and keep them away from the windows. And don't bother Manda. She's busy."

The whole day had been strange. Manda cooked and baked things they were not allowed to eat. Mama scurried around as if the missionary ladies were coming to lunch. Daddy rode off early and didn't come back for hours. Aunt Remy never showed up at all. Lilly had planned to beg Mama to let her ride Chessie over to see Kate, but it was not a good time to ask for any favors. That was easy to see.

Finally, after Lilly was about to die from curiosity, Mama took her aside and told her what had happened during the night. Lilly was shocked. How could it be that Mama didn't know how to fix poor Adie? And if Mama couldn't, why didn't Aunt Remy? This was a new thing to think about.

Now Lilly shooed the twins and Jack into the back bedroom. She had a pair of scissors, a shoe box, some shirt board, a jar of mucilage, and last year's Roebuck catalog. They would make paper dolls. She could do the cutting, the girls could pick out the pictures, and Jack could do the pasting. She had tried jacks, but Molly kept flinging the jacks all over the room, and Jack bounced the ball so hard he nearly broke a lamp. Paper dolls were a good activity. It should keep them busy—and quiet.

The girls weren't very good at picking out models to turn into dolls, so Lilly got her watercolor set and let them paint the shoe box where the paper dolls would live. They weren't very good at that either, but they liked doing it.

"Here," she said, handing Jack a figure she had carefully cut out, "paste this on the shirt board."

Jack pounded the brown nipple of the upended mucilage bottle against the back of the doll. "This thing won't work."

Lilly took it from him and broke the glue seal. She pumped it a few times on the front of the catalog, then handed it back. "Try again. Just a dab—not the whole bottle."

She could hear a wagon roll into the yard and Daddy John's voice. She couldn't tell what he was saying. Someone answered, but she couldn't understand him either.

Lilly went to the window. Out of sight behind the curtain,

she chanced to peek out. Mama had said to keep the kids away from the window. She didn't say Lilly couldn't look.

A man sat on the wagon seat. He had a long beard and longish dark hair. A woman sat beside him. She had on a high-necked rusty black dress and an old-lady bonnet that hid her face. When Daddy John pointed, the stranger flicked the reins. The wagon slowly rolled out of Lilly's sight. Aggravation! She would have stomped her feet, but that would set off the kids. Then they'd flock to the window.

With no to-do she slipped out the bedroom door. The children didn't seem to notice, so she hurried to the sickroom from where she could see the little house. The stranger was maneuvering a long, oblong wooden box from the wagon bed. Daddy John was helping. They carried it to the house and sat it on the porch. The man took a lid off the box and leaned it against the wall. He went inside. Daddy John followed. The lady stayed in the wagon. Lilly pushed the window up a little ways so she could hear better.

Mama came out of the house and stood in the yard. Aunt Remy came behind carrying a blue bundle Lilly knew was the baby. Mama and Aunt Remy walked together to the wagon. The lady reached down. Aunt Remy handed her bundle up.

Daddy John came backward out of the house. He was carrying his half of something. Carefully he backed across the porch. Lilly sucked in her breath when the stranger appeared in the doorway. They were carrying Adie's body! The box was a coffin!

Daddy and the stranger stood beside the box, then

shuffled around until Adie's head was in the right place and her feet were in the other. Mama hurried up the one stone step and into the house. She brought out an odd flat pillow and a smallish white quilt and put them in the coffin before the men laid Adie down.

Daddy John helped put the lid on. The stranger went to the wagon and fetched a hammer and some nails. He knelt at the coffin with the nails in his mouth. One by one he tapped them into the rim of the lid with the hammer. Three taps each. The lady in the wagon kept her face straight ahead. Lilly understood. She wished she had never looked, but now her eyes were stuck to the window, tight as the top to the glue bottle.

When the man finished nailing the lid on the coffin, he and Daddy carried it to the wagon and slid it across the wagon bed. The screeching sound made the hairs on Lilly's arms stand up. Manda came up with a woven laundry basket. A white tablecloth was tucked down around the top of the basket. Her arms bowed from the weight. Daddy took it from her and set it beside the coffin. The stranger lifted up the tailgate and fastened it shut. He didn't offer his hand to Daddy and he didn't speak to Mama, just hopped up on the seat beside the lady and drove away. He never looked back, but the lady did. Lilly thought she could see a smile on the lady's face. She hoped so. She hoped the lady was happy about the baby.

Lilly's stomach felt funny as she went back to check on her brother and sisters. Even before she opened the door, she knew there was trouble. Mazy had two paper dolls glued to her forehead. The doll's flimsy legs hung down over her eyes.

"Watch, Lilly," Jack said. "Blow, Mazy; blow."

Mazy stuck out her lower lip and puffed. The legs of the black-and-white dolls danced in her eyes. The twins dissolved in laughter.

"It took me forever to teach her that," Jack said, innocent as a kitten.

Lilly hastened to peel the paper from Mazy's forehead. "Jack! There's mucilage gummed in her hair."

"It wouldn't stay stuck to the skin. Hair's better."

Lilly sank to the floor and pulled Mazy into her lap. A glop of paper and glue remained in Mazy's golden curls. Lilly tugged. Mazy cried. Molly cried. Jack slipped out the door. Mama brought him back.

"What's going on in here?" Mama said with a level gaze at Lilly.

"Things got a little out of hand," Lilly said. She couldn't meet Mama's eyes.

"So I see." She took Mazy's hand and led her toward the kitchen. Lilly followed with Molly. Mama sat Mazy on the kitchen table. She took the lid off the butter keeper, pinched off a tablespoon-size piece, and worked it through Mazy's bangs. "Now you try," she said to Lilly.

Kneeling on a chair, Lilly followed suit. The glop of glue gave way and slid right into her fingers.

Mama swung Mazy up and kissed her cheeks. "Oh, you

smell good enough to eat." She sat Mazy on one hip and drew Molly up onto the other. "I think we'll go rest awhile. Jack, you help Lilly clean up the mess you made. Lilly, you watch out for your brother."

Lilly didn't say a word. She didn't even fuss at Jack as she washed watercolor paint from the bedroom floor and picked up bits of paper.

"Sorry, Lilly," Jack said.

"That's okay. I shouldn't have left you alone."

"Wanna go to the creek?"

"No, not today." Lilly crammed the mess into the shoe box. "Come along. I'll push you in the swing."

Jack drooped in the swing seat. Lilly pushed him half-heartedly. She wished she could go to the little house and help Aunt Remy. She needed to feel like she was in some-body's good graces. She tried to think about her upcoming trip to Lexington, but the image of Adie's body being lowered into the coffin blocked out the happy thoughts.

"Want to look for worms?" Jack said. "We could go fish-ing if we just had some worms."

"Sure, why not. Go get the coffee can from the shed."

They followed the path the wagon had taken. The wheels had left runnels in the tall grass and weeds. To the side of the path they found a good-size flat rock. Lilly helped Jack turn it over.

"Yippee. There's thousands of them," Jack said.

Lilly watched the night crawlers writhe against the newly exposed ground. "More like a dozen." She picked one up and dropped it with a plunk into the can. "We forgot to put dirt in. They'll shrivel up if we don't have dirt."

Jack found a stick and started poking it in the ground. "You catch the worms and I'll dig the dirt."

Soon the wiggle worms had a new home. Jack wanted to look for more, so Lilly went along. It was something to do, but after three rocks she tired. "Let's go back."

"Can we go fishing now?"

"Maybe tomorrow would be better. It's getting late."

"What's that?" Jack raised his arm and pointed.

Lilly looked but didn't see anything unusual.

Jack ran ahead on the trodden path. Half the worms bounced over the side of his coffee tin. He stopped beside a tree.

She hurried to catch up. "My goodness. We'd better go tell Daddy."

# 14

IT WAS NO use. Copper couldn't sleep. The turmoil of the long day looped through her mind like the notes of a song she couldn't get out of her head. She kept wondering what she could have done—what one little thing might have made a difference. John would say she shouldn't have gotten involved with the Stills in the first place. He asked—no, he told her not to go over to the Still house. That had really got her back up. No man, not even John, was going to tell her what to do.

She swung her legs over the side of the bed and sat up. Maybe John had been right this time. Knowingly, she had exposed herself and Remy to a dread disease, sure that she and she alone knew what was right for Adie. Now doubt undermined her surety. Was she becoming haughty—too confident of her medical prowess? Well, she'd gotten a double dose of humble pie last night. Adie wouldn't be any deader if she had stayed at home. There was the rub. Copper pushed the tumble of red curls out of her face and groped in the dark for her robe.

Down the hall she looked in on her children. Just as she suspected, Jack was sprawled across the foot of Lilly's half bed. Though he had a room to himself, they were yet to break him of wandering to the girls' room in the middle of the night. Molly and Mazy were tangled like vines in their bed under the window. Lilly slept curled on her side. She had forgotten to take off her necklace before bed. The gold, heart-shaped locket held two pictures: one of Lilly's father Simon and one of her daddy John. Lilly took special delight in springing the tiny latch and showing off her two daddies.

Padding across the floor in her bare feet, Copper went to the kitchen and eased out the door into the cool of the night. She stopped at the wash bench and dipped a cup of well water, which she carried across the yard. A big silver moon illuminated her path to the little house. The windows and door stood open, blank and staring like sightless eyes. Remy had been in there all day scrubbing like a fiend. The lingering odor of vinegar stung her eyes when she stepped inside.

The moonlight gave a silvery sheen to the room as if it were lit from within. The bedstead stood sans corn-shuck mattress in the corner of the room. Its very presence seemed a dark reproach. She ran her hand over the smooth tabletop. In the center she felt the knitting needles she had brought to Adie. These needles had knit the blue blanket and bonnet baby Lorne went home in. Grief overtook her. Trembling, Copper pulled out a chair and sat down. She wished she had brought her Bible. She could have lit the coal-oil lamp and read some comfort.

Adie, pitiful Adie. Her life seemed so short, so full of suffering.

A tap-tap-tap on the wooden porch alerted her to a visitor. Remy swung through the door on her crutches.

"Both crutches? You should have left the heavy cleaning to me."

Remy hooked one crutch over the knob on a ladder-back chair. She fell into the chair, her legs sticking straight out. She pointed with the other crutch. "I seen a whistle pig digging under yon side of the porch. John'll need to smoke him out afore he sets up housekeeping."

Copper slid her cup across the table to Remy. "Why are you up so late?"

"I come to share your burden."

Copper had a strong desire to lay her head on Remy's shoulder, let Remy stroke her hair and pat her on the back. Her soul yearned for the soothing touch of a mother or a sister. But Remy's way was different. She elbow-greased her grief right into the ground, never giving it time to fester.

Copper stood and paced the room. "Less than twenty-four hours since Adie died—it seems like twenty-four years."

Remy took a sip of water and scooted the cup toward Copper's place. "What'd John say about the basket?"

Copper sat back down. "Oh, he was hopping mad. I wish the children had never found it. All that food wasted after Manda cooked all day." Leaning forward, she rested her left elbow on the table and her chin in her cupped hand. "Actually, it wasn't wasted. John took it over to the Heatons'. You know that new family that just moved to the ridge? He thinks Mrs. Heaton is in the family way. I've never met her, but I'll make a call soon."

"Did he leave the milk?"

Copper's mind was fogged. What was Remy talking about? Suddenly she brightened—the formula. The baby's boiled, diluted, and sweetened cow's milk. "Why, no, the jug was not in the basket; nor was my written instruction for making more."

"Humph."

"Exactly," Copper said. "That's a good sign—don't you think? It gives me reason to believe I could go calling at the Still house. You know, just to check on the baby's feeding."

"Are ye asking me my take on the matter or are ye asking me to approve your notion?"

"I'm asking for your honest opinion."

Remy pointed a crutch at Copper like an extended index finger. "You'll rue the day ye mess with the likes of Isa Still, and I'll tell ye for why I think so. Ye can tell the manner of a man by the way he looks upon the world." She paused as if gathering her thoughts. "Isa Still's wild outen his eyes, puts me in mind of a distempered dog."

Copper nodded. "I know you're right. I just feel so bad that I lost Adie."

Remy hauled herself up with the help of her crutch. "Weren't in your power. Adie Still was wore-out and used up long afore you got tangled with them. At least her young'un was borned alive—thanks to you."

When Remy nearly lost her balance, Copper unhooked the other crutch and helped Remy position it under her arm. "I never thought of it that way. That makes me feel some better."

"Aye, we did all we could, I reckon."

From underneath the porch, the rustling sound of dry leaves followed their steps. Remy pounded a plank with the tip of one crutch. A high-pitched squeal rewarded her effort. "Ha!" she barked.

"Remind me to tell John about the groundhog," Copper said.

As dawn broke, Copper woke her oldest daughter. "Lilly," she whispered, "get dressed. Come to the barn with me."

Yawning hugely, Lilly crawled over Jack's still form. "Why?"

"I've got something to show you. Something you'll like."

In the kitchen, while Lilly put on her tall barn boots, Copper added a tablespoon of strong black coffee to a mug of milk.

Lilly's eyes widened as she was handed the cup. "Coffee for me?"

Copper held the door open with one hand and carried her own cup in the other. "If you're old enough to be productive this early in the morning, you're old enough for coffee."

"Am I milking Bertha?"

"Would you like to?"

"If you hold her tail so she won't slap me in the face." Lilly started down the steps. A slosh of coffee-colored milk spattered her white apron. She stopped on the second step, brushing at the faint stain.

"If you're going to work in the barn, you're going to get dirty. It doesn't matter. Clothes are washable."

"I know, but my apron looked so nice." She sipped her milk coffee. "Ah, this is good. Is Bertha my surprise?"

"Wait and see." Copper leaned her shoulder into the barn door and shoved. "This door is so stubborn."

The morning's first light barely penetrated the dark interior of the barn. Bertha bawled from her stall.

Copper fetched her milk bucket. "Get two stools."

Lilly got the T-shaped wooden seats and followed her mother into the stall. Copper folded her skirts tightly around her, then hunkered down on the short stool. Lilly mimicked her.

"Now watch," Copper said, stripping the cow's teat with a practiced squeeze and pull. Milk pinged against the side of the bucket. "It's all in the fingers. It's easy once you get the rhythm going."

Lilly leaned in and wrapped her hand around the teat. She yanked but nothing came out.

Copper put her fingers over Lilly's. "Let your fingers go loose and feel mine." Milk trickled in a tiny stream. "Try again."

Lilly finally got the hang of it. Taking turns, they milked the bucket full. "How do you know when you're finished? When the bucket's full?"

"When all four teats have been stripped and there's no more milk to be had. It's important to empty the udder; otherwise Bertha could get sick."

"You know what? Bertha didn't slap me once."

"That means you did a good job. Bertha likes a gentle touch." She patted Bertha's hip, then led her to a side door and out to pasture. The cow's bell clanked dully as she walked away, stopping every few feet to mouth a bunch of new green grass.

"Now for the surprise," Copper said. "Take one of those little berry buckets down from the peg."

Lilly brought a blue one to her mother.

Copper tipped the milk bucket and filled the berry bucket half-full.

"What's this for?" Lilly asked.

Copper unfastened the door of the stall next to Bertha's. "Come and see."

A mother cat and four tiny kittens nested in a bed of sweet timothy.

"I found them this morning when I first came out," Copper said.

Lilly knelt in the hay beside the cat. The cat eyed her

warily. Lilly clicked her tongue. "It's all right, kitty. I would never hurt you." Taking the battered tin pie pan her mother handed her, she slowly poured a stream of rich yellow milk into the pan. She set the tin beside the nest and backed out of the stall, slipping a loop of heavy twine over a board to keep the door closed. The door did not meet the ground, so the mother cat could easily come and go.

Copper and Lilly peered through the cracks in the door. The mama didn't move for the longest time, but she was hungry. You could tell by the way her nose twitched as she smelled the milk. After several minutes, she stood and stretched. One kitten hung from the cat's teat for a second before it plopped back onto the hay.

Lilly clasped a hand over her mouth to stifle her laughter. "Where did she come from?" she asked in a stage whisper.

"I don't know, but she sure picked a good place to have her babies, didn't she?"

Lilly shot her mother a sideways look. "So are we keeping her?"

"If nobody claims her and she wants to stay. It's good to have a cat in the barn." Copper brushed a strand of hair from Lilly's eyes. They hadn't taken time to tie it back before they left the house. "I was thinking you might pick one kitten for a house pet. We'd have to give the other kittens away, though. We can't have five cats."

"Really? I can have one for my own?" Lilly wrapped her arms around her mother's waist. "We haven't had a cat since Old Tom died."

"I know. That's probably why I found a mouse in the grain box yesterday. He'd gnawed a hole right through. Your dad will have to plug it." Copper picked up the milk bucket, loving the heft of it—not bad pay for a half hour's work. Lilly had slowed her down, but it was a valuable lesson for her daughter to learn. Every woman should own a cow and know how to take care of it. It bespoke a type of independence. With a cow, a few chickens, and a vegetable garden, a woman could raise a family alone if need be. She would need to teach Lilly that it was okay to get dirty. That might take a while.

"Why are you smiling?" Lilly asked as they walked to the springhouse.

"I was just wondering how many starched aprons you would need in a day's time if you started milking and mucking out Bertha's stall."

Lilly stopped midstep and seated her fists on her hips. "Mama! I am not a baby. I could do a lot if you would let me."

Copper was taken aback. There was truth to what Lilly said. Copper slipped out of her work shoes, then stepped into the springhouse. Lilly followed, leaving her boots perfectly lined up outside the door.

Copper poured the milk through the cream separator, explaining every move to Lilly. "We have more milk than we can use or give away right now. Manda will take this cream to town for me. It will fetch a pretty penny."

"And the eggs," Lilly said.

"Yes, eggs too. And sometimes truck from the garden, but usually we can anything extra. Milk and eggs won't keep."

"I love being in here," Lilly said, leaning back against a wall and spreading her arms wide against it. "It's so cool and peaceful."

Copper knew what she meant. The walls of the springhouse were constructed from thick slabs of rock chinked with clay. It straddled a free-flowing spring, a tributary of Troublesome Creek. John and Dimmert had chiseled holes in the solid stone floor through which containers of milk or butter or cheese could be lowered into the cold water for safekeeping. If the heavy wooden door was kept closed, the temperature inside was nearly constant, somewhat like a cave. When you were within its walls, the burble of water flowing over ancient rocks made the outside world fade away.

Crouching by one of the holes in the floor, Copper lowered the milk bucket into the spring and let water flow in. When she was satisfied with the amount, she hauled the bucket out and scrubbed it and the cream separator with lye soap. She washed and rinsed, then set the bucket and the separator upside down to drain. "This is all part of milking. You're not finished just because the cow is."

Lilly still leaned against the wall of the springhouse. She was staring at the floor. A curtain of hair hid her face.

Copper could tell her child was troubled. She chose her words carefully. "Do you have questions about what you saw yesterday afternoon? questions about Adie?"

Lilly pulled a ribbon from her apron pocket and with a

twist of her wrists pulled her hair away from her face and secured it with the ribbon. Her movements were practiced and graceful. Copper could see traces of the young woman she would grow to be. "I'm sorry I disobeyed. I'm sorry I was looking out the window when they put Adie in that box."

Copper cupped Lilly's chin and looked into her eyes. "And I am sorry I didn't prepare you for what happened. You're old enough to be included."

"What I really want to know is why didn't we keep the baby?"

"He wasn't ours to keep. His father wanted him."

"Was that old lady his granny? Will she take care of him?"

"The lady is Mr. Still's mother. She helped with all of Adie's other children. I don't think you need to worry about little Lorne Lee."

"Still?" Lilly twisted a lock of hair around her finger. "I didn't know that was Adie's last name."

"The Stills are neighbors, but they like to keep to themselves. You wouldn't have met any of them."

Lilly nestled into Copper. "Lorne Lee—that's a different sort of name."

Copper wrapped her arms around her daughter as tightly as she could.

Lilly pulled slightly away. "You're squeezing my lights out."

Copper squeezed her again. "Let's go to the house. Manda's sure to have breakfast ready."

Lilly swung Copper's hand as they walked across the yard. "So if we keep the cat and a kitten, does that mean we can't have a dog?"

"We need to talk to your daddy about that. I'm not sure he wants a menagerie."

"*Menagerie*? What's that mean?"

"Look it up. That's what the dictionary is for."

Lilly skipped ahead. She looked like a little girl again. "I'll wait until I get back from Lexington to talk to Daddy about getting a dog. He might forget if I ask him now."

Copper sighed. She wished Lilly would forget about Lexington. As much as Copper hated to, she had made arrangements as Alice asked. Lilly would travel to the depot by coach with Kate and her mother. Mrs. Jasper would see Lilly on the train and talk to the porter, and Alice would meet her at the stop. What could go wrong?

Copper determined to see the trip through her daughter's eyes. She didn't want to spoil the adventure for Lilly.

# 15

MANDA WAS HEADED to town in Miz Copper's buggy
with a load of cream and eggs and a bushel basket of new
potatoes on the floorboard. She had dressed this morning in her second-best frock. If not for Miss Remy's eagle
eye, she would have worn her yellow dress—the one that
matched her hair. But the last thing she wanted to do was
raise suspicion.

The brown gingham was okay, she supposed, but it made
her feel like the maid she was, whereas the yellow made her
feel special. She had worn it Sunday last, first to church,
then to the picnic. She flushed to think of the excitement
of that day. Oh, she fairly loved a gathering. . . .

When church let out, there was dinner on the grounds. Makeshift sawhorse tables groaned under the weight of sugar-cured ham, chicken and dumplings, fried chicken, and all the trimmings. Women spread quilts under shade trees, where babies napped and old folks waited to be brought a plate. Men played horseshoes as children ran amok, calling, "Tag! You're it!"

Manda's Sunday school class naturally congregated at one end of the tables, shunning the spread blankets of family gatherings. They were all young and unattached, and there were no children for them to chase and no plates to fill except their own. There were seven of them, four girls and three guys. It was Fred Estep who suggested going to the spring, but Manda herself who egged them on. And surprise, surprise, it was Gurney Jasper who suggested hiking to the top of Devil's Eyebrow with a stop at the spring on the way down.

Manda took a second look at Gurney. And for sure she knew he looked more than twice at her. At one point in the climb, as the girls squealed and giggled on the slippery slope, Gurney took Manda's hand and helped her over a moss-slicked rock. The gesture made her feel special, and she gave Gurney's hand an extra squeeze.

There was a hot zephyr across the ledge. It whipped the girls' skirts and loosened hair from pins. They all laughed hysterically when Fred's hat sailed out over the eyebrow and on to parts unknown. Manda could scarcely remember when she had had so much fun.

She and Gurney led the pack as they hiked toward the

spring. Behind them the other girls sang teasingly: "'Where, oh where, is sweet little Manda? Where, oh where, is sweet little Manda? Where, oh where, is sweet little Manda? Way down yonder in the pawpaw patch.'"

The guys joined in for the second verse. "'Where, oh where, is charming Gurney? Where, oh where, is charming Gurney? Way down yonder in the pawpaw patch.'"

Gurney's ears flamed at the second verse, but she noticed a smile on his face. And when he took her hand, she didn't jerk away. Holding hands wasn't anything serious, she didn't think. Besides, she liked everybody taking notice of her. This finding true love stuff was sure confusing.

Manda hadn't forgotten the middling man, however, and when they got to the spring, she examined the fallen log. There was nothing unusual there. While the others took turns drinking from the spring, she walked over to the ancient black walnut tree. The grass was not matted around its base. There was no trace of tobacco there. If not for the daisy-shaped button tacked with blue thread to the ribbon on her chemise she would have thought the other day was a dream. Just a dream and nothing more.

She stood for the longest time looking off across the meadow where wild violets and white field daisies swayed gently in a warm breeze. From somewhere a fiddle tune drifted her way. It played in perfect harmony with the rhythm of the dancing grasses and flowers. She imagined that she was part and parcel of that tune. Though she strained to hear more, the music faded away, light as dandelion fluff on the wind.

Gurney touched her shoulder. "Why are you over here all by your lonesome?"

"I'm watching the flowers," she said. "Look how prettily they dance."

"They don't hold a candle to you."

"We're going," Fred called out. "You two lovebirds can catch up."

Manda looked at Gurney. He was a handsome man once you stopped to study his square-jawed, honest face. She felt a thrill of delight just like Rose Feathergay in the magazine story. Was this rush and tingle what falling in love felt like?

Gurney reached out. She closed her eyes and tilted her chin—waiting—nearly faint with anticipation.

Gurney touched her cheek and ran his fingers through her hair. "You've caught a twig," he said, plucking it out.

The dreaded heat of a blush rose from her chest and blossomed across her cheeks. She felt naked as a jaybird standing there with her need displayed for him to see.

"Are you okay? You look a little peaked."

She wanted to slap his face but couldn't rightly figure why. "We'd better go. The others will wonder what we're up to."

"I'll go first," Gurney said when they reached the narrow, one-cow path. "Put your hand on my shoulder. I'll keep you from falling."

Another time she would have stomped around him and hurried away with no regard to his feelings. Instead, she let him guide her down the mountain.

His hair was cut short, neatly cupping the back of his

head. Where his farmer's tan met the collar of his shirt, a thin strip of pale flesh was revealed. The muscles in his shoulder were as solid as a ledge rock underneath her hand, but that little flash of white made him seem strangely vulnerable to her.

Her emotions swirled like tea leaves in a cup. There was something about Gurney that made her feel safe and protected. But what if she had misread the taking of her hand, the touch on her shoulder? The middling man made her feel desired, if overwhelmed and not a little frightened by his boldness. Shouldn't she at least try to see the exciting music man again? What if he was her one true love?

Manda had answered yes to her own question on Sunday, and now she was on her way to finding out the answer. If the music man was anywhere to be found, that is. Taking the cream to the Cream Station and the eggs to the grocery store gave her the perfect opportunity to look for him. Plus, she'd make some money. She and Miz Copper worked on the halves. That was only fair, since it was Manda who candled all the eggs and wiped the shells clean. She didn't see the need to candle the eggs since she had gathered them herself and knew they were fresh, but Miz Copper was particular. And Miss Remy—good grief, that woman put a damper on everything.

Last evening whilst Manda was in the shed, preparing the eggs for market, here the old biddy came putting her two cents in.

"Ye missed a spot." She held up an egg with the tiniest bit of downy fluff stuck to one side.

Manda took the egg, wiped it clean, and handed it back, admiring her own patience.

"This here's a pullet egg," Miss Remy croaked in her odd, rusty voice. "Do ye know the difference?"

"No, I can't say I do."

Remy sorted through several eggs. "See here? See the zig-zag mark on the end of this hen fruit? That quirl means this here's a rooster." She held out one egg and then another. "This smooth one is a pullet. Most likely you'll find a dozen pullets to every rooster."

Like Manda cared. She shrugged.

Miss Remy took the hint, backing slowly out of the shed on her crutches.

Manda breathed a sigh of relief.

Miss Remy stopped. "Ye might need to know that iffen ye ever plan on raising chickens. Else you'll have a yard full of roosters and no laying hens."

As soon as Miss Remy was out of sight, Manda helped herself to a dozen eggs she left out of the count. Her conscience told her not to, but she ignored the still, small voice. What did it matter? There were plenty, and no one would ever know.

Manda thought of last night's conversation as she headed to town. It struck her funny bone, and she laughed. She wouldn't mind to be the lone pullet in a yard full of roosters right now. She could just see them strutting around in that

frozen-toed rooster way, hoping she would notice their particular beauty, hoping she would pick one of them to set up
housekeeping with. Well, with any luck, today would be the
day she decided what rooster she wanted in her henhouse.

"Giddyup," she called to Chessie, slapping the reins before
she remembered the eggs and slowed the horse to a trot.

As luck would have it, the grocery store where she sold the
potatoes and the eggs was on the alley beside the hotel. That
was where she had spotted the music man the last time she
was in town. The Cream Station was on the next street over.
It would be easy enough to walk down the narrow passage
with the cream. Although there were several folks sitting on
the bent-willow benches that fronted the hotel, she was sure
no one would think twice about her choice to do just that.

Manda placed the empty potato basket in the buggy and
tested the lids of the tin cream cans, making sure the ride
from home hadn't loosened them. Then, leaving Chessie
secured to the hitching post outside the grocery, she strode
with purpose down the murky alleyway. Despite herself, her
heart quickened as she approached the garbage bin where she
had watched the exchange of moonshine.

She flinched and stepped back when a rat as big as a squirrel darted up the side of the large container. The vile thing
teetered on the lip of the bin, its beady eyes seemingly trained
on the buckets of cream. The rat's whiskers twitched, and its
clawed feet scrambled to keep from losing its perch.

Manda set the buckets down and picked up a rock. She
flung it at the bin. The rock pinged off the side and landed

in the dust at her feet. To her ears it sounded loud as gun-
shot. Nervously, she looked around, sure she would attract
a crowd. But nothing stirred in the dark shadows—nothing
except the rat, whose long, hairless tail disappeared over the
side of the sour-smelling bin.

She picked up her tins and walked on, keeping her eyes
focused on the light at the end of the alley. A movement
there caught her eye. Someone waved a small brown flag.
The flag shifted in and out of view like a taunt. Moving
closer, she could see the flag was actually a small brown paper
package.

Suddenly a man blocked her way. The middling man put
his arms behind his back. "You looking for something?"

"I, um . . . I, uh . . . I found the button," she stammered,
making no sense to her own ears.

"Did you now? Well, fancy that." He swayed gently on his
feet just like the dancing daisies last Sunday. She could not
look away. He was dressed in pressed dungarees and a stiff-
collared boiled shirt. A black cravat was knotted at his throat.
His boots were pointy-toed and polished. His dark jacket was
like a suit coat, but he wore it open. He smelled faintly of
alcohol and rich spices. "Whatcha got in the buckets?"

"Cream . . . I was headed to the Cream Station."

His tongue darted out, and he licked his bottom lip. "Let
me help you with that." He smiled.

She stared.

"You stay right here," he said as he relieved her of the
buckets.

She did. Her feet were frozen to the spot. It didn't take long for him to come back. As he rounded the corner of the building, he folded a paper bill and stuck it in his pocket. He placed a few coins in her palm. She didn't even count, just dropped them into her linen sack.

He took her hand and with his thumb massaged the red print left by the handle of the cream bucket. "Hands like this ought not to be doing heavy lifting."

He pulled her along by that same hand until they were halfway down the alley, just where the trash bin sat. The bin was not snug against the wall. He went in there first, leading her.

"I got a little something for you," he said, taking a small package from his coat pocket and tucking it into her purse. "You ought to be careful where you leave things."

"I will," she said.

He caught her chin and tipped her head. His eyes were black and hot, like the last bit of coal smoldering in a fireplace. "Is there any other little thing I can do for you?"

Her blood had turned to water and her knees to jelly. She had not one smidgen of will left. What could she do but close her eyes and offer herself?

His kiss exploded in her brain and coursed through her veins like liquid fire. She felt the rough brick of the wall press against her back and was glad for it, else she would have surely fallen in a heap.

The very air surrounding her seemed thick with his presence. If she had a spoon, she could have tasted him. He put his hands on the small of her back and pulled her close. He kissed her mouth, her cheeks, her fluttering eyelids, and the soft triangle at the base of her neck where her pulse beat wildly. Then, quick as a vapor in the morning sun, he was gone, leaving her stunned and trembling.

She didn't note the garbage bin nor the metallic skittering sound of the rat's claws as it scavenged bits of rotting food. She didn't see the gloomy shadowing of the alleyway nor fear she might be seen. She stood for several minutes settling herself. Now she knew—she knew what love felt like.

Coming out from behind the bin, she looked up and down the alley. It seemed like everything was off-kilter, like the world had tilted. But she had to go to the Cream Station and claim the tins. She couldn't go home without them.

A woman came out from the back as Manda stepped into the store. She wiped her hands on a linen towel and took her place behind a waist-high counter.

"I've come for my tins," Manda said.

"Two, right? I've got them washed for you." The woman leaned her ample bosom on the counter. "Listen, miss, you don't want to be messing with that—"

Manda cut her off. "My tins, please."

The lady put two clean buckets and two clean lids on the counter. "Forewarned is forearmed."

"I didn't ask for nothing but my tins," Manda said, seating the lids on the small buckets. She marched out the door. She could feel the woman's eyes burning a hole in her back. "Old maid," Manda muttered under her breath, "withering on the vine."

Her anger fueled her as she took the long way down one street and back up the other where the buggy waited. No way was she walking down the alley so the busybody could run to a side window and watch her every move with her prying eyes.

This time the middling man was playing a mouth harp in front of the hotel. There were a few folks leaning against a banister, listening. As she passed, he made a long sound like that of a train whistle with his mouth against the harmonica.

Manda felt like he had just told the world she was special. She put the tins in the buggy beside the empty potato basket and unwrapped Chessie's reins from the hitching post. As she watched him from the seat of the buggy, he slapped the harmonica against his leg and commenced to play "Fair and Tender Ladies."

She guessed it was their song.

# 16

SUNDAY EVENINGS WERE special in the Pelfrey household. Supper was whatever was left over from dinner. There were no chores other than what were absolutely necessary, like milking the cow and feeding the chickens. Manda wouldn't be back until Monday morning, and Remy generally spent weekends in her own cabin.

Copper loved these times when it was just she and John with their children. In the winter they would pop corn and gather at the hearth. John would tell stories or she would read from *Treasure Island* or *Alice's Adventures in Wonderland* or some such book, always ending with a Bible story. But in the summer, like tonight, they sat on the porch and enjoyed the dimming of the day.

Lilly was sitting on the top porch step in her long nightgown, brushing her hair with the silver-backed brush from the vanity set Alice had given her. She did a hundred strokes every night.

"What memory verse did your Sunday school teacher give you this week?" Copper said from her rocking chair.

Lilly huffed. "It's from the First Epistle General of Peter, chapter 5, verse 9."

"Don't be smart-mouthed when you're talking about the Bible, Lilly Gray," Copper said, then softened. "Would you like me to read it to you before it gets too dark?"

"I won't need it. I'll be going to church with Aunt Alice and cousin Dodie next Sunday."

"Why does that exclude your memory verse?"

Lilly slapped her brush down on the step beside her. "Because I won't have to recite the verse in Sunday school. Nobody will know the difference."

Copper was glad John was out in the yard chasing lightning bugs with the little kids. He wouldn't like Lilly's disrespectful tone, and the last thing Copper wanted was discord with her eldest tonight. "You don't learn your verses for your teacher. You learn them for your own instruction."

"I know that."

"Lilly . . ."

Lilly jumped off the step and put her vanity set on the rustic grapevine table beside Copper's chair. "I'll brush your hair while you read it to me. How's that?"

"I believe I left the Bible on my bedside table."

Back with the Bible, Lilly stood behind the rocker, removing pins and combs from Copper's hair. She lined them up beside the hand mirror set on the table.

"What book does Peter follow?" Copper asked.

"Peter follows James. James follows Hebrews. Hebrews follows Philemon."

"Lilly Gray Corbett, there's no getting the better of you."

Lilly pulled the brush through Copper's hair. "I like to know things. Read the verse, Mama."

"I'm going to read verses 7 and 8 first. They set the stage, so to speak. 'Casting all your care upon him; for he careth for you. Be sober, be vigilant; because your adversary the devil, as a roaring lion, walketh about, seeking whom he may devour.'"

"This is your verse. Verse 9. 'Whom resist stedfast in the faith, knowing that the same afflictions are accomplished in your brethren that are in the world.'"

"What's *staid fast* supposed to mean?" Lilly worked a tangle with the comb. "Those two words don't go together. Sounds like Peter is saying slow down and hurry up."

"*Stedfast*, not *staid fast*. It means to be firmly fixed in place. I believe this Scripture admonishes us as Christians to remember that we will be visited by the same afflictions that befall others."

"Like the verse that says it rains on the just and the unjust alike."

"Exactly. Here's what verse 10 says, 'But the God of all

grace, who hath called us unto his eternal glory by Christ Jesus, after that ye have suffered a while, make you perfect, stablish, strengthen, settle you.'"

"Maybe my teacher picked 1 Peter 5:9 for Kate. So she'd be steadfast with her toothache."

"Oh, dear. I thought she was better. Mrs. Jasper didn't mention it when we talked again this morning about your going to the depot on the coach with them."

"She's better. It doesn't hurt all the time. Hand me the rattail comb."

Copper handed the long, thin-handled comb over her head.

"Mrs. Jasper is going to take her to the dentist when they're in Cincinnati. Kate's scared. She's never been to the dentist."

"I wonder if Mrs. Jasper knows there's a dentist coming to town. He bought the old law office."

"Do they really knock your tooth out with a hammer and a cut nail? That's what Kate told me."

"Barbers used to do that. They were sort of like dentists, and they called it tooth-jumping. I'm sure the new dentist is much more humane."

"Good thing it's not a front tooth," Lilly said. "That'd be awful. I'm sure glad I'm going to Aunt Alice's and not to the tooth-jumper."

Copper winced. "Ouch. Be more gentle."

"Your hair is so twirly, it's like trying to unknot a clematis vine. Hold up the mirror."

Copper peered in the mirror at the long strand of hair Lilly held up. "I've never been described as 'twirly' before."

"I meant it as a compliment. Why didn't I get your beautiful hair instead of Jack? Boys don't need to be pretty."

Copper laid the Bible on a bench, then patted her lap. "Come here."

"I'm too big."

Copper patted her lap again. "You're never too big to be my baby."

When Lilly snuggled down, Copper held the mirror in front of Lilly's face. "Do you like the girl you see there?"

Lilly pulled the mirror closer. "She's kinda pretty. But I wish I looked like you."

Copper rocked slowly, savoring the moment. "Who do you see besides yourself when you look in the mirror?"

"I never thought about it. I guess, maybe Aunt Alice?"

"Open your locket."

Lilly released the tiny latch and tucked her chin to see the pictures, one of John and one of Simon.

Copper's heart squeezed painfully. It seemed impossible she and Lilly had never really talked about her father. "Do you want me to unfasten the chain so you can see better?"

Lilly swept her hand under her fall of hair and lifted it so Copper could reach the clasp securing the thin gold chain. Lilly flipped the picture frame open and removed the tiny circular picture of Simon. She held it out as far as her arm would allow, then slowly brought it closer. "Was Daddy Simon's hair black like it looks in the picture?"

"Yes, it was."

"Did it have a silver streak like mine?"

"No, you take after Alice in that. Remember she was your daddy's sister. There was a strong family likeness between them. See? You all have the same nose and the same mouth."

"Was she his little sister?"

"Alice was ten years older than Simon. In many ways she was like his mother."

"My daddy was a doctor, right?"

Copper cleared her throat. She was very close to tears. "Your daddy was a doctor, a very good one."

Lilly drew her legs up under her nightdress. Copper put an arm around them.

"Tell me about my daddy," Lilly said.

*Where to start?* Copper wondered. "What would you like to know?"

"Where did you meet him? I know he came to the mountains and found you all poor and uneducated, and then he rescued you and took you to Lexington, where Aunt Alice taught you everything you know."

"Hardly everything I know. If you remember, your grandmam is a teacher. She taught me and my brothers. I had a diploma for all twelve grades before I ever met Alice."

"But you were poor, right? Aunt Alice said you didn't even have shoes."

This conversation was not going as Copper intended. Alice Upchurch was getting under her skin, and she wasn't even present. "Having shoes and liking to wear them are two different things. I'd still go barefoot if I weren't a grown-up lady."

Lilly played with Copper's fingernails. She liked to snap them with her thumb. "Mama, you're a sight."

"It was a night much like this one when I met Simon Corbett. Your uncle Daniel was just a boy then, and he got bitten by a copperhead. It scared us all silly. We thought he would surely die. But someone remembered hearing of a doctor visiting relatives in the vicinity. Your daddy rode up on a horse to save Daniel, but the horse wasn't white.

"We courted long-distance—your father wrote the most beautiful letters—for nearly a year before we married. I was seventeen when I left these mountains to live with my husband in the big city. Oh, I was green as grass. I didn't even know what a water closet was. The first time I pulled the chain, I thought the water would ruin the ceiling of the room below."

Lilly laughed. "Poor little Mama. What else didn't you know?"

"It wasn't so much what I didn't know but what I did that got me through those first rough weeks. I knew my faith would sustain me, and I was confident of your father's love."

Lilly twisted around so she could look Copper in the eye. "Do I remind you of him?"

Copper closed her eyes and let her first young love wash through her mind. Early on, after his passing, every memory had had a painful aura—like dazzling shards of glass strewn in her path. But now the remembrance was softly blurred like an out-of-focus picture, sepia-toned and bearable. In her mind's eye she saw Simon in his study surrounded by bookcases full of leather-bound tomes.

"He was so smart and so curious. He had a very tidy way about himself—always organized. He was calm but not without a certain temper if he thought things were unfair. Does that remind you of anyone you know?"

Lilly pressed a crinkled ribbon on the bodice of her nightgown between her fingers. "All except the temper part," she said, then giggled. "Am I more like my father or Aunt Alice?"

"Definitely your father for his mind and charm and Alice for your feminine ways and beauty. Let's just say you got Alice's good parts."

"Don't you like Aunt Alice?"

Copper took a moment. She wanted to answer her daughter without deception or manipulation. "Things have not always gone smoothly between your aunt and me. We're both stubborn women. I would say I have affection and respect for Alice." She breathed in the scent of Lilly's hair, a mingling of chamomile and mint. "Sometimes I'm afraid she's going to steal you away from me." She tried to say this lightly and with humor, but her voice broke on the hidden truth.

Years rolled away when Lilly turned to catch Copper's face between her hands and squeezed until Copper's lips pouted like a fish. "I love you more than birthday cake. More than apple butter," she said, reminding Copper of the game they used to play. "How much do you love me?"

"I love you more than rain on a hot day. I love you more than long sweetening."

Lilly flung her arms around Copper. "I love you a bushel and a peck and a hug around the neck."

"You are my sweet, silly girl. I think I will rock you to sleep."

"You used to rock me every night, right?"

"Every single one. It was the highlight of my day. Goodness, where did John and the kids get to?"

"It's pitch-dark. Daddy took them in while we were talking. Didn't you notice?" Lilly slid off her lap and stuck out her hand. "Here, I'll pull you up. Let's go looking."

Barefoot, Copper and Lilly walked around the house in a summer night ritual. They stopped outside Lilly's room. In the window a jar of lightning bugs twinkled with a luminous glow. All around the house they went before coming to Jack's room on the other side.

"Jack's jar is so full, it looks like he took a bite out of the moon," Lilly said.

"We'd better get to bed ourselves. This is going to be a busy week getting you ready for your trip."

Lilly did a happy dance. "I know. I'm sooo excited. I can't wait for Wednesday."

"I could," Copper said. "I could wait a month of Sundays."

"Now," Lilly said, kissing Copper's cheek, "just you remember I'll always come back."

*She didn't even have to tiptoe to kiss me,* Copper thought as they walked across the porch. *When did that happen?* "Good night. Sleep tight."

"I have to let the lightning bugs out of the jars before I go to bed, else they'll be dead by morning," Lilly said.

Copper held the screen door open. "Don't forget to include Kate in your prayers."

"I won't. And I'll memorize my Scripture in the morning. You never know when you'll need a good verse to keep you company."

# 17

COPPER STOOD AT the cookstove, flipping corn cakes in a cast-iron skillet, while Lilly hopped around the kitchen on one foot, obviously too excited to sit at the breakfast table.

"I can't believe this day is finally here," Lilly said. "What time do we meet the coach?"

"Just as I said before, we'll leave here at eleven forty-five. It's no more than a ten-minute walk to the crossroads. The driver will wait if he's early but not if we're late. Now sit and eat."

Molasses mixed with melting butter as Lilly tipped the pitcher and poured the long sweetening over her cakes. She sliced a bite with her fork, then jumped up before tasting it. Going to the pegs behind the door, she took down an apron and tied it around her neck like a bib. "I don't want to get anything on my new corset."

Alice had sent Lilly's traveling frock along with the button-front, lightly boned girl's corset. Underneath the corset she wore a cotton chemise with puffed sleeves and a drawstring neckline threaded with pink ribbon. Her new petticoat had a flounced eyelet hemline also threaded with pink ribbon.

Manda was pressing the outing suit Lilly would wear on the train.

"Do you want some more corn cakes, Manda?" Copper asked.

"No, ma'am. I'm full up." She held out the cocoa-colored, cape-collared suit jacket for all to admire. "I love the plaid trim on this, Lilly. You're going to be the best-dressed lady on the train."

"I know." Lilly pushed back her chair. "Let me get my hat."

"I'll take more," Jack said, licking molasses from his plate. "I've still got room."

"Jack, don't lick."

Jack made one more pass with his tongue, then put the plate down.

Copper slid two more cakes off the spatula and poured thick syrup for him. "More milk?"

Jack nodded. His mouth was already too full to speak.

Manda hung the jacket with the already-pressed skirt before spreading a yellow handkerchief-linen vest over the board. The vest would go under the short, buttonless jacket and over the white pleated shirtwaist blouse so just a bit of yellow would show.

Lilly flounced into the room like a fashion model. Her straw skimmer perched on the back of her head like a precarious bird's nest. The hat band exactly matched the blue and brown plaid bias embellishment on the jacket.

"I think you want to wear that more centered," Manda said. "I'll fix it for you after you get dressed. We'll need a hatpin."

"May I get one from your dresser, Mama?"

"After you eat," Copper said. "You can't start out on a long journey with no food in your stomach. You'll get sick."

"I have all that food in my hamper," Lilly said.

"We talked about this. The basket is for your supper. Don't eat it ahead of time. Now sit!"

Lilly laid her hat on the table and took her seat.

Copper scraped her cold cakes into the slop bucket. Lilly had cut them up into small pieces, so they wouldn't do to save. She gave Lilly a hot cake. "Please eat."

Jack reached for the hat.

"Jack!" Copper, Lilly, and Manda yelled in chorus.

"Why am I always the one in trouble?" Jack asked.

"I can't imagine, Son," Copper said, wiping his hands and face with a wet rag.

"Can I go slop the pig?" he asked.

"You know better than to ask to do that. Go wait on the porch for Aunt Remy. She'll be here directly."

Copper poured a mug of tea and sat across the table from Lilly. She had planned the morning so she would have some quiet time with her daughter before taking her to the coach. But even with John leaving before dawn to haul logs for pay and Molly and Mazy spending the night with Merky at Cara's, the morning was still busy as a beehive. At least Lilly was eating now and she had drunk half her milk.

"Mama! Mama!" Jack yelled through the screen as if Copper weren't sitting six feet away. "Aunt Remy's coming around the corner. Can I go get my fishing pole?"

"Ye won't need no pole, boy," Remy said from the yard. "We're going dry fishing. All we have need of is a knife and a poke." She opened the door and stepped inside. "Come hug my neck afore I leave, Lilly."

Lilly put her arms around Remy. "I love you," she said.

Remy patted Lilly's back. "You be careful on that there iron horse. Don't be leaning out the winders."

"I won't." Lilly wiped a tear. "I'll sure miss you, Aunt Remy."

"Can we go now?" Jack said, his nose pressed against the screen.

"Did you tell your sister good-bye?" Copper asked.

Jack tore in. The door bounced behind him. He caught Lilly around the legs. "Good-bye. Bring me a present. A big one."

Lilly unlatched his arms and swung him around. "Be good while I'm gone, Jack-Pot. Take care of the mama cat and the kittens. Don't let Mazy and Molly wool them to death."

Jack ran back out the door ahead of Remy. Copper needed to talk to him about that.

"So," she heard him say as he waited for Remy to descend the steps, "what kind of fish don't need water?"

Copper watched Remy rest a hand on top of Jack's head, using his sturdy body like a cane. Jack matched his steps to hers. Maybe he didn't need a lesson in manners after all.

"They's a kind of mushroom that puts you in mind of a closed pinecone. Dredged in cornmeal and fried in bacon grease, morel's as good as any fish you ever ate."

Jack dragged Remy's crutch behind him. It made little ruts in the yard. "Where will we find them?"

Remy pointed. "We'll climb yon hill and go around to the north side. They's several stands of poplar trees way up there. Land fish thrive under poplar trees."

"Do they bite? Do they have whiskers like catfish?"

"You'll see, boy. You'll understand soon enough."

Lilly came up beside Copper at the screen door and slipped her arm around her waist. "I'll miss you all. I'm starting to feel a little homesick already."

Manda folded the ironing board and put it in the pantry. "Your outfit is ready."

"Oh, thank you," Lilly said. The mantel clock chimed the hour. "It's nine already. Come help me get dressed, Manda. I can't wait any longer."

By nine thirty Lilly was all ready to go. Her valise was packed, and her hat was expertly pinned to the crown of her head. "How much longer?" she asked.

Copper set the wicker hamper on the table and flipped open the hinged lid. "Let me check this one more time." She pulled back the linen towel Lilly could use for a napkin or a bib. There was enough food in there to feed a grown man for two days. She had packed chicken drumsticks, boiled eggs, buttered biscuits, tomatoes and a cucumber picked just this morning, salt and pepper in twists of waxed paper, two fried apple pies, and two slices of chocolate cake. Lilly wouldn't starve for sure.

"Something's missing." Manda stood back, surveying Lilly. She tapped her cheek with one finger. "Your spats! You can't go without them. They make the outfit."

Manda rushed out of the room and returned with the high-topped, kid-glove spats. Kneeling, she buttoned them over Lilly's patent leather slippers. "There, now you're perfect."

"You can get a drink of water from the container at the back of your car," Copper said. "Remember from last year?"

"You turn the spigot and hold a paper cone under it," Lilly said.

"Don't drink too much," Manda said, "or you'll spend all your time in the ladies'."

Copper couldn't think of one more instruction for Lilly. They'd talked about every possible thing from keeping her valise tucked beneath her feet to only sharing a seat with a lady. Mrs. Jasper would make sure the porter on the train knew to watch out for Lilly. She would give him the gratuity Copper had provided. Everything would be fine. Lilly would be in Lexington before bedtime. Much as she'd like to, she couldn't raise Lilly under a bell jar.

Finally finished preening Lilly, Manda poured water over the breakfast dishes.

"I can dry," Lilly said.

"Oh no, you might spot your dress," Manda said, shaving a bit of soft soap into the pan. "They won't take a minute."

"Guess I'll go sit on the porch and watch the world go by," Lilly said.

Copper poured more tea. She hadn't managed to have more than a sip all morning. "I'll sit with you."

She had no sooner taken a rocker beside Lilly's than a buckboard pulled into the barnyard. She put the chunky white cup on the porch floor and shaded her eyes.

Mr. Morton jumped down from the seat and hurried across the yard. "Miz Pelfrey, can you come? Something bad's a-happening." His face was creased with worry.

Copper felt a frisson of disquiet. It was much too soon for Emerald's baby to be born alive.

Manda stepped out the door. "I can see to Lilly. I'll walk her to the coach."

Copper caught her daughter in a fierce embrace, rocking her in her arms before letting her go.

Lilly squeezed Copper's cheeks between her palms and whispered, "Just remember I'll be back soon."

"I'll go get my kit, Mr. Morton," Copper said.

After her mother left, Lilly stayed in the rocking chair, pulling her white knit gloves off and then putting them back on. This morning was lasting way too long.

Manda came out with a granite bucket. "I'm going to

feed the hog. We've still got an hour before we need to leave the house."

Lilly watched Manda walk around the side of the barn. The pigpen was in the back. Daddy built it there to keep the smell and the flies away from the house. He didn't like for the little kids to go around there. He told Lilly a hog was a dangerous thing, but Lilly liked to visit the pen, where the fat hog rolled in its mud wallow on warm days. She always took an apple or a carrot or some such treat. The hog would sniff the air with his flat pink nose whenever she approached, as if she were the one who smelled bad. Maybe to the pig she did. The porker was the only animal Lilly didn't name. She didn't like to think about what would happen to him when the weather turned hog-killing cold, and they had fresh sausage for breakfast.

Manda came back around the corner of the barn. "I need to check on something. You stay right there. I'll only be a minute."

Lilly waited for what seemed like hours but, according to the pocket watch pinned to the front of her jacket by a fob, was only a few minutes. She wished Manda would come on. It wouldn't hurt to be early. The porch got hot from the summer sun, so she strolled up and down the yard in the shade of the trees, switching the valise and the wicker hamper from one arm to the other, trying to decide the best way to carry them. Neither was very heavy.

Aunt Alice would have all new outfits ready for her in Lexington. It would be so fun to try them on. Some dresses were sure to match cousin Dodie's. Dodie was a little different.

She was as sweet-natured as the kittens, but it took her a while to catch on to things. Lilly didn't mind. She liked Dodie lots.

It was boring just waiting. She'd walk down to the creek and back with her luggage. That would be good practice. She'd have to be really careful, though. Aunt Alice wouldn't like it if she got to her house with sticktights on her skirt tail.

The creek was sparkly where the sun shone on it through the leaves, but the path beside the bank was shady and cool. Lilly swung her bags as she walked along, sure she looked like a well-traveled young lady.

From far away she heard the bark of a dog. She wondered if it was the beagle, though it didn't sound like a beagle's deep bay.

Turning back, she started for home. Manda would be looking for her. She heard the dog again. It was yelping now. Its cry was pitiful to her ears. What if it was the beagle? What if it was caught in a trap? She had to go and see. If she hurried, there was still plenty of time.

The frantic sound of an animal in distress pulled her farther and farther along. She was out of breath when she got to the rock fence that separated the Pelfreys' property from the Stills'. She needed to go back or else she would miss the coach. She wished the dog would stop! Just stop! But it didn't.

For a minute she thought of all she would miss—the train ride, the chocolate ice cream, and the circus clowns. Really, though, she had no choice. Leaving her valise and the wicker hamper on top of the wall, she climbed over the rocks and went to find the dog.

# 18

THE SLOP OOZED over the edge of the bucket and plopped with thick drops into the wooden trough. Grunting, the nasty pig snuffed up the leftovers like it was his last supper. Manda hated this part of her job. She'd just as soon let the hog starve as stand here with the stink of the pen rising up around her like a vile perfume. Her earlier sunny mood took a dark turn.

She couldn't figure why things happened as they did. Why wasn't it her wearing a new outfit, waiting to catch a coach to the city? It was not that she minded helping Lilly. She actually liked the kid. But when would it ever be her turn?

If Manda stopped to think about it, and she often did,

she was the one who'd paid the piper. Only stood to reason she should be the one to dance. Here Lilly had a life of ease with a mother who adored her and a father, even though he was a step, who saw to her every need. While Manda's own father hardly knew she existed and her stepmother ignored her needs, as indifferent as a lazy sow flopping on its piglet.

Manda slapped at a horsefly. The day was turning hot. At least it wasn't Tuesday. She wouldn't sweat buckets while she ironed the Pelfreys' clothes, and thankfully nobody occupied the sickroom, so there wouldn't be extra chores. Often whole families turned up for meals whenever a relative was laid up there. Manda thought they were taking advantage, but Miz Copper was too kind to notice. Like that Abe Sizemore, Tillie's no-account. That man could eat the leg off a mule and have the saddle for dessert. Manda had been glad to be shut of them.

Her emotions churned like the mud the pig rolled in. Stupid thing—happy to be living off the leavings of others. She couldn't quite get a grip on what was making her so tired of her station in life. She'd never really minded until recently.

She thought of Sunday last and what she remembered of Brother Jasper's sermon. *"Every man received his reward according to his labor."* Well, she did the work. Now where was her reward? She'd had a bellyful of waiting.

It seemed to her that she always got the short end of the stick. As a girl, growing up in a house where nobody looked ahead and where manna was hard to come by—no matter what her father preached—Manda learned to make do or do without. Too often it was do without. By rights she should be living in hog heaven by now.

Manda was determined not to wind up settling like Dance or Cara, who was so befuddled by love she didn't know what she was missing. Lost in thought, Manda crossed her arms on the top pole of the pigpen and rested her head. She jumped back and brushed at her sleeves when the hog rustled over and started rooting on the other side of the fence. Looking up, he leered at her while mud mixed with cornmeal slid down his snout. A cloud of gnats rose like mist from his black-and-white hide.

If she could have her dream come true like the lovely Rose Feathergay, it would be thus: She and the middling man, newly married, would travel by coach and then by train to Eddyville, where Darcy would greet them with open arms. For the journey, Manda would wear a purple taffeta calling suit adorned with beaded crystal swirls.

She would work with Darcy in her dress shop and he would . . . well, he would play his music, of course. In no time they would be wealthy and have a genuine brick two-story house. She could see it now: Mr. and Mrs. Whoever? She guessed she'd better ask him his name! They would be pillars of the community, solid as the white columns holding up the roof of their porch. Then Manda could forget about tar-paper shacks and thin walls layered with sheets of newsprint that failed its duty to keep out a cold winter's wind. In the last house she lived in before her mother died, you could see the ground through the cracks in the floor. At least there was a floor. They all thought they'd come up in the world to park their chairs on wood.

All Manda could count on during her childhood was a passel of mouths for her mother to feed. At least that proved her father was good for something. No wonder women got old before their time.

Oh, she was full of woe today. She didn't even like her own company. Better get to the well and pump some water to wash out the bucket, or the slick rim of slop would set like glue and she'd have to chip it out.

Manda turned from the pen—what a place to daydream— and started around the barn. The hog made a funny high- pitched sound—somewhere between a squeal and a whistle. Silly thing was probably strangled. It ate like a pig after all. This particular hog had a penchant for choking, which meant she'd have to take a board and thunk him between the shoul- der blades to restore his breath. She didn't have time for this. She was not about to let Lilly miss the coach.

A more musical note stopped her in her tracks. When she looked back, the middling man was sitting neat as a pin atop the rail fence as if her dreams had conjured him up. The pig nosed an apple core around the trough.

She laughed with delight. "What are you doing here?"

"Me? Why, I come to visit my girl."

"How did you know I where I was?"

He looked at her through hooded eyes and laughed. "I been watching you. You and everybody else in this house. I don't miss nothing."

She stood clutching the handle of the slop bucket with both hands as if it were a bouquet of flowers. What she wouldn't give for the purple taffeta dress right now. "Can you wait for me? I have to walk Lilly to the coach."

"Surely," he wheedled, "you can spare me ten minutes."

"Just let me tell her—don't leave. Promise?"

He crossed his arms over his chest, hooked his heels in a lower rail, and leaned back as if he were sitting at a banquet table and not on the top rail of a pigpen. "Baby, I'm yours."

Manda put the bucket in the shade at the side of the barn and waved to Lilly. "I need to check on something. You stay right there. I'll only be a minute."

Right across from the pigpen was a narrow back door to the barn. With fumbling fingers she unlatched it, and he followed her in. Dust motes danced in the scant light let in by the few windows. A freshly cut stack of timothy hay sweetly scented the air. The double front doors were closed. She was glad Lilly couldn't see her. The animals had been let out to pasture, so all the stalls were empty. The only witness to their tryst might be the barn cat.

Without preliminary, he caught her upper arms with a vise-like grip and drew her to him. His lips were hard and demanding. Hers responded, soft and yielding. They stood for long minutes in the middle of the barn kissing—such kissing. The kisses seemed to draw the very lifeblood from her bones. She thought she might fall in a puddle of yearning at his feet. She couldn't get close enough, and it seemed neither could he.

The world outside dissolved like so much sugar stirred

into water. His lips were at her throat. She was spellbound. With one quick and fluid motion he lifted her by the waist, swung her up, and set her on the feed box. Suddenly frightened, she edged away until her back was against the barn siding. Forcefully, he pulled her toward him.

The splintered grain of the feed box scratched the back of her legs. Her arms ached where he pinned them across her chest with his muscular forearm. He grew insistent. Her mind screamed—*Run!* She twisted in his grasp like a fish on the line. "Stop! No!"

He backhanded her. Her head bounced against the barn siding with the thump of an overripe melon. "Tease," he said with his mouth against her ear. "Like it rough, do you?" Then he hit her so hard she saw stars. When her lip split, she could taste her own blood.

With an effort she freed one hand and gouged his eye. He yelped and stepped back. It was her chance. The only one she might get. She scrambled off the bin, falling to her hands and knees. Finding her footing, she backed up to the hay, never taking her eyes off the man. He laughed but not in mirth. With a dip of her knees, she reached down to grab the tool she knew was at the base of the haystack.

He advanced with a look in his eyes that scarred her soul. She wondered if he meant to kill her. She swept the air with the pitchfork like a blind man with a cane. He put up his hands, palms out, still laughing that crazy-man's laugh. Manda's heart pumped pure fear through her body. She'd been entertaining the devil.

"Help me, Lord," she prayed aloud.

He took a step forward, his arms still surrendered. "Who're you talking to? Ain't nobody here but us. Come on, baby. You've been asking for it."

Manda screwed up her courage and struck out. She could feel the pitchfork make contact before it slipped from her sweaty hands. With trepidation she looked out the slits of her swollen eyes and saw him falter.

His eyes were wide with surprise. "You little rouser. You stabbed me."

They stood in the middle of the barn like actors on a stage. It was cool and shadowy and strangely silent. The middling man stood stock-still. The pitchfork dangled where she'd stabbed him. It made an ugly sucking sound when he pulled it out. It clattered to the floor. Blood as red as rose petals dripped from the perfect holes left by the tines.

Manda was rooted to the spot. If the barn caved in, she couldn't move to save herself. Shocked, she couldn't take in what she had just done or what he had tried to do.

He looked around and found his hat. He put it on his head. Pulling a red bandanna from his back pocket, he bandaged his wounds. He walked right up to her and tipped her chin. He kissed her tender as a lover. "I'll see you in hell," he said, then walked out the back door.

Like a wooden soldier, she moved to the double doors and tried to shove one open. It stuck as it always did. She nearly screamed in frustration, but when it finally slid on its track, she took a minute to compose herself. Nobody had to know what had just happened. There were only two witnesses, and he wasn't dumb enough to tell.

All she had to do was walk across the barnyard to the house, get Lilly, and take her to the coach. It was as simple as that. It was like a bad dream best forgotten. She felt renewed, saved from death—or worse.

"Lilly," she called when she got to the porch. "Let's start out. You don't want to be late." Her voice wavered weakly like that of an old woman. Lilly wouldn't notice, though. She was too excited about her trip.

Nobody answered.

Manda went into the kitchen. Frantically, she searched each room. The house was hushed as a funeral parlor. She could hear nothing but the twelve strikes of the mantel clock. Her stomach churned. Oh no. Lilly must have walked to the coach stop alone.

She calmed herself. It would be all right. She would run and catch up. Generally speaking, the coach was late.

She made it to the crossroads in record time. There was no one about. The intersection was as empty as the house had been. Way off, she glimpsed the unmistakable back end of the coach bouncing away on its oversize wheels. She stood in the middle of the dusty lane waving like a fool, seeing Lilly off.

# 19

COPPER HELD ON tightly to her supplies as Mr. Morton hurried the horse along. She hated not taking Lilly to the coach. But what was she to do? Thankfully, Lilly understood and Copper trusted Manda—most of the time, anyway. Lately she seemed distracted, even flighty, and just last week Copper thought she had caught her in a lie.

It was when Manda returned from town after taking some potatoes, eggs, and two tins of cream to market. Before, Manda had always marched right in when she got home, proud as punch of the money she'd made for Copper and for herself. But Friday she took an unusually long time unsaddling

Chessie, and then she hung around the porch talking to Lilly before she came inside.

She'd fumbled in the bottom of her linen bag before she brought out some coins and placed them on the kitchen table. "I hope that's right," she'd stammered. "I think I lost some money somewhere along the way."

"Didn't you count it as you were paid?" Copper asked.

"No, ma'am, I forgot. I guess I got distracted."

"You must be more careful. You don't want folks thinking they can easily take advantage of you." Copper counted the money and handed half back to Manda.

"You keep it," Manda said. "I shouldn't have been so careless."

Copper folded Manda's fingers over the money in her palm. "The lesson you learned is more valuable than the few coins you might have lost. Don't you agree?"

"Yes, I guess so," Manda said, her eyes shifting.

Their interchange left Copper with a disquieted feeling. After supper that day, while Manda was playing yard games with the children, Copper talked to Remy about it, which was probably a mistake. Remy trusted few people. And Copper knew she'd never cottoned to the hired girl. Remy wanted to do everything herself.

Remy'd leaned on her crutch and made one of her pronouncements. "Girl acts like a sheep in the wrong pasture. She bears watching, I suspect."

"I can't figure it," Copper said. "She's always been honest with me."

"All's I'm saying is she's up to something. Market day she took out of here fast as a pullet wanting to lay an egg. And she was all fancied up in a dress that fit her like the bark on a tree. Who fancies up just to carry some eggs to town?"

Copper had to smile. What did Remy know about being fancy? "She's young. Girls like to look pretty and be admired." She watched Manda run across the yard, dodging Jack's tag. "I think I'll let it pass this time."

Remy had nodded. "Bears watching, though."

Now the buckboard hit a rock, and Copper nearly bounced off the seat. "Mr. Morton, it won't do your wife any good if you turn this vehicle over."

"Sorry, but I'm that worked up over Miz Tierney and all. I'm telling you she's sick enough to die."

"Who?"

"Miz Tierney, Emerald's mother. She's real bad off. She won't let Emerald even open the door to her room. She says she don't want to mark the baby with her pain." He flicked the reins again. "And you can see why I can't go in there—me being her son-in-law and that. Miz Tierney is real modest."

The horse and buggy splashed through the small pond Chessie had faltered over. Copper was surprised Mr. Morton could get a buckboard over this precarious trail. She knew she couldn't have.

Ruby. It was Ruby who was ill. Copper had a momentary feeling of relief. Emerald wasn't in danger of losing her baby. "When did Ruby take sick?"

"I reckon I heered her about three o'clock this morning.

I got up real careful-like so as not to disturb Emerald's sleep and found her mother pacing on the porch. Soon as Emerald woke, Miz Tierney went in her room and ain't come out since. Finally she hollered through the door, 'Ernie, go see if Miz Pelfrey can come.'"

Ernie Morton pulled the reins sharply when they passed the bent sycamore. "Gee!" he hollered to the horse. "Gee."

Copper steadied herself with one hand against the side of the buckboard. "Can you tell me what her symptoms are?"

"Symptoms?"

"Did she say what she thinks is causing her pain?"

"'Course Miz Tierney wouldn't say nothing to me, but Emerald told me her ma's got plumbing problems. Rocks in her pipes."

"Ah, kidney stones. That explains the pain. They say it's worse than labor."

Ernie took off his hat before swiping his arm across his forehead. "I don't know how women stand their plight. It's just one thing after another."

Emerald was waiting on the porch, still dressed in her nightgown. She was crying and wringing her hands. As soon as Ernie helped Copper down from the buckboard, Emerald ran across the yard and grabbed Copper's hands. Her face was red as a beet. "You're here. Oh, thank You, Lord, for bringing Miz Pelfrey."

Ernie retrieved the doctor's bag and Copper's valise and followed them to the house.

"Emerald," Copper said, "splash some water on your face and calm down. You're not helping your mother this way."

Ernie poured some water from the bucket on the wash bench into a small basin. He held it like an offering in front of his wife.

Standing in the middle of the porch, Emerald scooped up handfuls and dashed them in her face.

"Now," Copper said, "I want you to sit down and put your feet up. Your pressure's probably sky-high. I'll take care of your mother."

There were two doors off the kitchen of the house. It wasn't hard to tell which one led to Ruby's bedroom. It was the one from which long moans came. Copper cracked the door. "Ruby, whatever is the matter?"

Ruby was on her back on the floor with her knees drawn up. Her fingernails clawed at the thin piece of carpet underneath her. She turned her head to look at Copper with the pleading eyes of an animal caught in a trap.

Copper knelt at her side and brushed strands of sweat-soaked hair from her face. "I'm here to help."

Ruby caught Copper's hand with the clasp of a drowning person. "I think my innards are falling out."

"May I examine you? Would that be all right?"

Ruby arched her back and pushed her heels against the floor as a powerful contraction seized her.

Copper had seen this move before. She placed one hand on Ruby's abdomen. "I believe you're in labor."

Ruby rode the wave of the contraction, then looked at Copper as if she'd lost her mind. "That can't be. I'm too old."

"Evidently not," Copper said with a smile.

"I can't figure it," Ruby said, rolling her head from side to side. "I've been through the change."

"Look at it this way. It's much better than your innards falling out."

When she began to check her patient, she saw an alarming sight. A loop of navel cord protruded from between Ruby's thighs. It could easily be mistaken for an intestine.

Emerald was so overwrought, Copper was averse to involving her. She didn't need two deliveries today. Ernie would do. Still kneeling, Copper cracked the door behind her. "Ernie, bring me water—hot, if you have it—lye soap, a basin, and clean linen. Hurry!" With her foot she pushed the door closed. Copper helped Ruby into the knee-chest position. That should buy a little time by easing the compression of the cord. She jerked a quilt off the bed and draped Ruby for modesty.

There was a light knock at the door. "Here's your stuff," Ernie said.

"Just set it down out there. I can get it. Stay close by, though, so you can hear me if I need you."

Copper gave Ernie a few seconds to get away. Ruby would die of mortification if she was seen in such a position. As Copper retrieved the things, she saw him sitting in a kitchen chair just a few feet away. His back was to his mother-in-law's bedroom. "Thank you, Ernie," she said.

"You're welcome and all."

There was no time for her usual antiseptic technique. Lye-soap scrubbing of hands and tools would have to suffice. From her kit she took her ankle-length apron, her hair covering, the ligatures, and the scissors. Poor Ruby seemed to doze a minute with her face twisted sideways on the rug.

Copper touched her back. "Let's get that baby out of there."

# 20

MANDA STAGGERED BACK to the house. She made it nearly to the porch before she collapsed, trembling and crying. She lay there for the longest time trying to get ahold of herself before someone came home.

She got to her knees and crawled to the steps. She sat on the top one with her head in her hands. Considering that Mr. John was off logging with just about every other man on Troublesome and Miz Copper was gone on a mission, the first one back would likely be Miss Remy. No way was she going to let Miss Remy see her like this. She'd die first.

She shook herself. *Think!* What should she do? Her mind clicked with reasoning. First go to the barn and see if there was any little thing out of place, anything that someone might question. It took all her courage to walk back to that barn. Dread accompanied each step, souring in her stomach like green apples.

The closer Manda got to the door, the sicker she felt. Her head whirled like a child's top until she emptied her stomach in the grass. Now she'd have to clean that up too, as well as the slop bucket. It seemed like years ago since she'd blithely set it in the shade of the barn.

The door was standing open. Was it supposed to be? Her mind spun backward. She recalled thinking she was glad it was closed so Lilly couldn't see her with the middling man. That was right, so when she finished checking the barn, she should close it tight again.

The most obvious thing out of place in the barn was the pitchfork. She was nearly sick again when she picked it up and saw blood drying on the tines. Had she really stabbed a man? How could that be? She had never intentionally hurt another living being. What if he went to the sheriff with some made-up story? She could be in jail before nightfall.

"Think!" she said out loud this time. She took the fork outside and thrust it into the ground over and over. It came out clean as ever. Back inside, she tried to figure exactly where the tool had been in the haystack. She stuck it far into the base so it wouldn't fall over.

"What else?" Manda asked as she looked around. The feed box—she'd have to check the feed box. It loomed like a beast in the shadows, but she forced herself to go to it. Her heart nearly stopped when she spied a piece of white muslin caught in the splintery grain on top of the bin. She checked her petticoat and saw the jagged tear. It was nearly her undoing. Her head whirled again and she saw, as if through his eyes, herself sitting atop the grain bin.

A flash of white-hot anger fueled her. She wished he would come back. This time she'd stab him through the heart! Her shoulders slumped. No, she wouldn't. The Bible said vengeance belonged to the Lord. The middling man would get his eventually. What she needed to do was protect herself and her reputation and figure out how she let this thing come about in the first place.

Carefully, she removed the small piece of fabric and stuck it in her pocket. She walked around the inside of the barn but couldn't find another thing worth her attention. She closed the double doors and took the slop bucket to the well and filled it. Tipping the bucket, she splashed water over the place where she had lost her breakfast, then went to the well again, filled the bucket, and left it to soak.

Back at the house she stood and looked across the yard to the barn. There was nothing out of the ordinary. Tucking her blouse into her skirt, she went inside. It was only one o'clock—such a little bit of time had passed, but in that little bit her life was changed, nearly ruined. What that man had almost done to her was the thing every woman dreaded. It would have marked her for life. No other man would want to touch her if that had happened. She would have been branded a fallen woman—no matter the circumstance.

Manda poured a cup of cold, strong coffee and drank it black. Memories scratched at her conscience. She tried to ignore them, but they continued picking at her, as irritating as chigger bites. She saw herself flirting with the man, preening for him, begging for his attention. How could she have been so stupid? She'd set her own self up—and she didn't even know his name!

Hot tears sprang from her eyes. She slapped both hands over her mouth to hold back the sobs that threatened. She began to pace around the room, beating her fists against her legs. Where was she to find solace? To whom could she turn?

She'd just have to rely on herself like she'd always done—act normal and carry on. That was the only thing that would get her through.

That decided, Manda thought she would go to the garden and gather some vegetables for supper. On the way out the door, she grabbed a bonnet from a peg and glanced at the mirror over the washstand. She caught her breath. Her hair stood out like a dandelion gone to seed. Her eyes were nearly swollen shut, and her upper lip was split. Dried blood flaked in the corners of her mouth. One sleeve was hanging by a thread.

Miss Remy and Jack could be back any second. She needed to buy some time. There was a piece of scrap paper in the middle of the kitchen table and a yellow lead pencil. It looked like Lilly had been copying a Bible verse. Manda tore the page in two, shoving the used part into her pocket.

Her fingers brushed the muslin fabric. She leaned over the table and began to write.

> *I have gone to visit Darcy. Will catch a ride. Miz Copper is at the Mortons'. Mr. Morton came for her. Saw Lilly off. Be back before too long, good Lord willing.*
>
> *Yours,*
> *Manda*

She propped the note against the sugar bowl, then went to the sickroom. Under the cot where she slept weekdays was the tattered carpetbag she used to haul her clothes back and forth. She reached under and pulled it out, checking to make sure her treasures—the stash of wages and egg money and the album of pressed flowers—were still inside. The baking powder tin where she kept the money felt comforting in her hand. She shook it. The small roll of paper bills stifled the clinking change. Counting last week's wages, she'd finally saved enough to get to Eddyville with some left over.

Taking a moment, she opened the album, her eyes hungry for something serene and beautiful. Ever since she was a girl, she had collected and pressed flowers. When she lived with her parents, she dried the petals between the pages of the heavy family Bible. Once she began to work for Miz Copper, she slipped the roses, marigolds, daisies, zinnias, strawflowers, and black-eyed Susans behind the proper letters of the dictionary that rested on a wooden stand in the living room. Miz Copper had gifted the album to her. It had velvet covers the color of moss and solid vellum pages. The gift had made Manda feel special. Now she felt like a husk of a girl as dried out as the once lusciously blooming flowers.

Grief for her young and innocent self washed through her. Just this morning at the pigpen she had belabored her boring life. Now she'd give anything to have that sense of safety back, that sense of things in place—boring or not.

What if she walked into the kitchen and took a seat at the table and let whoever came home first find her there? What if she just told her story straight up as it happened? She could see the hue and cry that would cause. Mr. John would go get Dimmert and Cara and Dance and Ace. Someone would go to town and bring back the sheriff. She would have to tell the story again and again. The sheriff would round up a posse. The men, probably even Gurney, would ride off seeking vengeance, tracking the middling man like a rabid animal. Every tongue up and down Troublesome Creek would soon tell the sad tale of Dory Manda Whitt—Manda the fallen woman.

No, she should stick to her story, telling no one but her sister. Darcy would understand better than anyone else. When her husband was arrested, tongues wagged, relishing the story for weeks, until someone else's tragedy became the latest gossip fodder. But Darcy had overcome her hardship, and so would she. It was like digging a tunnel with a bent teaspoon, doable if the spoon held out and you lived long enough.

Of course, Miz Copper would help her given the chance.

Just the very thought of seeing the kindness and concern on her benefactor's face made the tears stream once again. Manda didn't think she could stand any sympathy right now. And what if Miz Copper started looking at her differently? She really couldn't stand the thought of that.

The screen door slammed. Jack laughed. They were home.

Hurriedly, she emptied the two dresser drawers designated for her use into the bag, atop the baking powder tin and the mossy green album. She shoved the dresser drawers closed with her hip, slipped out the sickroom door, and headed for the little house.

She didn't dare go around to the front. Someone might see. Manda crept to the back of the cabin. She pried a window open and crawled over the sill.

There was a fresh corn-shuck mattress on the bed. Manda had stuffed it herself from the supply Miss Remy had dried last fall. They kept the shucks in a wire bin in the washhouse. One of Manda's chores was to keep the shucks turned and aired so they wouldn't mold. Once she'd found a nest of mice in there. Miss Remy had blamed her—said she wasn't turning the shucks often enough—and made her sort through each husk looking for any sign a mouse had been nibbling. Manda must have thrown out half of them.

The corn shucks rustled dryly when she lay down. She would rest here until full dark, then walk to town and journey on from there. Maybe she would come back—maybe she wouldn't. It remained to be seen.

She sank deeply into the mattress. It rose around her like

a feather bed but without the softness. That was good; a bed of nails would have suited her just fine.

"Stupid. Stupid. Stupid. Stupid," she chanted under her breath.

Why had she fallen for the romantic notions in those magazine stories? Had she ever known a Rose Feathergay? or anyone who remotely resembled her? Hardly. Poor Rose would probably find out her woodsman was an ax murderer.

Life was just one long tedious road to nowhere. Manda touched her sore lip and winced. The middling man's words came back to her: *"You've been asking for it."* She decided Miss Remy had it figured out. Lead your own life and don't get tangled up with men. From now on that was what she intended to do.

It was hard to give up on your dreams, though. Tears leaked from her eyes and ran down the sides of her face like rain slides down a windowpane. How could she have been so stupid?

# 21

COPPER COOKED SUPPER for the Morton family. Ruby would have none of lying in bed, so she sat at the table with her newborn bundled in her arms. Everyone, excluding Ruby, grinned from ear to ear partly from happiness over the baby and partly from relief that Ruby was alive. Ruby looked stunned, like she'd been poleaxed. Copper kept turning from the stove just to look at the beautiful baby. In the rush to get out of the house, she had forgotten her scales, but she guessed him to be ten pounds.

"No wonder you had shortness of breath, Ruby," Copper said. "I can't believe I missed that you had a baby that big in your belly."

"You can't believe it? Mercy me, I feel such a fool."

"But aren't you happy?" Emerald said, taking the baby from her mother and bouncing him in her arms. "He's so beautiful."

"Should Ernie go fetch Mr. Tierney?" Copper asked.

"I reckon not," Ruby said. "I live here. He visits Sundays."

Copper looked at the chubby newborn lying in his sister's arms. Obviously Mr. Tierney did more than visit. She couldn't wait to share this story with John. But it would go no farther. She was scrupulous in guarding her patients' privacy. John was the guardian of her secrets.

"You done real good, Miz Tierney," Ernie said. "Why, this fine boy will be our baby's uncle."

"Ernie," Ruby said, "I hate to be a bother, but I crave a glass of cold buttermilk. Would you mind to go to the springhouse and get some?"

Ernie backed out the door, never taking his eyes off Emerald and the infant. "If that ain't a pretty picture."

Ruby craned her neck to make sure her son-in-law was out of earshot. "Miz Pelfrey . . ."

"Please call me Copper."

"Copper, really how did this come about? I ain't had my visitor for a year now. If I'd have had the barest inkling such a thing could happen, I would have told Mr. Tierney to keep his this-'n'-that at home."

Copper checked the new potatoes. She dumped in a bowlful of just-shelled peas. She'd let them cook a few more minutes. She tapped the fork against the lip of the pot and put the lid back on. "Turn-of-life babies are not that uncommon. It can be a very fertile time. It's like the body's not quite ready to give up on reproducing. I once helped deliver a set of triplets to a fifty-five-year-old woman. Like you, she thought the disorder in her health was from her turning a certain age."

Ruby slapped her own cheek. "Surely not."

"Yes, triplets and all over four pounds. It was the talk of the town."

"Was ary of them normal?"

"Fit as fiddles—the whole lot of them."

"Triplets." Emerald's face got dreamy. "Oh, I'd love me a set of triplets."

"Don't wish for such," Ruby said. "You'll bring trouble to this house."

Ruby was like many women up here in the mountains. She was stalwart and strong—always expecting the unexpected. Stories circulated of women dropping a baby at the end of a row of corn they'd just weeded and then going right on to the next, or having a baby in the middle of the night and then getting up to cook breakfast or do a wash. Many were poor as Job's turkey and couldn't afford the time to lie abed. And most, like Ruby, were too proud to be waited on.

Copper knew her own situation was unusual. Because of her first marriage, she had money of her own. John was a hard worker and often worked for wages, but having money in the bank afforded her family luxuries not available to most folks in the area. Having a nice house with room for her small clinic and a hired girl like Manda allowed her the ministry of midwifery God had led her to. It also helped that John was not arrogant. He didn't base his manhood on what she did or what she had. His only complaint was that he missed her when she was gone.

Copper dusted pieces of trout with cornmeal. They popped and sizzled when she laid them in the skillet. Her stomach rumbled. She hadn't eaten but a few bites of leftover corn cakes today. Supper would sure taste good.

Ernie returned and started filling glasses with buttermilk. Copper cut the corn bread. Emerald dished the food onto plates.

Ruby said, "I wish I'd known you were coming, Copper. I'd have baked a pork cake."

Everyone laughed as they took their seats.

"Another time." Copper sat with her hands folded in her lap. She would give Ernie an opportunity to offer grace. If he didn't, she would ask if she could. He didn't, but Ruby did.

"Lord," she prayed, "how can we thank You enough for the blessings of this day? For food on the table, this boy in my arms, for You bringing Copper to me in my time of need, for all these and more, we give You thanks. Amen."

The fish flaked when Copper cut it with her fork. It was moist and tender. "Ernie, this fish is delicious."

"Oh, I can't take credit," he said. "Miz Tierney's the fisherman in this house."

"I caught them last evening," Ruby said. "I went fishing before the pains laid me out."

Copper didn't know when she had enjoyed an evening more. This family was so full of kindness toward each other.

Ernie even insisted on doing the dishes. "You cooked," he said when Copper began scraping the plates. "I'll see to this."

Copper got Ruby settled with the baby. It took a lot of coaxing to get him to nurse. Fat thing just wanted to lie about being adored. Copper could have just carried him home with her—he was that delectable. As if Ruby would give him up.

Besides, if Copper's suspicions proved correct, she would be busy enough with her own in about eight months. She hadn't told John yet. She'd give it a couple more weeks to be certain. Hopefully, he would be as happy as she was. He had his reservations, she knew, but he would come around.

Emerald poked her head around the doorframe. "Your husband's out front."

She went out to meet John, surprised and pleased to see he had brought Jack along.

"Everything all right?" he asked, handing Jack down from the saddle.

She nodded.

"I got to steer, Mama," Jack said. "I'm good at it too."

John dismounted and sneaked a kiss to her cheek. "We brought Chessie with us so you'll have a way back tomorrow."

She nestled in his arms for the briefest time. Public displays of affection were not appropriate, and besides Ernie was right there.

"Thank you," she said. "You've met Ernie, right?"

John pumped Ernie's hand. "Yeah, that day in the church-yard. How's it going?"

"I'll just take Jack inside to meet the new baby," Copper said, "and leave you fellows to talk."

She held Jack's hand and cautioned him not to be loud and not to touch the baby. "Ruby, this is my son, Jack. He's come to pay his respects."

Jack looked the infant over. "Ma'am, you got yourself a whopper."

Rose smiled. "I sure do."

"Does he have a name?"

"Not yet. I haven't had time to think about that."

Jack leaned against the bed and looked the baby over. "We had a baby Mama called Jumbo, but he wasn't big like this. I don't know why Mama called him that. Can I see his feet?"

"It was the Sizemores' baby," Copper explained as Ruby unwrapped blankets. "Do you know Tillie and Abe?"

"Can't say as I do," Ruby said.

"I need to have a get-together once all the babies are big enough."

"Wait until I have mine," Emerald said.

Jack swung his head around to stare at Emerald. When he opened his mouth to speak, Copper tapped his shoulder. He turned his attention back to the baby. "Can I feel of his feet?"

"Sure," Ruby said.

Jack looked at his mother.

"Gently," she said.

With one finger Jack stroked the newborn's foot. The tiny
toes flared. Jack laughed and did it again.

"That's enough," Copper said. "Remember, he's not a toy."

"He sure is wrinkled," Jack said.

"Thank Mrs. Tierney, Jack."

"Thank you for sharing your baby with me," he said. "His
feet will probably straighten out one day."

"You're welcome," Ruby said. "You come back anytime."

"All right," Jack said. "Let me know when he's ready to
go fishing."

As Copper ushered her son from the room, Ruby and
Emerald's soft laughter followed. "That's one smart boy," she
heard Emerald say.

Copper couldn't help but be proud of Jack. She had
another story to share with John.

When they got back outside, Ernie took Chessie to stable
her for the night. Copper walked along with John to the head
of the trail that led back to Goose Creek and then on home.
Jack sat astride John's horse.

When they reached the trail, John turned and said,
"Listen, Manda's gone."

"What do you mean—gone?"

John handed her a crumpled bit of paper.

Copper smoothed it out and read what Manda had
printed. "I don't understand. This is not like Manda."

John shrugged. "Remy showed this to me when I got
back to the house this afternoon, said she found it by the
sugar bowl."

Copper read it again. "Forevermore, what was she think-ing?" She touched John's arm. "What should we do about the girls? I never thought to leave them so long with Cara."

John pulled her into an embrace. "They're fine, sweet-heart. I stopped on the way over here, and Cara said let them stay as long as we needed. But you'll be back tomor-row, right?"

"Yes, early afternoon, I'd say, if Ruby continues to do well. What will you and Jack eat? I don't want to make Remy think she has to cook."

"Remy and Jack had supper on the table when I got home today. Mushrooms and onions over fried potatoes. It was really good, wasn't it, Son?"

"Yup," Jack said, looking like he was going to nod off.

Copper put her arms around John's waist. "Thank you."

"For what? I'm just sharing the load."

"You make my life so easy."

He bent his head to her.

"You two aren't gonna start kissing, are you?" Jack asked.

"Turn your head," John said. "I'm going to plant one on your mother."

"Lift him down, John."

Jack slid from the saddle and hung suspended between his parents' arms. Copper kissed his cheeks until he squealed, "Uncle. Uncle."

Saddled up with Jack in front, John waited. "I'll just watch until you get back to the yard."

Copper walked backward, waving and blowing kisses as

far as she could; then she stood and watched her husband and son ride away. Her heart was full. Had a woman ever been more blessed? She thought not.

She thought of Mazy and Molly and was ever so thankful for Cara. She hadn't worried about them all day knowing they would be safe and well cared for in her friend's house. And Jack was with his father, not to mention Remy. Manda was a puzzle. Copper would never have thought she would go off like that. Of course she had seen Lilly to the coach first and she had a right to visit her sister, but something seemed amiss. It would be interesting to get Remy's take on it.

Lilly's train should be nearing Lexington by now. Copper wished she could be with her to witness her excitement. Alice was probably beside herself with anticipation. Selfishly, she still wished she hadn't let Lilly go. She liked tight apron strings—the tighter the strings, the lesser the worry. Well, there was nothing to do about it now but wait and enjoy all Lilly's stories when she returned.

For now she needed to get the newborn to eat and see to Ruby's comfort. In the morning, Ernie was going to fetch a neighbor lady to help out for a few days so Emerald wouldn't feel the need to do any heavy-duty work. Copper would be able to leave when she got there. Everything was in perfect order.

# 22

A SOUND LIKE a rasping saw startled Lilly awake, but she kept her eyes tightly closed. She didn't want to see where she was. The sound came in waves, speeding up and slowing down, then speeding up again. She was hungry and very thirsty, and when she rubbed her sore knees, they smarted like Mama had put stinging antiseptic on them.

She could feel something behind her, something like a wall, but it didn't seem like wood. Without turning around, she patted with her hands. It had ridges like a piece of tin. Was she on a roof? No, that didn't make sense. A roof would be under her if she was sitting on it, not all around her. She should have figured that out when the man dumped her here, but she had been too scared to notice anything. She wasn't going to open her eyes and look, though, because that would make it real.

Maybe she could keep from looking, but she couldn't keep from thinking. Kate would say that was Lilly's problem—she thought too much about serious things. Maybe Kate was right.

It had all started when she heard the dog barking. Who could ignore that pitiful sound? Not her. Scenes flashed behind her eyelids like lightning, scaring the wits out of her, until she settled on remembering things as they had happened. It was important to keep everything in order so she could deal with it one thing at a time.

Manda told her to wait on the porch, but she got bored and walked down to the creek. She heard the dog and went to investigate. When she got to the rock wall, she set her valise and the wicker hamper on top and climbed over. She remembered the dog's bark turned to whines and then to crying—if dogs could cry. She decided they could. The cry seemed to come from beyond a garden filled with corn. It was just a short way from the stone fence to the field. She started walking between two rows. The green stalks stood tall and straight with budding ears of corn tickling her face with their silky tassels. She tried to run but it was hard. The rows were too close together.

Something stopped her when she got to the end of the rows. She stood in the shadows of the cornstalks and looked out. A man was at the edge of a pond. A beagle was running around on the bank acting all frantic. It looked like the dog she fed the pieces of biscuit to. The man heaved a gunnysack into the water. It made a big splash. The dog jumped in after it. The man whisked his hands together like that was that and walked away.

Lilly held her breath. When she could no longer see the man, she ventured out of the cornfield. She ran to the edge of the pond. A thick patch of cattails obscured her view. Dragonflies buzzed her head. Watching her step, she parted the cattails. One burst and sent seeds flying around her.

The dog flailed in the water.

"Here, girl," she said but not too loud. "Come here."

The beagle paddled over and climbed up onto the shore. Droplets flew everywhere when the dog shook herself. Her big brown eyes looked up at Lilly. They said, "Help me."

Out in the pond, the bag was sinking. Lilly had a sick feeling about what was inside.

She searched among the fuzzy brown cattails for a stick. When she found a long, narrow piece of driftwood, she waded into the murky water, Daddy John's warning playing in her ears: *"Ponds are dangerous. The muddy bottom will suck you in, and you might not be able to get out."*

She could see what he meant, for it was like walking in cold molasses. Before she'd gone ten steps, one of her new shoes was stuck. She pulled her foot out and continued on, leaving the shoe in the mud. The water lapped at her waist. She leaned as far forward as she dared, jabbing with the stick.

She could feel the burlap bundle with the end of the spindly pole, but she couldn't catch hold. She needed to go farther out into the water. Using the stick, she probed the bottom of the pond. If she walked another two feet forward, she'd be in over her head, and she was not a good swimmer.

This called for praying with your eyes wide open. "Heavenly Father," she prayed aloud, "I'm in an awful fix. I'd be ever so grateful if You'd show me the way out."

Streaming behind the bag was a length of heavy twine she hadn't noticed before. Gently, gently, gently she used the end of the stick to turn the bag around and snagged the twine where it was coiled around the mouth of the sack. The bag was nearly submerged, but she saw victory coming her way. So close. So close—and then the stick snapped. She could have cried with frustration, but she didn't have time.

"I'm serious, Lord," she prayed again.

The water splashed behind her. The beagle swam by. Using her stocky legs like sculls, the dog propelled herself through the murky water. She grabbed the sack by her teeth and began swimming toward her.

Lilly reached for the burlap bag and caught it by the twine. The weight of it nearly pulled her under, but she held on and struggled back to the bank.

Kneeling by the bundle, she worked on the tie with her muddy hands. The dog ran circles around her, barking. "Shhh," she said as the twine came loose. There were four brown and white puppies inside the bag. She lifted them out and put them on the bank in the sunlight. Her heart was grieved.

The mother beagle nosed them all before settling on one. They all looked dead to Lilly, but the mother held out hope. Lilly put her hand where she thought the puppy's heart should be. She could feel a beat. When she touched the others in the same place, their tiny chests were still. Oh, it was so sad.

The one puppy's belly was so full of water, it jiggled. She picked it up by the heels like Mama said she did with just-born babies. She smacked its behind but not very hard. Dirty water gushed out of the puppy's mouth. It made a meager mewling sound. That made her so happy she wanted to dance before she remembered where she was and what she'd seen. She held the puppy close.

"Let's get out of here," she said to the beagle.

But before she had a chance to turn around, a rough arm grabbed her from behind. It closed around her midsection, nearly cutting off her breath. "You bunch of meddling no-goods," a man hissed in her ear. "I've had my fill of the lot of you."

Every time she tried to scream, he tightened his hold until her head was swimmy and her ears popped. It seemed he carried her a good long ways before he climbed a wooden ladder, opened a short but wide door, and tossed her in. She landed on her knees. The puppy plopped from her arms onto the floor with a soft *oof.* She hadn't realized she still held it.

The door closed. Her ears rang, but she could hear the man descend the ladder. The sound gave her some relief. She lay on her side and pulled the puppy close. It curled into her like the twins had when they were babies.

She heard the mother beagle's frenzied howling. The howling stopped on a sharp yelp of pain. She squeezed her eyes tightly shut and stuck her fingers in her ears. She didn't want to think about what was happening to the dog.

Even with her fingers in her ears, she could hear the thump of the ladder against the bottom of the doorframe. The door opened with a screech, and the mother beagle sailed across the floor, landing on her feet like a cat.

"Here's ye some company," the man said. "Cur ain't good for nothing no way."

The door screeched shut on rusty hinges. Lilly could hear something shoved against the door. "See how you like two or three days up here," she could hear him say as he descended. "Teach you lot to mind your own business."

She cried really hard but not very loud, for she didn't want the man to hear her. Who knew if he was still about? All she could think of were those three puppy bodies lying on the bank.

The beagle sat in front of her with her head cocked. She watched Lilly for a while, then came over and licked her tearstained face, like she was sorry to get her in this mess.

Lilly put her arms around the dog's neck. "That's okay. It's not your fault." She wiped her nose on the back of her hand. "At least we saved one baby."

She lay down again. The mother dog sidled up really close and then sort of fell against her. It almost made Lilly laugh. The puppy nursed. It seemed no worse for wear. Though she never thought she would, Lilly slept.

Now it was hours later. Lilly could tell by the change of light in the room. Even with your eyes closed, you could tell light from dark. She guessed now it was twilight. The waxing, waning, sawing sound shrilled like a thousand locusts caught in a jar.

Locusts! That was all it was. She'd just never heard so many at one time. From the climb up the ladder, she surmised she was in a sort of tree house. That was what made the bugs so loud; they were up in the trees as well.

She was uncomfortable, but try as she might to get her mind off her bladder, it would not be denied. "Oh, bother," she said and blinked.

She had guessed correctly. The walls of the round room were made of tin. The low roof seemed to be some kind of thatching. Narrow beams crisscrossed the room where a ceiling would be. Lots of stuff hung from the beams by hooks: splayed woven baskets and cracked dried-out harnesses, two chairs without seats, several moth-eaten suits of clothes, assorted pots and pans all with dings and chips, and if that didn't beat all—a chamber pot. With any luck it wouldn't have a rusted-out spot in the bottom. All she had to do was figure out how to get it down.

"What if I lift you up and you unhook it?" she said to the dog.

The dog wagged her tail. She seemed eager to help.

"I was just funning you. That only works if you have thumbs."

Stacked against the wall were several wooden boxes. Lilly

eased the top one down. It wasn't too heavy but it was awkward. She managed to get it to the floor. Lifting it was a different story, so using her legs for leverage, she scooted it until it was just under the necessary. Standing on top of the box, she unhooked the pot. From her vantage point she looked around the room. There was one door and two high-up windows on either side. One window was directly over the boxes. They reminded her of windows built in forts—windows designed to keep arrows out. She guessed that was one thing she didn't need to worry about.

For now what she needed was privacy. Although she was about as alone as she had ever been, she felt as if the walls had eyes. She went back to the boxes and pulled the stack out from the wall at an angle, creating just enough room for a privy. That was pure relief.

Perusing the hanging closet, she looked for the lid to the thunder mug. There didn't seem to be one. Maybe that was why the pot was here instead of still in use. After moving the box again, she took down a round basket missing a handle. Upside down it made a fine cover for the pot. The floor seemed kind of springy when she walked on it, like the floorboards were too thin. It was a good thing she was not overweight else she would have to balance on the joists.

The dog walked to the door and looked back as if to say, "You're not the only one with a need, sister."

"Silly," Lilly said. "If I could open the door, you couldn't climb down the ladder."

But maybe she could open the door. She hadn't even

232

tried. She peeked through a crack where the frame didn't quite match up to the door. There was nothing out there but trees. Below, she could see where tall weeds had been mashed down. It seemed like this place was not often used. The door didn't have a knob but sported a carved handle. On either side of the door were metal pieces that were bolted into the doorframe. They looked like they would hold the piece of lumber that leaned against the wall. More than likely that was just like the one she had heard the man fix in place from the other side. Her heart sank, but she tried anyway, throwing all her weight against the heavy door until her shoulder was as sore as her knees. Like the narrow windows, the door was meant to keep things out— or in, as the case might be.

The dog pleaded with her eyes.

Lilly scavenged about. There was a stack of old newsprint tied up with string. She slid several sheets out and lined a spot for the dog.

The beagle just looked at her.

Lilly stood on the paper. "Come."

The beagle stayed by the door. She rolled her eyes.

She made her voice sound stern. "Come!" she said and motioned to the paper.

The beagle ambled over and sniffed the fusty newsprint.

Lilly scooted the dog's tail directly over some fellow's faded picture. She stood right in front of the dog, not allowing her to step off the paper. "This is a perfectly fine lavatory. Haven't you ever heard beggars can't be choosers?"

Finally the dog got the picture in more ways than one. Looking as relieved as Lilly felt, the beagle went back to the puppy.

The puppy didn't seem as active as Lilly thought he should be. She sat beside it on the dirty floor and looked it over. Its belly looked much better, but its little eyes were just slits. She wondered if that was normal until she remembered Jumbo and how hard it was for him to see the light. Besides, maybe the puppy didn't want to know where it was any more than she did.

In a few minutes it would be full dark. It looked like they would be spending the night. Lilly wasn't hungry anymore. Mostly she was thirsty and scared.

"I'm sorry," she said when the beagle licked her hand. The dog's tongue was as dry as hers. "We'll do the best we can tonight. Daddy John will find us soon. You can bet on that."

Why, Daddy might even come tonight. As soon as he got in from work, Manda would tell him Lilly had missed her ride. She was sure he would remember how much she liked to walk by the creek. That would be the first place he'd look.

When Daddy found the valise and picnic hamper on the rock wall, it would be just like Hansel and Gretel leaving the trail of crumbs on their way to the witch's house. He would think she was a very clever girl, although she'd have to admit she hadn't meant to leave such great clues.

He might get Mama before he came. Mama would have to wait until Mrs. Morton's baby was delivered before she left. That was probably why they hadn't come for her yet.

Her bottom was numb from sitting on the floor. She might as well make herself and the dogs comfortable while they waited. It might be morning 'cause Mama said babies often picked the middle of the night to make their way into the world. Lilly wasn't worried even though she was probably in major trouble for leaving the porch in the first place. Oh, well, it couldn't be worse than the trouble she was already in.

Looking up, she saw that the legs of the moth-eaten suits of clothes hung down far enough for her to reach. She jerked them down and made a thick pallet against the curving wall farthest from the door. She sat down Indian-style with her back against the tin. The mother dog lay at her feet. The puppy nuzzled and nursed.

Lilly determined to keep her eyes open all night. "I'll teach you a bedtime prayer, puppy," she said as tears dripped from her chin. "Now I lay me down to sleep. I pray the Lord my soul to keep. If I should die before I wake, I pray the Lord my soul to take. Amen." She said all her God blesses, not skipping or hurrying like she sometimes did. She blessed everyone she could think of, including the mailman and her favorite clerk at the dry goods store, the one who always saved her a peppermint stick. She prayed for Kate and asked God to spare her from the tooth-jumper. She prayed for all the animals and even the snake that lived in the rotten log by the creek.

Her voice grew as raspy as the locusts that had finally stilled for the night, but she kept on. It seemed to comfort the dog. Her eyes grew heavy like they were full of sand, and despite herself she fell asleep, still sitting.

She didn't know how long she had slept when she heard the rusty door hinges protesting. It was dark, but a golden moon backlit the man who blocked the doorway with his head and chest. He set something on the floor. She didn't dare to breathe. It seemed each noise he made was magnified by the darkness. She heard each one distinctly. The door closed. The bar dropped. The ladder thumped. The man swore. His heavy footsteps receded.

Lilly hugged her knees, then winced and let go. Maybe it would be best to wait until morning to see what he had brought. What if it was the dead puppies? She had dreamed of dogs frolicking in fields of wildflowers. Probably that was puppy heaven. Lilly was sure God saved animals too—she thought they were the least of these the Scripture mentioned. It lightened her mood to think so.

She tried to say the verse aloud, but her lips were too dry to form words. Maybe thinking the words was just as good. *"Verily I say unto you, Inasmuch as ye have done it unto one of the least of these my brethren, ye have done it unto me."*

Where was that Scripture in the Bible? It bothered her that she couldn't place it. She should have paid more attention to her Sunday school teacher like Mama had told her a thousand times.

Her brain was foggy and she felt feverish. The words *verily* and *inasmuch* echoed from the round tin walls as if someone were chanting them.

*Verily. Inasmuch. Verily. Inasmuch,* she heard and decided the words were beautiful.

When she married, if she had twins like Mama did, she would name them Verily and Inasmuch.

The dog uncurled herself from around Lilly's feet and stretched. She went to the door and woofed. Lilly could have cried. She didn't have the energy to drag the animal to the paper again. The dog came back to her and nudged her arm.

Her legs felt like a swarm of sweat bees stinging when she tried to stand. It was dumb to sleep Indian-style. She lifted one foot and shook off the pins and needles, then did the other. She went to the paper. The dog went to the door. She pointed as if it could see her in the dark. The dog woofed and won. She'd have to carry or drag her to the piddling spot.

In the faint beam of moonlight filtering in around the doorframe, she could see the dog's nose pressed up against a half-gallon jar. Water, it was precious water. She lifted the jar, unscrewed the zinc lid, and drank until she was nearly sick.

Squatting, she dribbled water into her cupped hand until the beagle had her fill. She wondered about the puppy— should she give him some? Deciding the mother dog had more sense than she did, she put the lid back on. The dog stood back and woofed again. At the beagle's feet Lilly discovered a small package wrapped in paper.

"Potatoes and corn bread," she said when she undid it. It was cold and smelled greasy. She wasn't hungry anymore. "Let's save it for breakfast."

The dog begged. Lilly gave her some food, then wrapped the rest back up.

Having slaked their thirst, they joined the puppy on the pallet. Lilly lay down, but a button poked her in the back. She refolded the jacket so the buttons were inside.

Lilly felt much better. The man wouldn't be giving her nourishment if he meant to kill her. He was trying to teach her a lesson. Well, he would find out she was a fast learner. Given a little time, she'd get herself and the dogs out of his hidey-hole. In the morning she would make a plan. Just as the beagle had shown her on the bank of the pond, there was always hope.

# 23

COPPER STOPPED AT Cara's on her way home from the Mortons'. "I've come to collect the girls," she said as she dismounted and wrapped Chessie's reins over the hitching post. "Did they wear you out?"

Cara was sitting on her porch with her whittling knife. She made intricate handles for ladies' fans. Darcy would sell them in her dress shop. A small pile of shavings lay at her feet. The girls were playing with Merky's dolls. They had made three little pallets in the shade of the purple morning glory twining up the trellis at the far end of Cara's porch.

Mazy put one finger to her lips. "Shh, Mama, babies sleeping."

Copper shared a smile with Cara. Was there anything cuter than little girls playing house? While their babies slept, Merky poured air tea from a doll-size china teapot into three teensy cups. Mazy and Molly copied her every move.

"Looks like Merky has the twins in line," Copper said.

"We've had the best time." Cara shaved a strip of wood from her project. It curled from her knife like an apple peel. "How did Mrs. Morton's delivery go?"

Copper laughed and shared Ruby Tierney's story—all but the confidential parts.

"My, my," Cara said. "A turn-of-life baby. Maybe there's hope for me yet."

Copper pulled up a chair and sat beside Cara. She felt her friend's sorrow at not being able to have a baby of her own. "I'm sorry. I hope I didn't make you sad."

"No, of course not," Cara said. "If I had birth children, I might not have Merky. I couldn't even imagine not having that little ray of sunshine in my life."

"I sure thank you for keeping Mazy and Molly last night."

"They're well-behaved children." Cara set her carving basket aside. "They've wagged those dolls around ever since they got here. I was wondering—would you like me to make them some?"

"Oh, would you? They would love that." Copper watched the girls a minute, soaking them in. "Did you hear about Manda?"

"Mr. John told me when he came by last evening. What do you make of it?"

240

"I don't know. It's not like Manda to up and run off. I wish she had waited to talk to me."

"I guess it puts you in a bind," Cara said.

"We'll be fine. I'm more concerned about her. Remy thinks she's been acting odd for a while, but I don't know. . . . She's just young."

"Whatever happened with her and Gurney Jasper? I thought he was sweet on her."

"I think he was sweet on her, but I don't know that the feeling was reciprocal." Copper smiled. "You've got to have that spark, you know, that certain something that draws a man and a woman together, not to mention keeps them together."

"Maybe Manda will find her spark in Eddyville," Cara said. "Evidently she's gone off to Darcy's."

"That's what the note said. I guess she took off right after seeing Lilly on the coach." Copper shook her head. "I've been praying for Manda's safety. Guess I'll add her happiness. She's such a good girl and a hard worker. She deserves the best."

Copper stood and massaged the crick in her lower back with both hands. It had been a long night, but the neighbor lady had shown up right after daybreak. Copper had finished up what she needed to do for Ruby and saddled Chessie. She and the girls should be home before ten.

⚬⚬⚬

Copper and Remy were just preparing the noon meal when they heard a horse approaching out in the barnyard.

"Hope that don't mean another baby's a-coming," Remy said.

"It shouldn't be," Copper said, untying her apron and hanging it on a peg. "I don't have anyone due."

She looked out the screen door. John walked out to meet the rider, whose horse was lathered up. "It's Big Boy Randall. It's not like him to let his horse overheat like that. Something must be wrong with Mary or the baby."

Remy came up beside her, and they watched Big Boy dismount and approach John. He said something. John staggered backward a few steps. Big Boy put out his arm and grabbed John's shoulder as if to steady him. He handed John a piece of paper.

John glanced at the porch.

Copper opened the door.

"Wait," Remy said.

But when John sank to his knees, Copper flew across the yard. Big Boy's face was a mask of pain and John's was white as skim milk.

"What's wrong, Big Boy?" she asked. "Has something happened to your wife or daughter?"

Still on his knees, John handed her a telegram.

She swallowed hard. The telegram was from Alice Upchurch to John Pelfrey. It read:

TERRIBLE TRAIN WRECK. STOP.
NO NEWS OF LILLY GRAY. STOP.
WILL MEET YOU AT FOUR CORNERS. STOP.

"Four Corners?" she said stupidly, as if that mattered.

"I'm sure sorry to bring you this news," Big Boy said, whisking his hat off his head.

"How . . . ?"

"I was over to the telegraph office sending a message to my sister Aloda in Lexington when this came over the wire. I told the operator I'd bring it your way. I'm awful sorry."

She turned to her husband. "What does this mean? Is Alice saying Lilly's train . . . ?"

John righted himself, his eyes swimming in tears. He put his arm around her shoulders. "It could be a mistake. It's probably all a big mistake."

Copper looked at Big Boy. She knew him to be a man of honor and truth. "Do you know anything else? If you do, tell us and don't sugarcoat it."

"There was a Teletype coming in, and I stayed to hear it. Evidently the Republic Railroad's Old Number Twelve collided with a freight train right near the station at Four Corners. Three of the passenger cars and a baggage car went over the side of a ravine. Old Number Twelve's locomotive, the tender, three other cars, and the caboose are still on the rails. The freight train is on the track but has major damage."

"Old Number Twelve was the train Lilly took," John said.

"Please, Lord, no," Copper begged God. She quivered all over.

"Now you got to have faith," Big Boy said. "You got to

stay strong. There are casualties, but that don't mean your daughter's not fine."

If John hadn't been holding her, she would have fallen on her face in the dirt. "Saddle the horses, John! We're wasting time."

Big Boy bent his knees until he brought his face in line with hers. "Listen to me. They've halted all trains using that piece of track for the time being, but they're sending out a relief train this afternoon. I begged you a ride on that. Considering the situation and the fact that you practice medicine, the engineer said he'd make room for you and John. You can be at Four Corners this evening."

"But I want to go now," Copper said.

"He's right," John said. "The train will get us there much quicker."

"That's settled, then," Big Boy said. "Now I know you got preparations to make before you leave. Is there anyone you want me to tell? anything I can do for you?"

"Let's see," Copper said. Her mind was a blank, but Big Boy was right. She had to see to the needs of her other children before she left. "Please stop by Brother Jasper's. We need powerful prayer."

"I'll do that on my way home. I'll need to tell Mary, but I'll be back in plenty of time to get you to the station." Big Boy headed with his horse toward the watering trough.

Copper clasped John's hands and prayed, "Surround Lilly with a host of guardian angels, Lord. Keep her safely in the shadow of Your wings. Be with all the folks who were on that train and with all their families. And give us strength for the journey. Your will be done, Father. Amen."

A loud popping noise caught Copper's attention. Jack was throwing green apples at the side of the barn. Had he heard? "John, you'll have to talk to Jack. He'll be upset at both of us leaving him."

"Shouldn't I go get Cara? Someone will have to stay with the kids. We can't leave Remy with all this."

Copper felt like screaming. How could she concentrate on anything but Lilly? Had the world not stopped? "That's a good plan. Take Jack with you."

"All right, and I'll ask Dimmert to see to the animals and milk Bertha while we're away."

Copper searched John's face. She saw fear and confusion. Whimpering, she fell against his chest. "I can't stand this. I'll be out of my mind before we get to Four Corners."

John held her tightly. "It's a matter of faith. You prayed God's will be done. Now we have to accept that what will be, will be. There's not a thing you can do by fretting to change one iota of what has already happened."

"But what if she's lying there hurt? What if she's calling for me?" Her voice rose shrilly. She felt close to panic.

John took her by the upper arms and held her out from him. He looked into her eyes. "Stop. Don't borrow trouble. Isn't it just as likely that she's sitting in the depot waiting for us to come and fetch her home?"

"But Alice said, 'No news of Lilly.' If she was safe, wouldn't they know?"

"Alice probably got word of the wreck last night because she lives in the city. I'm sure the officials hadn't had time to sort everything out by then."

"But Big Boy said casualties."

"He also said most of the passengers survived. Cling to that word, okay?"

"Yes, I will. I'll start getting ready for the trip. You go on and get Cara."

John pulled her close again. "That's my girl. You can do this."

She took a deep breath and turned toward the house. *Give me strength, God,* she prayed.

As they prepared to leave, folks began to gather around, offering whatever help they could. Half a dozen people from church knelt on the porch praying aloud. An elderly lady Copper didn't even know swept the front walk with the stub of a broom. Gurney Jasper went in the barn and came out with a hoe. He headed for the garden. Ace Shelton carried the one suitcase she had packed toward Big Boy's buggy. Dance and all her kids spread quilts under the apple tree. Mazy, Molly, Merky, and Jack joined them there. Several women brought food, which Cara tucked away in the pie safe.

Abe and Tillie Sizemore came with their boy. Tillie brought him shyly to the door. "I thought seeing Abe Jr. might offer ye some comfort."

Copper opened the screen door and took the baby. She laid her cheek against the little boy's fuzzy head. It brought tears to her eyes along with a fierce longing to have her first-born safe and sound in her arms again. "Thank you," she said shakily. "He really is a Jumbo now."

"Thanks to you. Abe and me—we pray for you every single night."

"Your prayers are precious to me. Please pray for Lilly."

Tillie ducked her head. Copper watched the young mother join Dance under the apple tree. Dance held out her arms, and Tillie gave her Abe Jr. Copper couldn't help but be cheered by that. People were coming together in a time of need, just like they always did here in the mountains.

John brought Brother Jasper into the kitchen. Brother Jasper carried his big black Bible.

Copper fought back tears. "Have you heard from Mrs. Jasper and Kate?"

"Not directly," Brother Jasper said. "Gurney will go to Jackson after a while and send a telegraph to her sister's. She'll want to know about Lilly."

Big Boy stuck his head in the door. "Ready when you are."

"Let's offer prayer," Brother Jasper said.

John, Copper, Cara, Big Boy, and Remy joined hands as Brother Jasper prayed a short but powerful prayer. He ended with a Scripture from Isaiah: "'Fear not: for I have redeemed thee, I have called thee by thy name: thou art mine. When thou passest through the waters, I will be with thee; and through the rivers, they shall not overflow thee: when thou walkest through the fire, thou shalt not be burned; neither shall the flame kindle upon thee.'" He clasped first John's hands and then Copper's. "God be with you, Brother and Sister Pelfrey."

Copper felt clothed with the full armor of truth. She was ready for whatever lay ahead. She followed the men out the door.

Remy stopped her and handed her the doctor's bag. "I put in everything I could find that you might need."

"Oh, I didn't even think of this. Of course I need it." Copper bent to hug her friend.

Remy allowed it and even gave a squeeze back followed by a broken sob. "I still can feel the poor little thing's hug around my neck," she said before she turned and fled to the back of the house.

John stood holding the door for her. Copper walked across the porch, down the steps, and toward the waiting horses. She stopped along the way to thank the old granny who was sweeping the path.

"I'll do ary thing I can to help," the lady said. She looked at Copper through eyes like round black buttons. "You might think you can't get through this, but I'm living proof ye can."

"Thank you," Copper said. "I'll cling to that."

Jack ran behind as they rode off in the buggy, his feet churning up the dusty road. "Good-bye, Mama," he called out. "Good-bye, Daddy. Bring Lilly home fast."

Dimmert came up behind Jack and lifted him to his shoulders. Jack's laughter buoyed Copper's spirit. It would have to last for a good long while.

# 24

WHEN LILLY GRAY woke, she prayed for a miracle. On her tender knees, she fervently asked God to whisk her away from the place where she was confined and back to her own clean sheets and fluffy feather pillow, back to Mazy and Molly and Jack hogging half her bed, back to the smell of biscuits baking and bacon frying. Instead, she saw the same ugly ridged tin walls, the same old junk hanging from the same old beams and breathed in the same musty air.

For the first time she noticed her mud-stained skirts and missing shoe. "A perfectly beautiful outfit ruined," she said to the dog.

The dog wagged her tail and came up for a pat on the head.

"You're glad to be here, aren't you, girl? You're feeling safe and happy this morning." Lilly bent over her knees and unbuttoned her spats. It was a tedious job without a button-hook. "Just look at this." She held the kid-leather spat out for the dog's perusal.

The dog tugged it from her hand and began to chew.

"Enjoy your breakfast," she said. "You might as well eat them. They can't be saved."

She took off her other spat and shoe. Her stockings had long laddered runs and bloodied holes in the knees. Her skirt was stiff with mud, and she had no idea what had become of her hat. She was a mess, a complete mess. And the dog was not much better. Her short fur was matted, and little bits of mud flaked off her feet when she walked.

Maybe she'd use some of the water to wash up a bit so she would be presentable when Daddy John came to get her out. Oh, he was going to be so mad. That awful man who drowned the puppies would pay for stealing her. He would pay. And Mama—well, that mean-spirited fellow didn't want to face her mama.

Anger helped get Lilly up off the pallet she had made. Moving the puppy from one side to the other, she straightened their bed as best she could. The puppy mewled in its puppy way, and the mother licked it all over with her slurpy tongue.

"At least one of us will be clean," Lilly said.

Looking about the room, she decided she would pull one box off the stack to use for a table. They could keep their water there and the packet of potatoes and corn bread. Her stomach growled. Should she eat it all now or try to save some? Would the man bring more? She guessed he wouldn't have brought the first packet if he meant for her to starve to death. She went to get the water jar.

Right inside the door, Lilly found the answer to her prayer. Her own little miracle—comfort from home. How could she have missed her valise and her wicker carryall last night when she saw the jug of water? She would swear it wasn't there, which meant the man had come a second time and she hadn't heard the squeaking door. That wasn't good. She didn't want him to catch her sleeping. Maybe she should throw the latch on this side of the door and lock him out like he locked her in. But, no—then he couldn't bring more food and water. Oh, she was mad enough to spit.

She decided she was wasting her energy on the man. Here she'd just received a blessing, and she wasn't taking time to appreciate it. She took her miracles back to the box table. The smell of fried chicken was enough to make her mouth water. But she wasn't about to eat at the table without first washing her hands. Using her box stool, she stood on it and unhooked two battered granite pans. One would do for a washbasin, and one would do for the dogs' water bowl.

There was a quandary in the midst of many quandaries. She couldn't very well wash up on the same table she ate on, and she didn't want to take another box from her privy wall.

Then it wouldn't be private. She burst into tears. Why did everything have to be so hard?

Her tears upset the dog, so Lilly blotted her eyes on her sleeve. If she and Kate were playing house, what would they do? Seeing the obvious answer, she went to the privy wall and moved the wooden boxes around until one stuck out, making a sort of shelf. She put her washbasin on it. Perfect. Just as she'd marked out the rooms on the flat rock beside the creek where they'd played house, Lilly had her living quarters arranged. There was the box that served as a kitchen table. There was the bedroom where her "baby" slept contentedly. Here was her washstand and there was her privy.

She poured some of the precious water into the pan and washed her face and hands. Lifting her skirt, she found a clean bit of petticoat and dried herself.

"There, much better." Unfastening the wooden toggle that held the lid of the wicker hamper together, she lifted the lid and feasted her eyes on fried chicken, hard-boiled eggs, red ripe tomatoes, sliced cucumbers, biscuits, cake, and pie. She clapped in delight. "We've got a feast, doggy, a veritable feast. What should we sample first?"

She guessed they'd best start with the chicken. Everything else would keep. She picked up a drumstick and sniffed it suspiciously. The grease it had been fried in smelled stale, but the meat hadn't turned. She ate the two legs but gave the dog the breast. She needed it more than Lilly did since she was nursing a puppy. They also ate most of what was left of the potatoes and corn bread from the brown paper packet.

Tears threatened again when she saw Mama had packed her toothbrush and a tin of Colgate's dental powder in the bottom of the hamper. Mama never let her eat one meal without cleaning her teeth afterward.

She washed her hands again in the same water. That was disgusting, but she didn't want to waste it. After she wet her toothbrush and sprinkled on the clean-tasting powder, she went as far away from her bed as she could and brushed, rinsed, and spat there. She used the linen towel from the hamper to dry around her mouth. When she finished, she spread the towel over the top of the box. It looked cheery there with its embroidery of bright yellow daisies and spread-winged bluebirds.

Next she looked through the valise. She had one day dress, one petticoat, one nightgown, several pairs of pantalets, several pairs of clean hose, and her everyday shoes. Also she'd packed her hairbrush, some ribbons, and a comb. No need to be less than tidy. She laid the dress along with clean undergarments across her bed. Best of all was finding her small Bible. This she laid atop the towel beside her brush and comb and the watch and fob she'd unpinned from her jacket. The watch didn't tick but sloshed when she shook it. Everything looked right at home on the table. The things she didn't need right now were packed back inside the valise. She closed it and put it beside the door in case she had to grab it in a hurry when Daddy came.

Before she changed, she looked through the crack beside the door. There was no one out there, but still she changed

lickety-split. It felt good as anything to get out of that corset. She liked to be fashionable as much as anyone, but this
was not the place. She folded the traveling outfit around the
corset and left them on the floor. She never wanted to wear
them again—not even if Aunt Remy washed them with her
homemade lye soap.

She walked around the room liking the feel of her comfortable, broken-in shoes. This was a boring place. How
would she spend the rest of the day? Maybe she should clean
up the dog's spot. Then she'd have to wash her hands again.
How much water was left? Only a third of a jar. She tried to
save it, but she was so thirsty and the beagle was also. She
could watch for her daddy to come. It probably wouldn't be
long now.

The dog watched every step she took. "Don't worry. I'm
not leaving you or your baby here in this dreadful place.
You'll like my house. I've got a brother and two sisters and a
cat and kittens." She shook her finger in the dog's direction.
"Promise you won't chase the cats? or the rooster? He'll turn
on you if you do." She knelt beside the dog and pointed to a
teeny round spot on her forehead. "See that? There's where
I got flogged once. Mama threatened to make rooster stew,
but I cried and begged her not to."

With a huge, bored sigh she flung her arms wide and fell
backward on the pallet. "That rooster's living on borrowed
time."

Her fall startled the mother dog. She jumped and, tucking her tail, cowered in front of her.

Lilly stroked the top of the dog's head and her ears. "I'm sorry. I didn't mean to scare you." She started laughing. "Besides, I cracked my head. I forgot I wasn't on my bed at home."

The dog lay down beside her. The puppy, ever hungry, wriggled their way.

"I'll bet we make a pretty picture—a girl with a cracked head and a dog with pointy fur. When you get finished with this feeding, I'll comb the mud out of your hair. How's that?"

The dog pointed her long nose at the wicker basket and whined.

"It's not time for dinner. You can tell by the light it's not nearly noon yet. Besides, my largesse only goes so far."

The dog rested her head on crossed paws, feigning interest.

"*Largesse*? It's from the French *largesse*. It means giving generously. It's the opposite of stingy. *Largesse* was last week's new word. Before that the word was *cipher*." She twirled a lock of hair around her finger. "*Cipher* has two meanings actually. It could mean an insignificant person or figuring numbers. It's a pretty word—don't you think? If I have triplets when I grow up and get married, I could name them Verily, Inasmuch, and Cipher. I'll bet in the whole history of the world there's never been triplets with those names. But enough of that. You need to stop paying attention to me and feed your baby."

Lilly's eyes grew heavy. She was having trouble keeping them open, as if there were itty-bitty fishing sinkers attached to her lids. Sitting up, she shook her head. She needed to stay alert. What if Daddy walked by and she missed him? After all he didn't know she was up in the treetops.

The dog yawned mightily.

"Thanks. That helps a lot." Lilly yawned too. She lay back down and stroked the puppy's soft fur. It felt like Aunt Alice's fancy coat. Her eyes closed. She would rest them for a minute.

Lilly woke hours later bathed in perspiration. The sun was bearing down on the tin shack like a furnace. If it weren't for the deep shade provided by the trees, Lilly figured they'd be toast. It would only get hotter as the day wore on. She needed to do something. There had to be a way out of this place.

She drank some more water and topped off the dog's dish. The dog shouldn't have to beg. There was only a quarter of a jar left. She made her way around the room pushing on each tin panel—one might be loose. No such luck.

Tipping her head way back, she studied the roof. If she had a pole, she could poke it through the flimsy-looking thatch. But she didn't have one, and besides, what good would that do?

Frustrated, she went around the room again until she came to the door. Leaning up against the wall was the piece of wood that blocked the opening of the door from the inside. She fiddled with the latch to see how it worked. It was simple enough—a length of wood lay between two heavy metal pieces that were screwed to the wall and acted as notches to hold the wooden bar. Through the crack she could see a bit of the outside bar. Could she lift it from inside? All she needed was something to slip through the opening and pry the block up.

She went around the room again. It was making her dizzy. How did she expect to find the right tool when she didn't even know what she was looking for? She climbed up on her step box for a different view. There was something long and polelike lying atop the rafter that she hadn't been able to see from the floor. She moved the box in front of where the pole should be and tiptoed to grab it. The box tipped and she fell. Her chin hit the corner of the shelf she'd made on the privy wall. Wash water splashed her face when the basin slid off.

Lilly held her chin with both hands. It stung like fire, and there was blood on her fingers when she dared to look. If she kept this up, she would be maimed like the poor beggar children in India she had once seen in a book in Aunt Alice's library. The blood on her fingers made her feel as dizzy as walking around the room had.

She took her valise back to the pallet and got out her comfy cotton nightgown. She ripped the ruffled flounce off the bottom of the gown, then tore the rest into large squares. After pouring a bit of water over one square, she used it to dab her chin. The flounce she tied around her chin and knotted atop her head like Mama had done Kate's flannel. Thinking of Kate made her think of her teeth. What if she'd knocked one out? With the tip of her tongue she felt each one. All were in place and none was loose. Thank goodness for that.

To get her mind off her trials, Lilly ate a piece of chocolate cake. It was so good she licked her fingers. The dog got a but-tered biscuit and the rest of the potatoes from breakfast.

Undeterred in her quest, she moved the box for better balance and climbed back up. Her fingers wouldn't quite grasp the pole. As she stood on the box with her hands on her hips, she pondered what to do. This was getting tiring. Jumping down, she went to the table box and got her brush. With it in hand she could move the pole. Straining, being careful not to fall again, she shoved it off the other side of the beam. The pole hit the floor and rolled all the way to the pallet. The dog nosed it suspiciously. Lilly felt like she'd won the hundred-yard dash like the boys at school ran on field day. She deserved a blue ribbon.

The pole was actually a sawed-off broom handle—or maybe a hoe handle. That didn't matter as long as it would move the bar that barricaded the door. When she looked outside, it was quiet and still as a graveyard after dark. She shoved the pole through the space between the door and the frame. It went in, but the fit was so tight she couldn't move it up and down. Now what? She jerked it back and forth. This was very hard work, but she was making progress. The frame and the door now had grooves from the pole. It seemed to take a very long time, but finally she could slide the handle under the outside bar and move the handle up against it. It didn't matter, though. The bar was too heavy. She couldn't budge it.

Something tickled her brain. Her daddy came to mind. She once saw him pry a heavy rock out of the ground using a pole and a piece of wood he called a fulcrum. That was what she needed—a fulcrum and something to position it on so it would be higher than the heavy bar on the other side of the door.

The old chairs might work. From atop the box, she lifted them down one by one and lugged them to the door. Though the seats were missing, the frames were intact. She spaced them a few feet apart so she could situate the wooden bar across them. Her jaw clenched in frustration. The chairs were not tall enough for the piece of wood to be used as a fulcrum. Narrowing her eyes, she stood and surveyed her creation. She wasn't giving up. This was a puzzle to be solved and she would solve it.

Two trips to the privy wall answered her problem. Two of the wooden boxes set on end were exactly right. Why hadn't she seen that before she got the chairs down? No matter. Standing behind the fulcrum, she levered it up against the outside bar. The bar moved! She shouted for joy. She could taste freedom, and it was as good as chocolate cake.

Her celebration was short-lived when the broom handle was jerked from her hands. Her heart thudded to a stop. She always wondered if you could really die from fright; now she knew you could. The door screeched open, and she stepped backward to the pallet.

The bushy-bearded man was on the ladder. He set a jar of water just inside the door. "I ought to knock your silly brains out. I ain't never seen the like—don't appreciate nothing."

His head disappeared below the threshold, then like an afterthought reappeared. "I'll give you fair warning. I'll leave this door swung wide so's you won't roast in here like a pig on a spit, but if I see hide nor hair of you, I'll nail this door shut and you'll have a fine tin coffin."

Lilly held her breath as he climbed down the ladder, then jumped in fright when his head bobbed up again like an apple in a dunking tub.

"And another thing, missy. Iffen you hear anybody calling for you, you keep still else I'll drag you to the pond and let you watch that there dog trying to swim outen a gunnysack. Don't think I won't." He slapped another paper packet on the floor. "Enjoy yore fine queezeen."

"*Cuisine*," Lilly couldn't help but whisper in his absence, "from the Latin *coquere*, 'to cook.'"

The dog stuck her wet nose against Lilly's arm as if to say, "For pity's sake—shut up."

# 25

COPPER WAS WORKING on nothing but fear. The relief
train had delivered them to the site of the wreck just a short
time ago. Their approach had been so calm it was eerie.
The last half mile of undamaged serpentine track winding
through hills of bucolic farmland and apple orchards in no
way prepared her for what she was soon to face. But just as the
train rolled puffing and blowing across a rickety trestle that
spanned a deep ravine, she could see and smell the smoke.

The scene they walked into was right out of a nightmare. A
long length of track stuck up from the rails like a ladder leading nowhere. Back down the rail, three undamaged cars and a
caboose sat placidly on the tracks as if they were waiting for a

porter to shout, "All aboard!" A pile of lump coal lay burning itself out on the bank, sending up puffs of dark smoke like signals of distress. Debris was everywhere—crates of smashed eggs, a busted drummer's shoe trunk disgorging boots and high-tops, coops of lifeless chickens, an upended safe, shattered glass, wooden benches, and a twisted pair of spectacles. Suitcases spilled their contents out onto the ground. Copper searched it all, looking for something familiar.

Straight ahead the locomotive sat, still hooked to another train car that dangled over the steep side of the ravine. At least she thought it was the engine—a head-on collision with another train had pleated it like an accordion. Beyond that was the other train. According to the conductor who had brought them to the scene, it was not a passenger train but a freight carrying supplies to Jackson, and one of its cars was loaded with dynamite. "Enough to blow us all to kingdom come," he'd reckoned.

Men scurried up the bank from the creek far below, hauling water to other men who manned the hand-operated water pumps hosing down a boxcar which Copper supposed held the explosives.

Copper walked with John to the edge of the ravine. She caught her breath when she saw the smoldering heap of mangled steel and shredded wood far below. A path wide as the beds of several wagons made the steep hillside look as if it had been scraped clean by a giant's sledge.

A burly, bearded man with a badge on his chest approached. "Hard to believe, ain't it? The force of the wreck whipped

them cars through the trees like they weren't no more substantial than a pat of butter. Looks like they was cleared by
the grim reaper, don't it?

"'Course, they weren't anything substantial, mostly saplings," the man continued. "The railroad keeps the right-of-
way pretty clean."

When no one replied, he elbowed John. "Say, you come
to work or what? We don't need no gawkers here. And if
you're searching for a loved one, you'll have to go wait in the
family tent with the others. It's only about two miles off-site.
You understand we can't have civilians milling about such a
dangerous place, slowing down our progress."

Copper exchanged looks with John. He stepped forward,
introducing them. "Yes, we're here to work. We came on the
relief train just now."

"And the little lady?"

"She practices medicine. We're ready and able—just show
us what you want."

The sheriff eyed John's broad shoulders. "You go on down
there." He motioned to the gully. "They can use more strong
backs."

"I work in timber," John said.

"We for sure need you, then. Did you happen to bring
your ax?"

"No, sorry."

"No matter; there's a supply wagon on up the line. You'll
find it easy enough. Just tell them Sheriff Tate sent you."

John squeezed Copper's hand, then started up the track.

She understood his intent. They would not call attention to their plight in front of the lawman. They would be of no help to Lilly or anyone else by waiting in the family tent.

The sheriff turned to her. "If you'll follow me, I got a fellow that needs some quick attention. They just brought him up out of that fiery pit of hell."

Copper matched his fast steps. With a hand under her elbow, he led her to the other side of the tracks and under a sugar maple tree where a man lay stretched out in the shade. "We've set up a field hospital in the depot yonder, but it's full and running over with folks in need of attention. I was just going to beg for help. You appearing so suddenlike is the answer to my prayers."

Copper folded her skirts under her knees and sank to the young man's side. His blue eyes were open and clouded with fear and pain. A light beard stubbled his cheeks and chin. A sparse mustache promised the manhood soon to come.

He gripped her hand hard. "Are you an angel?"

"Now, Billy," the sheriff said, "you ain't dead. This here's a sawbones, and she's going to make sure that don't happen."

"How old are you, young man?"

"He's coming up on sixteen," the sheriff responded. "He's my little brother. He's apprenticed to the brakeman on the Republic." He leaned over Billy and tousled his hair. "Learning the trade real good, ain't you?"

"I'm a-trying," Billy said. He attempted to lift his left arm. Between his elbow and wrist a bone protruded through muscle and skin. "This hurts like thunder."

"I'm a nurse. Your brother and I are going to fix you right up."

Copper soothed both the young man and his brother. "Would you take off his shoes and socks and unfasten his belt?"

Copper checked the boy out with her stethoscope and her hands, but it appeared he had no internal injuries. His lungs were clear; his heart beat steady; he didn't gasp or complain of pain when she checked for broken ribs, felt for crepitus along his collarbone, had him move his toes and the fingers of his good arm, and palpated his abdomen.

"We'll just need to stitch that gash on his forehead," she explained to the sheriff, "and splint his arm. He's going to be fine."

"See, what'd I tell you? Didn't I say you'd be right as rain soon as we got you some help?"

"I hurt, though, Bubby."

She spread a linen towel out on the grass and laid out scissors, forceps, tweezers, a round of gauze, and a small brown envelope containing a curved needle and silk sutures.

"What else do you need?"

"Water, soap, a basin, splints, and a bottle of whiskey," she said.

The sheriff rubbed his palm over his chin. "I could go for that too."

Copper gave him a look. "It's for the boy."

"Oh, sure, sure," he said. "I'll be right back. There are all kinds of stuff in the depot. We got two relief trains with medical supplies out of Lexington. Do you want me to see if there's a doctor to help?"

"If one's available, but I can do this. You can help me."

Copper took the white apron and head scarf that made her look like Florence Nightingale from her linen bag and shook them out. All the while she prepared for the task ahead, her eyes and ears searched for Lilly Gray. But except for the workmen, the site was surprisingly void of people. The sheriff was doing a good job. She knew John would be searching too by asking questions while he worked. Her fervent hope was that he didn't find her down in the gorge, where the worst of the wreck remained.

". . . lumbering noise, and my feet flying out from beneath me."

Copper pulled her wandering attention back to Billy. "So you were caught off guard?"

"Completely. Oh, ma'am, you can't imagine. The screeching of the brakes, the scream of the whistles, the thunderous crash—it all sounded like Satan was throwing open the very gates of hell. Next thing I knew the car I was in went sailing off the tracks. The trees didn't stop us, seemed like we was flying for a few seconds; then we hit the ground and started sliding toward the creek. I didn't know if I was on the floor or the ceiling, but I was grabbing for something to hold on to. Before I had time to think, a section of the car peeled back smooth as the bark on a tree and I was flung out into the elements. I landed hard on my side. Then the train car rolled over me, and I was trapped. I reckon my arm's broke." He raised his eyebrows in question.

Copper took his hand. "Your arm is broken at the radial bone, and you have a cut on your forehead. But there's nothing that can't be fixed. You're very fortunate."

"My ma prays for me every morning and every night."

"Well, your ma's prayers were answered."

"Here're your supplies, ma'am." The sheriff set the basin on the ground and poured water in.

Copper scrubbed to the elbows. "Did you bring the medicinal whiskey?"

The sheriff offered his brother a drink, and he slugged down a long draught.

"Take one more," Copper said.

Mixing a small amount of the spirits with water, she poured it freely over the wound on the forehead and on the arm where the radial bone poked through the skin, then patted the sites dry with sterile gauze. She picked grass and gravel from the forehead gash with the tweezers before flooding it again.

Billy's muscles lost their tension. He seemed to relax.

"I believe we can begin," Copper said. "Sheriff Tate, if you'll hold his head still for me, I'll have him stitched up in no time." With a needle shaped like a fishhook without the barbs, Copper closed the wound except for a small opening on one end. "I'll leave this in case the cut gets infected. It will act as a drain. Looks like the wound's bled freely, but you know to watch closely for lockjaw."

"Sad to say I do. I lost a boyhood friend that way."

Copper wrapped the closed head wound in gauze. "You'll need to have these stitches removed in a few days."

"Will do."

"We'd best get this break set while he's still got his happy juice on board. Let me see the splints."

The sheriff handed her two thin firm boards.

Copper measured them against Billy's arm from just below the elbow to the fingers. "This one is fine, but shorten this one. The inner one mustn't be so long that it presses at the bend of the elbow when the arm is flexed."

Once the bone was set back in position, it was a simple matter to fix the side splints in place with strips of gauze. She fashioned a sling from Billy's shirt and tied it around his neck, keeping his elbow fixed at a right angle.

Billy closed his eyes and soon was softly snoring.

"You'll need to get him to a doctor as soon as possible," Copper said while packing up her kit. "They'll want to put a cast on that arm."

"I appreciate you being so gentle with him. He likes to think he's a man already."

"Sheriff Tate, might I beg a favor?"

"You bet."

"My eleven-year-old daughter was on that train. I'm desperate to find her."

The sheriff sucked in his breath. "I'm really sorry to hear that."

"Do you know if any children . . . ?" Her voice faded away. She couldn't bear to finish her question.

"Do you want to go to the depot and have a look-see? I'm not supposed to do this, you understand, but hang it all, I don't care."

Copper took the arm he proffered and was thankful for it as he escorted her to the teeming depot. It seemed most every bench and chair was occupied by a dazed and moaning person. She hadn't realized she clutched his arm so tightly until he patted her hand.

"Some have already been taken to the hospital in Lexington," he said as they walked up and down the aisles. "These are waiting to go next."

"Is there some sort of roster? Is anyone keeping a record?"

"There is. The ticket seller has it in the cage. Do you want to look?"

Copper's heart trilled and her knees went weak. "Might you get me a cup of water?"

The sheriff led her to an unoccupied seat. She closed her eyes and took deep breaths.

Sheriff Tate brought a paper cone of tepid water. Just like the one Lilly had been looking forward to drinking from. She drank it down and stood. He led her to the ticket seller's booth.

"Hey, Ed," he said. "We want to take a look at your roster."

The agent slid it under the glass partition that separated him from purchasers. "Updated it not fifteen minutes ago."

She scanned the list of twenty-five names or descriptions. Then went back to the top and read them again more carefully. The listed names were easy, but the descriptions took a minute. Male elderly; gray, handlebar mustache; deceased. Female young adult; brown hair; green dress; unconscious; dispatched to Lexington via relief train. And so on. With some relief she noted there were no children listed, male or female, none dead, none dispatched.

She slid the clipboard underneath the window. "Thank you," she said, her voice aquiver. Lilly must still be in the wreckage. She had to get down there. "What's the easiest way to the site?"

"It'll just cause a ruckus if you try to do that," the sheriff said. "It'll only distract the workers and slow things down. I know that's hard to hear, but it's hard on everybody. Best thing you can do is pitch in here. Nobody's going to stop you asking questions while you work, if you get my drift."

He was right, of course. At least she was here where she could be of some use, not sequestered in the family tent. She'd have to bide her time and pray.

"I've got to get back to work," the sheriff said. "Now just you remember Billy. He was down there through the night and most of today and he come out of it okay. Your little girl will do the same. It won't be long until they have everyone accounted for."

"Nurse," a woman called from a nearby bench, "can you help me?"

Copper smoothed her long white apron, tucked an errant strand of hair under her headdress, and went to work.

When night fell, lanterns were lit along the walls of the depot. Copper met other women in white and a doctor from the city. She flushed cinders from eyes, bandaged wounds, helped the doctor cast a leg broken at the fibula with woven lint and plaster of Paris, sent for Billy so they could do the same for his arm, and reassured a pregnant mother of three

270

that her unborn baby was in no imminent danger. All the while she worked, she questioned to no avail.

"No," everyone replied with pity in their eyes, "I can't recall seeing anyone who looks like that."

Around midnight Sheriff Tate brought her a cup of just-brewed coffee. She wrapped her hands around the hot mug and walked with him back to the edge of the ravine. She could hear an occasional shout and see the wavering lights of torches and lanterns far below.

"We're pulling the men off until first light," he said. "You can understand. Even with extra lanterns they can't see what they're doing. One slip and they could be under tons of steel. We can't chance them getting hurt or worse."

Copper nodded. Hopeless tears spilled unchecked from her eyes.

"They'll bed down in the cars still standing down the track, catch a break, and eat something hot. You wouldn't believe the food. Seems like every church up and down the tracks has sent something."

"People are good," Copper said, remembering the scene she'd left in her own yard. Was that just hours ago? It felt like years. It felt like this place was the only place that had ever been. "If you see my husband, would you tell him I'm in the depot?"

"I will," the sheriff said, "and I'll bring you a plate. If you don't eat, you'll be dead on your feet."

*I already am,* Copper thought.

# 26

MANDA WAS WEARY of listening to her sister. Darcy hadn't stopped nattering at her since she showed up on her doorstep early this morning. She hadn't been sure what to expect—maybe a sisterly hug, maybe some care and concern? maybe fewer questions?

She had barely had time to take her bonnet off, to the tune of Darcy's sharp intake of breath, when the nanny/maid showed up. Darcy tucked her son into a stroller and sent them off to the park. Manda supposed she was embarrassed to have the boy's sitter seeing her battered face. As soon as the squeaky-wheeled stroller rolled out the door, the interrogation began and soon had Manda crying buckets.

"How could you be so stupid? Don't you know those fiddle-playing bums drift from town to town preying on pretty girls? And your running away? Don't you know that just raises suspicion?"

Well, no, Manda didn't have a clue. How could she? And what made Darcy so high-and-mighty? Her husband was in prison, after all. But Manda knew the difference. Darcy could take care of herself and even her little boy while Manda was at the mercy of anybody who would take her in. Her sobs changed to moans.

"I'm sorry. I'm sorry. I'm sorry." Manda knotted and unknotted a clean hankie. "I didn't know what to do. I couldn't face anyone knowing what happened in that barn. All I could think of was getting to you."

Darcy sat down beside Manda on the fancy horsehair love seat in her parlor. She put a strong arm around Manda's shaking shoulders. Taking the hankie, she patted Manda's cheeks, then handed it back. "Blow your nose."

Manda settled her head on Darcy's shoulder. It felt so good to be in her sister's embrace. She couldn't help but think of all the times when they were kids and Darcy, being the older sister, would come to her defense. "Remember when I was sick that time and you fed me scrambled eggs? I didn't even know a person could scramble eggs. They were so good."

"You were seven and I was not much older. You had the red measles, and Mommy was afraid you'd go blind. Remember how she made you keep that cloth over your face so you'd be in the dark?"

"I'd forgot about the rag. Mostly I remember you taking care of me."

"I guess we children took care of each other. The eggs were scrambled because I didn't know you had to grease the skillet before you broke the eggs in. I was so embarrassed."

"Is that a true story?"

"True as true love."

"Don't call me stupid again, but I thought I loved that music man. I even thought he truly loved me back."

"I don't think you're stupid, and I'm sorry I called you names. I'm just hopping mad is all. I'd like to go after him with a pair of pinking shears." Darcy rose from the love seat and went to the shaded window where a fern the size of a bushel basket sat in the muted light. She turned the fern on the plant stand and plucked brown leaves from among the lush green fronds.

Darcy had picked up a few pounds, and they looked good on her. Manda thought she was beautiful standing there in a rose-colored dress, her hair caught up with mother-of-pearl combs. She must have just dressed for work when Manda barged in.

"I know all about true love," she said with a strange, sad smile.

Manda stayed on the settee, exhausted. She'd traveled all night to get here. "I guess I just remind you of your own sorrow."

"You? No, don't even think that. Every time I look at our son's face, I'm reminded that my husband is serving time for harming Ace." She went back and knelt at Manda's feet, looking up at her. "Henry Jr. looks just like him. My heart gladdens every time he smiles. Sometimes at night, I take a lamp and go to his room and stare down in his crib just to see him in sleep. He's the closest thing I have to Henry, and I cherish him."

Her words made Manda feel small. "I almost threw myself away. I almost let my foolish heart destroy my honor."

"Oh, honey," Darcy said, "you're just young. I'm going to draw you a nice hot bath. I had an honest-to-goodness bathtub installed in the lavatory since you were here last. You're going to love it."

Manda soaked for an hour after Darcy left for the dress shop. Every time the water cooled, she turned the faucet on and let wonderful hot water flow. She scrubbed and scrubbed and washed her hair before she began to feel clean again.

Darcy had said to make herself at home, so Manda slipped on the soft blue robe she found hanging from a hook on the back of the lavatory door and sat down to play with the creams and potions in the sparkly glass pots on Darcy's dressing table. With a puff she powdered her cheeks and around her blackened eyes. She looked like a raccoon. Sighing, she wiped the powder off.

She could hear Henry Jr. racing around downstairs and the nanny's quiet voice keeping him in line. Would she ever have what Darcy had? Her heart yearned to have such assurance as her sister possessed.

There was a light tap on the door. "Miss Whitt," the sitter said, "I've left a lunch tray for you in the guest room. Mrs. Thomas thought you'd like a nap afterward. Should I turn down the bedclothes?"

Manda's head throbbed. She should never have looked in the mirror. "No, thank you anyway."

The stairs creaked under the sitter's steps.

Manda made her way to the pretty bedroom. Every single thing in Darcy's house was pretty—even Darcy. An invalid tray holding a bowl of soup, some crackers, a cup of strawberries, and a glass of lemonade sat waiting in the middle of the bed.

The window was half-raised. Filmy white curtains blew out on a breeze. Manda removed the tray and placed it on the seat of a chair. The bed seemed so inviting. Without removing the counterpane, she lay down and gave herself to healing sleep.

Later, after Darcy came home from work, they ate side by side in the dining "nook" as her sister called the smallish area off the kitchen. The nanny/maid had prepared a simple supper of fruit and cheese before she left for the night. It was perfect for Manda's touchy stomach.

Henry Jr. smeared applesauce on the tray of his high chair. Though not much younger than Mazy and Molly, he seemed much more immature. He was a charming child with Darcy's quick smile and Henry's dark good looks.

Manda washed the few dishes while Darcy put her son to bed. "Give Aunt Manda some sugar," she said before she carried him upstairs.

Henry Jr. smacked his lips against her cheek. What a doll baby.

Standing at the sink, she could look out over her sister's yard. Across the back was a whitewashed fence where red roses climbed a trellis and lilies bent their heads under the weight of profuse orange blooms.

Back in the kitchen, Darcy picked up a towel and began drying the knives, forks, and spoons.

"Don't you feel like you've died and gone to heaven when you look out there?" Manda asked. "It's just so peaceful."

Darcy held a fork up to the light, then dropped it back into the soapy water under Manda's dishrag. Manda washed it again, dipped it in the rinse pan, and laid it in the wooden drainer.

"I've found I'm more content if my house is in order and if I have nice things around me. Remember how we used to not even have a place to hang our clothes?"

"What clothes?"

"You've got a point," Darcy said, holding the twice-washed fork up to the window before polishing it vigorously. She opened a drawer in the cabinet beside the sink and arranged the utensils in a caddy. Each type had a separate compartment.

"How clever," Manda said. "I've never seen such a thing. Miz Copper keeps hers in the pantry in a stoneware crock, and Cara's sit in the middle of the kitchen table with the handles sticking up out of a fruit jar."

"Bet you don't remember where Mommy kept hers."

"We had utensils?"

Darcy chuckled. "It wasn't that bad. We didn't eat our food with our hands."

"We had food?"

Darcy snapped Manda's arm with the dish towel. "You don't recall possum stew."

Manda pretended to gag. "You've come a long way, Sister. I'm proud of you."

"So have you, if you'd give yourself some credit."

Manda lifted the dishpan. "Do you want me to scrub the front stoop with this water?"

Darcy tilted the pan. The sudsy water swirled down the drain.

"That seems wasteful," Manda said.

With a twist of her wrist, clean water gushed from a faucet over the sink. "We have plenty. Plus, I have a woman who cleans once a week and also does the laundry."

"At the Pelfreys', that woman is me."

"I used to do the same. I never minded the work, and Miz Copper was so good to me."

Manda felt a pang of guilt. She'd left the Pelfreys in the lurch. She knew they'd think she'd run off on a lark. And Miz Copper would be disappointed in her, maybe even mad, if she found out Lilly had walked herself to the coach. Manda hadn't even told Darcy that part of the story. Lilly was a friend, though; she wouldn't tell on Manda. And really, it wasn't such a terrible thing to have happened. She was the only one hurt.

"Let's go sit outside and catch the breeze," Darcy said.

They went out back. Darcy had a nice brick-paved sitting area protected from the weather by a green- and white-striped awning. Clay pots filled with red geraniums sat along the edges. Her porch furniture was painted white. Comfy pillows in the same material as the awning decorated the chairs.

Manda took a seat, sinking into the cushion.

Darcy propped the door so she could hear Henry Jr. if he needed her. "Ah," she said when she plopped down. "It feels good to get off my feet."

"I wish I could visit your shop," Manda said.

"Come with me in the morning."

"I didn't think you'd want to be seen with me this way," Manda said, ducking her head. "I know I look a mess."

"Gracious, it's not as if you'd stop traffic. Besides, why should I care what someone else says?"

"I'm not as brave as you. I care a lot if folks talk about me."

"That's because you live in a small place where any news is big news. Here in the city people might talk for a bit; then they'll be on to something else. Believe me, I know." Darcy leaned back in her chair and put her feet up on a footrest. "So did you recall where Mommy kept the knives and forks?"

"We had that old dresser with the little drawers on either side of the mirror. She kept what few we had in one of those drawers."

"Remember it always stuck when it rained? Mommy would take the nub of a candle and run wax along the bottom."

"Poor Mommy," Manda said.

"She did the best she could," Darcy responded. As if no other words were needed.

Manda cast a sidelong look at her sister. What she was about to ask would change both their lives, and she wasn't sure what Darcy's response would be. Her stomach felt nervous. Maybe she should wait—or maybe she should pray about it. That would be selfish, though. God was way too busy for stupid girls like her.

"So," Darcy said, "what are your plans?"

"I told the Pelfreys I'd be back in a few days. I guess that's what I'll do—go back and work, try to save some money so I can strike out on my own," Manda said, while hoping her sister would come up with a different solution.

"What about that Gurney fellow, the one you wrote me about?"

"He's not the one. If I'd truly cared about him, I wouldn't have got messed up with that scoundrel." Manda traced the healing cut on her lip with one finger. "I'm swearing off men for good."

"It seems like us Whitt girls like a man who's trouble," Darcy said. "You with that man, me with Henry, and Dance with poor old Ace."

"I believe Ace got the trouble there," Manda said, a giggle bubbling up.

"Ha! You might be right," Darcy said. "You know, I never thought of it before, but out of all us girls, Dance is the one most like Mommy."

"That's probably why our father was always on the road."

"Mommy did—"

"—the best she could," Manda finished her sister's sentence. "You always say that. It seems like you don't care about all the heartache we went through as kids."

Darcy reached over and took Manda's hand. "You need to let Mommy's failures go. Eventually you have to grow up—accept the way things were and the way things are. If you spend your life blaming her, the past will always haunt you."

Manda sniffed back a tear. "How did you get so smart?"

"When something untoward happens to me, I ask God what the lesson is—what it is He wants me to learn. That keeps me from worrying overmuch. The Bible says God chastens those He loves. It keeps us on the straight and narrow."

"What do you reckon my lesson is?"

"I don't know. That's for you to figure out. I do know that you have to pray and listen for His answer with an open heart and an open mind." Darcy stood and fluffed the pillow in her chair. "Why don't you think about staying here with me and Henry Jr. for a while? I've plenty of room and I could use your help at the shop."

Manda's heart flipped. She couldn't believe her ears. God had answered her prayer, and she hadn't even been on her knees. Maybe He did care about her. "But what about the Pelfreys?"

"You can write to them and explain that I've offered you a job. You know Miz Copper'll want whatever's best for you. She won't have any trouble getting another hired girl."

Manda went to bed with a light heart. Everything was working in her favor. Darcy's offer was the answer to everything. No one need ever know what went on in that barn. It could be as if it never happened. Regardless of what Darcy said, some lessons were best left unlearned.

# 27

COPPER FORCED HERSELF to eat a bite of breakfast though it tasted like sawdust and tightened her throat. She wouldn't be any good to anyone if she keeled over, but it seemed impossible to swallow. She and John sat under the tree where Billy had lain. All of the victims she and the others had cared for yesterday had been transported to the city for further care if needed or to catch another train if not. Now the depot was ready for whomever the men brought up today. Copper feared it would be little more than a morgue after all this time. A day and a half had passed since the accident. How long could anyone live under all that rubble?

She handed her sausage biscuit to John.

"Copper, you have to eat."

"I'm all right. You're the one who's doing the heavy lifting."

John washed his breakfast down with coffee. "I just knew I'd find her last night. When it got too dark to fell trees, I went to the site and searched until the section foreman made me leave."

"I know," she said wearily. "You told me."

John tossed half her biscuit to the birds. A blackbird cawed and swooped down, snatching up a bit of bread. "I've got the funniest feeling, like Lilly's not here, like this is all in vain."

Copper didn't know how he was able to feel anything. Her brain was dead, and her heart was dying. Once she'd helped put the last of the injured on the rescue train bound for Lexington, way after midnight, she'd given in to his demands that they try to catch some sleep. She had wanted to set vigil over the ravine. They'd borrowed blankets from the supplies and come up here under the tree to rest. He was snoring before she had even wrapped up in the scratchy woolen Army blanket. Thoughts of Lilly dead or dying kept her tossing and turning most of the night.

At daybreak, a woman had come around passing out sausage and biscuits and cups of coffee. She looked like a farmwife. The skin around her eyes had deep crinkles from the sun, and the hands that offered food were spotted and worn. They told of years of service. Her dress was homespun and her apron a popular feed-sack print. Copper had one just like it.

"Thank you," Copper had said when the woman poured

coffee from a granite pot into cups she carried on a tray. "This is so kind of you."

"My church wanted to do some working prayer," she'd said. "This is a terrible thing. Terrible."

Now finished with his respite, John was tying his bootlaces and getting ready to go back into the fray. He tested his theories. "Maybe she was dazed by the accident. Maybe she hit her head and wandered off to a farmhouse or something."

"Oh, John, wouldn't someone know by now if that happened?"

He cupped her chin. "Don't give up hope. God will bring her back to us. I just know it."

Later that morning, Copper was assisting in the treatment of burns. A man had just been carried into the depot on a canvas stretcher. He'd been pinned by the legs underneath the rubble, but he was alive and the burns were not too deep. They were painful, though, and the man cursed loudly whenever he was touched. Under the direction of a physician, Copper moistened the ugly wounds with water.

The man spat out an expletive.

"I'm so sorry," Copper said.

"Can I sit up?"

They assisted him to a nearby chair. Grunting and groaning, the man positioned his legs across the stretcher. When Copper sprinkled finely powdered, common cooking soda into the wounds, his face stretched in a grimace. Ugly words streamed like sour milk from his mouth.

The doctor caught Copper's arm midshake of the cooking soda tin. "I'll finish. You don't have to listen to this."

"I'm not offended. It's the pain that's talking."

The doctor turned a steely look on the man. "We'll have no more of that."

Taking the heel of one foot in the palm of his hand, the doctor lifted one leg and then the other in order for Copper to wrap strips of wet linen from ankle to thigh.

The man relaxed in the chair. "Man, that feels better. Sorry, lady."

"That's okay," she said. "I'll be praying for you."

"You're a fine nurse," the doctor said. "Where'd you take your training?"

"I'm not formally trained," Copper replied. "I'm just observant."

"Well, you're a natural," he said, already turning to the next case.

Any other time the doctor's observations would have meant something to Copper. His words were the same ones Simon had told her years ago. Now all she wanted was a chance to help her daughter. There'd been only three litters brought up this morning, and with each one her hope was rekindled, then dashed when none bore Lilly Gray. With each hour that passed, Lilly's chances of survival dimmed.

She was dribbling teaspoons of water into the corner of the burned man's mouth, going slowly so he wouldn't throw it up, when she heard a way-too-familiar strident voice and saw the sheriff blocking the path of a way-too-familiar woman.

"Let me pass!" Alice Corbett Upchurch demanded. "I have rights!"

"Can you finish this?" Copper asked another helper. Giving the cup and teaspoon to the aide, she went to meet her sister-in-law. In all truthfulness, she hadn't given Alice a passing thought until this moment. And in all truthfulness she didn't want to give her one now. She didn't have the patience for it.

"How long were you going to let me sit in that hovel with strangers, Laura Grace? Why, it's no more than a tent, and there are no amenities."

Copper winced at the formality of her given name. The one Alice insisted on calling her. "I'm sorry. I didn't think—"

"Of course you didn't. You're too busy running around taking care of everyone but Lilly Gray. Thoughtless." Alice tapped her perfectly polished shoe against the depot floor. "You've always been thoughtless."

Alice looked like she'd just stepped out of a bandbox. Not a wrinkle nor a smudge marred her clothes. The feather on her hat was dyed to match her royal blue promenade dress. Regal as a queen visiting her subjects, all she needed was a scepter. Copper noticed a freckle-faced girl with gingery hair standing reverentially a few feet behind Alice. A suitcase hung from one hand and, of all things, a hatbox from the other. Alice probably had her heating a sadiron on a camp stove this morning in order to press her outfit.

"How did you get here?"

"My butler brought me. You remember Joseph. He's

tending to the carriage and the horse. As soon as we collect Lilly Gray, we're heading back." Alice glanced around the depot, lifting her skirts the slightest bit and wrinkling her nose. "Now where is my niece?"

Copper bit back a hateful retort. She understood Alice's need to control the situation. Her fear must be as great as Copper's own. And she had probably sat in a folding chair all night hoping against hope for word. "You must be exhausted. May I get you a cup of coffee?"

"Indeed not. We brought our own supplies. Some woman brought food around this morning. I refused. Amy ate." With a toss of her head, she indicated her maid. "But you know the working class—their stomachs are stronger than ours."

"Alice!" Copper said more sharply than she'd meant to. "We haven't found Lilly." Her voice broke on a sob. "I don't know where she is. I'm so afraid—"

"Don't carry on so. I brought money; we'll pay someone. There has to be a way."

"I don't think you understand. Leave your things here and come with me."

The maid set the suitcase and the hatbox on the floor.

"Amy, for pity's sake, don't put those down. Someone will steal them."

Copper found Amy a seat. "Wait here," she said.

Alice stepped delicately over rubbish as Copper led her to the ravine. They stood watching men maneuver the wreckage. They could hear the ripping sound of crosscut saws before a tree crashed to the ground.

"John is over there." She indicated a heavily wooded hillside. "They're cutting a path so they can haul the debris out that way. It's not as steep as coming straight up the side of this gorge like the rescuers have to do."

Alice hadn't said a word. She seemed to be in shock.

Copper knew just how she felt. "See what we're up against?"

A discreet cough and then a quiet moan escaped Alice's throat. "First my brother and now this. I simply cannot bear it."

Copper slipped an arm around Alice's perfectly corseted waist. "I know. I know."

Alice produced a handkerchief from under the starched cuff of her shirtwaist and blotted her cheeks. "This makes no sense. She's only a child. This can't be happening."

"Wait," Copper said when she saw two men struggling up the steep grade with another canvas stretcher. She stepped over the edge, slid in the dirt, fighting to keep her balance on the steep grade, and met them halfway up. "Please."

The men stopped and let her lift a corner of the sheet that covered the body's face. Whoever it was, she was unrecognizable in death. But the long wavy hair that spilled over the canvas was auburn. Copper took the side of the stretcher, bearing some of the weight.

"You don't need to do that, ma'am," one of the men said from behind the bandanna covering his mouth and nose. "It ain't fittin'."

"I'm a nurse. I've seen death before," Copper said, climbing with them to the top.

"Then we thank you," he said.

Alice rushed over, blocking them. "Is it Lilly?"

Copper waved Alice away. This would shock her sensibili-ties. At the summit of the long incline, they clambered back onto the bank. The stretcher tipped. One thin, bluish arm slipped off the canvas. The lifeless hand dragged in the dirt before Copper noticed and tucked it back underneath the dirty sheet. Alice clamped both hands over her mouth and turned her back.

As she watched the men carry their burden toward the station house, Copper thought of what would be added to the roster: *female adolescent; auburn hair; brown dress/ white collar; deceased.* She despaired. Some mother's pre-cious daughter reduced to a single written line on a register in a ticket seller's cage.

The July sun was bearing down. Heat shimmered off the tracks. A bird took a dust bath beside the rail. The heat magnified the odor of decay. Alice raised her black parasol. Beyond the standing cars, a locomotive screeched to a stop. Two men jumped out of the cab and began to hook up the caboose that was still fastened to the other cars.

Copper shaded her eyes to watch. She had a sudden desire to search those cars before the men hauled them away. She grabbed Alice's free hand and dragged her along the far side of the track where the cars' doors stood open. "Give me a boost," she said when they reached the door of the first car.

Alice didn't protest but carefully furled her umbrella

before linking her hands to make a step. "You are being fool-ish," she said as Copper receded into the gloom of the car.

"I have to look. Something of Lilly's could be in here." She heard an odd noise at the door.

Alice was hanging by her waist, half in and half out. "Well, don't stand there gawking. Give me a hand."

Copper pulled her in. "I'll go to the last car and come this way. You look in here."

She hurried to the last car before the caboose. She searched each bench, getting on her knees to look under. Surprisingly there was little out of place. She supposed there were not so many injuries in this last car. Folks would have taken their possessions with them when they stepped off.

She went outside and across the wooden platform that sat over the knuckle couplers which connected the cars. The second-to-last car was much like the other. It had taken her about ten minutes. She needed to hurry back to Alice else they would be hauled off along with the tail end of the train.

She pushed the connecting door open, crossed the plat-form, and entered the first car. There was much more damage there. Alice was sitting on a bench seat, holding a baby in her arms. Copper couldn't believe her eyes.

"Some little girl's doll," Alice said. "Look at the battered head. This is all so pitiful."

Copper's heart stopped thudding. *A doll, just a doll.*

"It makes you wonder if the child's head looks the same," Alice said.

Copper let her sit there with her sorrow while she pulled

clothing, shoes, and still-fastened suitcases out from under wooden benches. But there was nothing there of Lilly. Underneath her feet she felt the buck of the car. The locomotive let out a tremendous belching noise, and the train whistle blasted.

"Alice! We've got to get off!" She sat in the open door with her legs dangling in the air, gauging the drop. Pushing off with the palms of her hands, she planted her feet on the ground.

"I can't do that. I'll snap my leg bone." Alice clung to the side of the door. Her eyes were wide with fright.

The train was picking up steam. Copper had a good mind to let her go—let her roll right on to Jackson. "Jump, Alice!"

Plopping on her stomach, Alice kind of shimmied out backward, falling on her rump, her legs sticking out of a fluff of petticoats. She looked stunned. If the situation hadn't been as it was, Copper would have burst out laughing. It wasn't often she saw her sister-in-law looking foolish.

"For pity's sake," she said. "Help me up. I think I've injured myself."

Copper hauled her up and dusted her off. Though Copper was sure Alice would be sore as a boil tomorrow, the only thing broken was the heel of one shoe.

"Get my umbrella."

Copper raised it over Alice's cockeyed hat, giving Alice shade as they walked along the track.

"I simply must have another pair of shoes," Alice said, limping. "I can't be expected to carry on in these."

"What size?" Copper asked, laying the parasol aside and sorting through a drummer's busted barrel.

"Six," Alice said.

Copper raised her eyebrows but played along. She held up a pair of size-six walking boots for perusal.

"Well, perhaps an eight," Alice said, joining in the search. "This is just like an end-of-season sale at a department store."

"Lilly loved the new shoes and the spats you sent for her to wear with her traveling outfit." A picture of an excited Lilly posing in the kitchen in the fawn-colored suit popped into Copper's mind. She remembered how she dreaded Lilly's leaving, how she'd packed and repacked the wicker hamper, trying to offset any possible problem. "I didn't want her to come, you know."

Alice balanced on one foot, trying mightily to unfasten her stylish alligator boots without tipping over. Her face flushed. "Are you blaming me?"

Copper bent to work the buttons on Alice's shoes. "I want to. I want to so badly." She jerked off one dress boot and then the other. Alice steadied herself with her hand on Copper's head. It was easy to slip the size-eight patent-leather pumps onto her elegant arched feet.

"Why can't you just leave us alone? Why must you interfere?" Doubled over, resting her hands on bent knees, Copper heaved sobs from deep in her being. She cried until she couldn't breathe.

Alice patted her back. "Laura Grace? Laura Grace, please."

Alice's voice sounded distant to her ears. The air sparkled

with tiny pinpricks of light that faded to dark, blissful night. She was a child again. Caught up in her father's arm, she was safe. The nightmare was over.

Coughing and sputtering, Copper inhaled the familiar scent of ammonia. Her nose stung, and her eyes smarted like fire. A nurse waved an open glass vial under her nose. She pushed the hand away.

"There we are," the nurse said. "We're coming around."

"Let her breathe," the doctor said.

Slowly reality sank in. She was in the depot, but she was the patient. Alice waved a folding fan in her direction. The doctor held her wrist at the pulse point. The nurse wet a towel and dabbed Copper's temples. The sheriff stood back, a look of dismay on his face.

"What happened?" she asked, still woozy.

"You fainted," the doctor said. "The sheriff carried you here. I'd say not enough food and too little rest."

Copper struggled to stand. The room spun and the floor tilted. She backed up into the chair. The air was dense with a wet, oppressive heat. She felt like she was smothering.

"Do something," Alice demanded, right in the doctor's face.

"She'll be fine," he said. "She just needs a little rest and some food in her stomach."

"I'll sit here a minute," Copper said. "I got too hot. That's all. I feel better already."

"No more work for you today," the doctor said.

Alice crooked her finger. Amy hurried over. "Have Joseph bring the carriage around."

The girl started off with the suitcase and hatbox in hand.

"Put those silly things down," Alice barked.

*Poor Amy,* Copper thought, resting her head against the tips of her fingers.

Soon Alice's butler pulled the carriage up to the back door of the depot. Despite her protests, Alice got her into the carriage.

"Drive out into the country," Alice said. "Stop at the first nicely shaded spot you find."

Joseph stopped beside a creek and spread a blanket under a copse of hickory trees. Copper lay supine on the tartan throw. Overhead, leaves danced to the tune of a pleasant breeze. The sweet smell of honeysuckle cleansed the overwhelming odor of death that had permeated each breath she'd taken since she'd come to the scene. Water rushed swiftly by in the nearby creek, calling her to step in.

"Let's go wading," she said.

Alice sat ramrod straight on another blanket, an exact replica of Copper's. "Close your eyes, Laura Grace. Rest."

"An hour, no more," Copper said. "Promise?"

"I'll wake you in one hour. Now hush."

Alice woke Copper to tea and coddled eggs. The eggs were finely dusted with paprika. There were stone-milled crackers spread with strawberry jam to go along. The homely scent of sassafras wafted her way from a campfire built on the bank of the creek. Upstream, Joseph filled canteens with fresh water. It was an idyllic picture reminding her of better times.

Alice folded her blanket and began reassembling the picnic supplies. "Put out the fire, Amy."

Copper finished every bite and even had a second cup of tea. "Let's pray before we go back."

Alice bent her head.

"Joseph, Amy, come pray with us."

Alice raised one eyelid in question as the servants joined them and Copper had all join hands. Copper prayed fervently, asking for God's protection and His mercy. She thanked Him for Alice and Joseph and Amy and for their ministry to her.

Joseph surprised her with a prayer of his own. "Father God, we bow lowly as the worms we are before You." His rich voice was like a serenade. "We have a mighty need, Lord, and we ask You to answer by finding Lilly."

Alice joined in. "Lord, You know our needs. We don't need to beg, but there will be an extra offering in the collection plate if You will give Lilly back to us unharmed. Amen."

Copper knew she should be appalled by Alice's tactless entreaty, but she couldn't be. She'd put out a fleece of her own, promising to give up everything but her other children if Lilly was just restored to her. She was weak, not strong like Abraham, and she prayed God wouldn't test her faith that way. While lying awake last night, she'd determined that the greatest sacrifice she could offer, outside her children, was her practice. Maybe this was all to show her that she was spending too much time tending to other people's needs and not enough on her family. She was ready to lay it all at the Savior's feet.

They'd no sooner stepped out of the carriage than the sheriff approached. "There's a man looking for you," he told Copper. "He says he's got to talk to you right now."

*John,* Copper thought. *He's probably worried sick. I should have found him before I set off with Alice. But, no, the sheriff had met John the night before, so he would know if it was him.* "Didn't he tell you his name?"

"Tell you the truth, I didn't ask. I figured if he was looking for you, then he was an all right fellow. I brought him here but you were gone. Doc said you'd be back shortly. If it helps, he said he was a preacher, and he was toting a big black Bible. Hey, there he is—yonder with your husband."

It was Brother Jasper hurrying her way with John. Seeing her minister gave Copper no comfort. She took a step backward, bumping into Alice. "I don't understand. This can't be good."

John grabbed her shoulders. "Listen. Lilly is not here. She was never on the train in the first place."

Copper couldn't get her mind around what he was saying. It was as if John were speaking in tongues. She looked to Brother Jasper for an interpretation.

"Do you need to sit down?" the preacher asked.

She swayed on her feet. John circled her shoulders with his strong arm, steadying her. "No . . . I'm all right, but what do you mean Lilly's not here?"

"Remember I said I was going to send a message over the wire to my wife's sister's house to let her know about the train wreck? Well, I did, and then I waited and waited until I got the reply. She said Lilly didn't meet the coach to go to the station with her and Kate."

Copper felt a lightening of spirit. "This is wonderful! That means Lilly is all right."

She watched Brother Jasper's face for the news she needed to hear, but all she saw was consternation. "What?"

"I went by the house on my way here to see Lilly for myself. I hate like fire to tell you this, but she's not there either."

"Then where is she?"

"I don't know. I spoke to Miss Remy, and she said they hadn't seen Lilly since day before yesterday."

"But Lilly was going on the coach. Mrs. Jasper was going to look out for her."

"I know," Brother Jasper said. "I don't know what to tell you about that except Kate's jaw was swollen up big as a muskmelon that morning. She'd spent the night crying in pain, and her mother was desperate to get her to Cincinnati."

"Is Kate all right?" Copper asked.

"The telegraph didn't say. I'm going there after I leave here, but I had to see you and John first."

"We appreciate it," John said. "We could have been here for days yet."

"What did the note say, John?"

"What note?"

"The one Manda left on the table. What was in the note?"

John scratched the top of his head. "Let me think. It was something like Mr. Morton came to the house for you, Copper—then something about Manda going to her sister's—"

Copper shook his arm, interrupting. "Lilly. What did the note say about Lilly?"

"I don't know the exact words, but I know the note led me to believe Lilly was on that coach."

A great emptiness swept through Copper's very being. She thought that finding Lilly's broken body in the mass of twisted steel would be the worst thing she could ever face, but she'd been wrong. Having no body to find was worse. Losing a child to death would break your heart, but losing a child entirely would steal your soul.

Alice cornered the sheriff, taking over. "You'll need to commandeer one of the relief trains. We need to get to Jackson as soon as possible."

Copper looked at John. He read her eyes.

Tenderly he took Alice's arm. "I'm sorry, but you can't come with us. It would be best if you go home to wait. You'll be more comfortable there, and I promise I'll send word as soon as we know anything."

Alice seemed to crumple at his touch. "Either way?"

"Either way," he said.

Copper and Alice embraced for an awkward moment, but there were no words of sympathy. Copper knew the blaming went two ways. It was a time for forgiveness, but she couldn't muster up the energy. It seemed Alice felt the same.

When Alice turned away, so did she. Alice could wait—for now Copper needed to focus on the long way home and what she might find on Troublesome Creek.

# 28

LILLY ROOSTED LIKE a homing pigeon atop the restacked boxes under the narrow window. Curiosity had overcome her fear now that the man was gone. She hadn't dared to go to the open door yet, but she would. What she saw outside the high-up window was a complete surprise. There was a house with a big flat rock for a stoop and a weedy packed-dirt yard. The door to the house stood open, and there was no screen to keep out flies or mosquitoes. The house looked deserted, but there were a dozen or so rags pinned to a sagging wire clothesline, and a few chickens scratched about in the dirt.

A barefoot boy came out of the door swinging a bucket.

She couldn't believe her eyes. "Tern!" she yelled before she thought. "Tern Still!"

She nearly fell off the stack of boxes when Tern whirled around to the sound of her voice. He held one finger to his lips and shook his head.

She ducked down. Everything started making sense. The reason she knew the beagle was because the dog belonged to Tern, who was the son of the man who stole her, who was the husband of Adie, who was the woman who died in the little house.

Boy, she was in big trouble. Mr. Still was mad at her family. He probably believed in an eye for an eye and a tooth for a tooth.

*Ping! Ping!* She heard what sounded like pebbles hitting the tin siding. She peered out the window again.

There stood Tern trying to look like a man. "You ought not be hollering out that window."

"Who are you to tell me what to do?"

"My pa's the toughest man there is. That gives me rights."

Lilly snorted. "Are you going to get me out of here or not?"

Tern jerked like he'd been hit with a rock, then put his finger to his lips again. He ran back to the stoop, where he'd left the bucket, snatched it up, and ambled around the side of the house.

Lilly soon saw why. A buckboard drew up in the yard. Mr. Still helped a woman who was holding a baby down off the seat. Several boys climbed out of the bed and raced each other to the house. "Last one in's a rotten egg," one yelled.

The old lady looked the same as she did when Lilly saw her the day they brought the coffin to the little house. Same stiff, black bonnet hiding her face, same black dress so old it looked rusty, same stooped, shuffling walk. Lilly's eyes widened; she was coming her way. The shuffling continued until the lady reached the clothesline. With one hand she held the baby, and with the other she unpinned a square whitish rag. Mr. Still reached for the baby. The lady slapped his hand away.

"Ma," he said, "I don't know why you're so het up."

"You don't know?" the grandma said, whipping at him with the rag. "You don't know much, Isa Still. You're just like your no-account daddy."

"Don't I take care of you the best I can considering the circumstances?"

"The circumstance is all I'm considering. Here's the circumstance spelled out for ye. You stole a neighbor's gal. She's up there in that old building where your daddy kept his moonshine makings. The circumstance is that rotten shack could give way at any time—it ain't fitting for occupation. That gal could be kilt, and then your circumstance would be setting in the county hoosegow."

Lilly watched her pull the rags off the line. She was a little old thing, but she stood taller with every word. And with every other word, Mr. Still appeared to shrink. His neck retreated like a turtle's until his hat seemed to be sitting on his shoulders.

"So what's that do for my circumstance?" the lady said.

"Why don't you tell me that? Who you reckon's gonna take care of all these young'uns whilst you're toasting your toes on the county dole?"

Lilly jabbed the air with her fist each time the grandma made a point. "Take that," she whispered. "Take that."

"I'm sorry. I didn't think—"

"Of course you didn't. Don't I always say, 'Talk it over with your ma before you do something stupid'? Don't I always say that?"

"Yes. But there she was fishing my dogs out of the pond. There wasn't time to ask you. Besides, weren't nobody home but me and Tern. You was gone to your sister's."

Mrs. Still's exasperated sigh sailed all the way up the tin siding and rushed through the narrow window. "It ain't like I don't know where I've been, boy." She started hanging the rags again, like she forgot she'd just taken them down, punctuating each sentence with a thrust of a clothespin onto the rusty wire. "Here's a nugget for ye. If you can't talk it over, then just don't do it!"

Lilly could see her cheeks turn red under the brim of the black bonnet. Without unpinning it, she tugged a rag back off the line. The clothespin shot straight up. Mr. Still ducked.

"I'm sorry. But you know how I've been stewing since Adie died. I finally just biled over." Mr. Still's voice dropped, and Lilly strained to hear. "Weren't none of any of them Pelfreys' business."

"I know and I agree. But none of that was done in spite.

306

Don't you see that? Right or wrong, Miz Pelfrey was trying to help."

"So what do we do now?"

"I believe this move of yourn is even more foolish than that skunk farm you had and probably harder to deal with."

"But you liked that pretty cloak I made for you, right?"

"Isa, Isa. When am I ever going to have a need for a big-city costume?"

Mr. Still's mouth spread in a big smile. "I'll line your coffin with it."

The grandma laid the baby on his back in a patch of grass. Expertly, she removed one diaper and applied another. Shaking her head, she smiled up at her son. "You know, that would be nice. Probably ain't nobody hereabouts had nothing so fancy lining their oak-board overcoats. Sometimes you remind me why I fell so hard for your good-for-nothing pa."

Mr. Still helped her up and then picked up the baby. Lilly could swear the old lady's knees sounded loud as the rusty hinges on the short door.

"So what'll we do about the girl?"

"Smart, is she?" Mrs. Still asked.

"I reckon so. She had a lever in there prying the bar offen the door."

"Then I say we pack up and head out. They ain't gonna let you off on a few *sorrys*. No matter your gift of gab." Mrs. Still seemed to survey her surroundings. "I'm right tired of this place anyhow."

"What about the girl?"

"If she's as smart as you say, she'll figure it out. Besides which they're sure to find her sooner than later. I'm surprised they haven't already."

Mr. Still tapped the side of his forehead. "Probably because I threw them off the trail."

"How so?"

"The girl's hat was caught up in the weeds at the pond. Nearly gave me a stroke when I saw it. But then I set to thinking it over."

"Chaw it slow and spit it out. We ain't got all day for your pronouncements."

"I figured I'd use that hat to confuse anybody looking for the girl, so's I took it yon side of the creek and up past the churchyard. Left it right beside the road in plain sight."

"Good thinking, Son. Sometimes you surprise me." The old lady reached up and patted Mr. Still's face. "Still, that won't work for long. We'd best get out while the getting's good."

"When are you thinking?"

"Tomorrow. If they'd have been looking today, they'd already be here. For now, put Tern over by the rock fence. He'll know if anybody's a-coming, and we'll light out like Snyder's hound."

"I'll get the dog, then."

"Isa, think! What do beagles do best? Track. Track and hunt. It's liable to come right back here and then lead the law straight to you. Leave it be!"

"I reckon the girl can have it for her trouble," he said. "But, man, I sure do hate to leave my fishing pond."

"Ye can make another. Ain't that hard. All it takes is a shovel and a strong back." The old lady stacked the diapers across her shoulder and took the baby from him. "Ye got a shovel, don't ye?"

Mr. Still didn't seem to take offense at his mother's retort. He just carried the used diaper pinched between two fingers and followed her across the yard.

Lilly was sorry to see them go. She hadn't realized how hungry she was for somebody else's words, even scary words, even scary words directed at her. At least she knew Mr. Still wasn't going to snap her neck or drown her like he drowned the puppies.

Since she knew he wasn't watching, she went to the open door. He really was as dense as his mother said if he thought she wouldn't take the first chance she got to climb down that ladder. All she had to do was figure out how to take the dog and the puppy with her. Her hopes drained away when she saw the ladder lying on the ground. She was high up in the treetops. It was much too far to jump.

If they really left her here, could she ever escape? She needed to come up with a plan. But first she went to the hamper and took out the boiled eggs, the little waxed-paper twists of salt and pepper, and the red ripe tomato. The dog ate from Mr. Still's greasy packet while tomato juice dripped down her chin.

A gloom settled over her. Why hadn't her daddy come? Didn't anybody even miss her? And why hadn't her heavenly Father answered her prayers? She rinsed her hands and took the Bible off the table. At least she could memorize her Sunday school Scripture while she had the time.

Turning to 1 Peter, she read about being steadfast in difficult times. God promised there would be suffering only for a while and that the suffering would strengthen and settle you. She guessed she could remain steadfast through one more night if that was what God wanted her to do. She would bide her time until she knew the Stills were really gone, and then she'd get out of here one way or another.

She eyed the valise and then the dog. When Mr. Still put the ladder up before he left, she could put the dog in there and carry her down, then come back for the puppy. It was like a riddle waiting to be solved. The beagle put one paw on the grease-stained paper, anchoring it while she licked. She wanted to enjoy every last bit.

Lilly took the paper away. "You're not a billy goat."

The dog wagged her tail. Her brown eyes looked happy.

"Are you a happy girl?" she asked, scratching between the dog's ears. "I think I'll name you since it looks like you belong to me." Lilly studied the dog's face, searching for clues. "I think Steady would be a good name for a dog such as you because you have been so steadfast in your suffering." The puppy lay sleeping like a fat little blob. "We'll wait until your baby gets some personality before we pick a name. Don't you think that's a good idea?"

Lilly sat cross-legged on the pallet and lifted the puppy into her lap. Through the open door she could see storm clouds brewing in the distance. Thunder rolled across the far mountains, and a sudden breeze cooled the air. The old lady's words came back to her like a portent of things to come: *"That rotten shack could give way at any time. . . . That gal could be kilt."*

As she stroked the puppy's soft ears, she thought of all the times her family had gathered on their tin-roofed porch to enjoy a summer storm. When Daddy John saw the first bolt of lightning strike or when the thunder boomers followed after another, he'd herd everyone into the house. She and Mama would draw chairs up to the screen door and listen to the rain tap-dancing on the roof. It was the safest place in the world.

The light outside the open door turned greenish black. Tree branches thrashed and scraped against the walls. Rain fell in dark sheets. Lilly settled one arm around Steady and one around the puppy. Was her mama on the porch looking to the mountains right this moment? Was she wondering where Lilly was? Were her tears falling like the rain?

Suddenly the door slammed against the facing. The wind shifted and sucked it back open like an unseen hand. Marble-size hail bounced across the floor before the door banged shut again. The hail ricocheting off the tin-walled hut was so loud Lilly couldn't hear herself think. The puppy nuzzled her arm, looking for his mother.

Lilly bent her head. She'd never been so alone.

# 29

DARCY WAS RIGHT. Hardly anyone gave Manda a second glance as they walked to the dress shop. It was such a beautiful morning, and Manda was so excited to be there that she almost forgot her troubles.

Darcy twisted the key in the lock on the door and ushered Manda inside. Right in the middle of the room was a big oblong table where Darcy measured and cut the cloth to order. Floor-to-ceiling shelves held meticulously labeled bolts of fabric: serge, cheviot, silk, velvet, ladies' cloth, tweed, polished cotton, melton, kersey, and even beaver, among others. The fabrics were so varied and rich-looking, Manda wanted to wrap herself up in them.

The room was feminine but also serviceable with a seating area featuring delicate, curved-legged chairs under a crystal chandelier. Darcy's desk was a Victorian writing table. Ferns like the one in Darcy's parlor hung in the two windows that faced the sidewalk.

"You want folks strolling by to notice but not really be able to see inside. It gives the ladies shopping here some privacy," Darcy explained. "Plus, the plants mute the light coming in. Sunlight devastates fabric."

Manda wanted to touch everything. There were dozens and dozens of cards of buttons and frogs, yards and yards of lace, ribbon, braid, and gimp trims, so much it put the dry goods store at home to shame. A glass-topped display case held folding fans adorned with feathers, gloves with tiny pearl buttons, handkerchief cases, and ribbon bags.

"Take a look at these. I just got them in yesterday." Darcy set a white cardboard box on the table and pulled back a piece of tissue paper. "This is a Russian appliqué collar. I ordered a dozen. Did you ever see anything so elegant? Of course you can't tell how very beautiful it is until you remove the muslin foundation. See? It's worked upon the wrong side. Imagine how tedious."

Manda was afraid she might drool on it. "Who in the world could afford to wear these?"

"Anyone with a wealthy husband or old money," Darcy said, holding one up to Manda and cocking her head. "These wide collars are not becoming to every figure, but this would look nice on you."

314

"What if a customer wants it, but you think it doesn't flatter?"

"Well, I try my best to steer the portly ladies to something else." Darcy pulled another box from a stack of boxes on a long shelf under the table. "For instance, a vest and cuffs in point lace like these or perhaps a collar of dainty ribbon stock and bow."

Holding the appliqué collar under her chin, Manda tilted a cheval glass and stared at her reflection. She looked like death warmed over. "But surely these are more expensive. Wouldn't you make more money if you encouraged them?"

"Don't you think that would be dishonest, Manda?"

Manda felt small as a worm. What would Darcy think about the eggs she had taken from Miz Copper without asking?

Darcy looked over Manda's shoulder and into the mirror. "Thankfully you didn't inherit Mommy's double chin like I did. See how pretty you look?"

A single tear tracked down Manda's cheek. "I don't look pretty. You know I don't."

With her index finger, Darcy lifted Manda's chin. The light on her face shifted, defining her high cheekbones and lessening the purple shadows under her eyes. Even her split lip didn't look so bad when your eye was drawn to the Russian collar.

"Did you know our great-great-grandmother on Daddy's side was Cherokee? That's where your cheekbones come from and your pretty straight nose. If your hair was dark instead of yellow, you could pass."

Manda fitted the collar back in the box and smoothed

the tissue paper in place. "I can see why your shop is so suc-
cessful. Every woman wants to feel beautiful—whether she
is or not."

Darcy tapped her foot on the floor like she always did when
she was aggravated. Uh-oh, Manda had pulled her chain.

"Dory Manda, beauty is easy to find if you look through
kind eyes."

Shame coursed through Manda's veins like hot blood.
The things she'd done to lead her to the ugly scene in the
barn loomed large in her mind's eye. She'd flaunted herself
shamelessly, she'd stolen and lied, she'd abandoned Lilly, she'd
hurt Gurney for no good reason, she'd been rude to Miss
Remy, she hadn't touched her Bible in months . . . The self-
condemning list went on. There was no beauty inside herself
to shine out on anyone else.

Darcy went to the door and turned the sign to Please
Come In. She looked at the clock on her desk. "Let's get you
started on some piecework before my first appointment. I've
got things set up in the back room."

Manda spent a quiet morning with needle and thread.
Darcy's designs combined machine stitching with hand,
which produced durable goods with great attention to detail.
No wonder her shop had been bustling all day.

Manda was just finishing a hem on a dress with a bell-
shaped skirt when Darcy came to get her.

"We'll walk home for lunch," she said. "I can't wait to see
little Henry."

Manda fitted the garment over a dress form.

JAN WATSON

Darcy lifted the skirt and perused the hem. "That's good work. Mrs. Jones is going to love this."

"How do you keep the dress forms straight? I couldn't find a label on any of them."

"Ah," Darcy said with a twinkle in her eye, "you don't want your customers to compare their shape to another's. If the forms were named, then matronly Mrs. Jones, for instance, could see that she is more full-figured than young Mrs. Smith. Even though every woman's figure changes with children and age, one doesn't like to admit it. I know which form to use the minute a patron walks through the door."

Darcy flipped the sign to Closed. "We should collect Henry Jr. and take him to the park."

Manda walked along, window-shopping. "I feel so at home here with you. I'd really like to take you up on your offer."

Darcy grabbed Manda's hand and swung it like they were girls going off to pick blackberries or jump in the creek. "I'd love to have you. Sometimes I get so lonesome I could cry."

"Surely you have lots of friends here, you owning your own business and all."

"When your husband is in prison, folks tend to shun you. Don't get me wrong—everyone is nice. Nice and cool in a kind of sorry-for-me way." Darcy's sunny, round face clouded. "I never could stand pity. It gets my dander up."

"Boy, not me. I can use all the sympathy I can get."

"Sympathy's one thing. Pity's another," Darcy said.

"How so?"

"Sympathy says, 'I understand. I've been through it too.'

Pity says, 'That will never happen to me. You brought it on yourself.' Sympathy shares. Pity's haughty."

"You've changed so much since you came here. You don't even talk the same. Your words are more particular."

"I would hope so," Darcy said, pointing out a drugstore. "We'll stop here on the way back after lunch. They have all kinds of paper and envelopes to match. You can pick out something for your letter to Miz Copper."

"I won't know what to say. I'm afraid Miz Copper's mad at me."

"You'd have to do something really bad for that to happen. I'm sure she's just puzzled and probably concerned. I'll help you. As soon as it's in the mail, you'll feel 100 percent better."

Manda hoped it was so.

⸻

They chose to picnic on a bent-willow bench under the shade of a sugar maple tree. The park was sparsely populated today, but Manda couldn't help noticing a young couple strolling by the lake. "Wish that was me," she said.

Darcy unpacked cheese and bread and red grapes. "Give it time. Your turn will come."

Manda took off her bonnet and laid it on the bench. She plucked a grape and popped it into her mouth. "You're so lucky to be here."

Darcy threw a red bouncing ball and Henry Jr. chased it, laughing and bringing it back to his mother. "It's not this

place that blesses me. It's this boy. As soon as Henry has
served his term, we're out of here."

Manda was surprised. "But why? You have your shop and
your house. It all seems perfect for you."

"The house and the store are rented. Everything I own
can be packed and moved at a moment's notice. I even kept
the box the chandelier came in."

"That might be a long time coming, though, right?"

Darcy fed Henry bites of cheese. "I trust you as my sister
to keep what I'm going to tell you to yourself."

"I will. I promise."

Darcy looked across the water as if weighing her thoughts.
Then the old Darcy smile spread across her face. Manda
thought she looked like a girl again. "Henry's name will come
up for a possible pardon from the governor next spring. I'm
very hopeful."

Manda almost choked on a grape. Pardoned? What would
that do to her plans? Henry Thomas wouldn't want her hanging around once he came home.

"If that happens—pray it will—we'll be starting over,
probably in Chicago. Henry has connections there. And it's
a big city—you wouldn't believe it." Darcy bounced the ball.
Her eyes were shining as she turned to Manda. "You could
go with us." She swept the air with her hand. "If you think
this is grand, you should see the parks in Chicago."

"Chicago?" Manda felt like her brain was doing cart-
wheels. Just a few minutes ago she thought she'd had her life
figured out. "I don't even know where that is."

"It's in Illinois. Not so very far away. I lived there for a short time after Henry and I wed. You've forgotten."

Manda folded bread around a piece of cheese. She felt very small for thinking of what she wanted over what would obviously make her sister happy. It was so hard not to be selfish. "Why would the governor care about Henry?"

"This is how the Lord works. I've prayed and prayed for Him to find a way for Henry to come back to me. Then out of the blue, I got asked to make several frocks for a woman who would be going abroad. This was all hush-hush. I was intrigued. Plus, the money was good. Nobody told me who she was, but I was asked to go to Frankfort to take measurements. I closed the shop for a few days, left Henry Jr. with the nanny, and hopped on the train. They paid for everything."

Looking around to see if anyone was listening, Darcy's voice fell to a stage whisper. "That woman is the governor's wife. A friend of hers wore one of my creations at a fancy ball, and she simply had to have one like it, only different of course. I was there for several days, helping her select fabrics and fitting her in muslin mocks."

Henry Jr. leaned against his mother's knee, rubbing his eyes and fussing. Darcy started packing up the remains of their lunch. Pigeons cooed and jockeyed for position at her feet as she shook their napkins free of crumbs.

"She is a very gracious woman, and she was interested in me. That's rare, I'll tell you. Usually women of means act like I'm invisible, like my only life is sewing. But the governor's wife is not that way. For some reason, I felt compelled to tell her everything. And the rest, as they say, I hope will be our history."

Darcy stopped at the hall tree on their way out the door and took two umbrellas from the tin umbrella well. "Looks like we might need these," she said as gray clouds scuttled across the sun.

Manda's mood darkened with the day. Nothing looked as bright and charming as it had this morning before Darcy sprung a pardon on her. They were passing the drugstore before she noticed.

"Let's stop and get your stationery," Darcy said. "You can write your letter at the shop, and we'll post it on the way home. You'll feel better once that's done. And, oh—don't let me forget to buy a newspaper."

Manda hated to buy a box of paper and matching envelopes when one of each would do. She counted her change and picked out the cheapest box available.

"I'll get this," Darcy said. "What you don't use, I will. Besides, I owe you for the work you did this morning."

Manda put her money back in her small drawstring purse. "Thank you. Don't forget you wanted to get a newspaper."

As soon as they got to the shop, Darcy made tea and poured two cups. She took hers to her desk and unfolded the paper.

"What should I do now?" Manda asked.

"Hmm?" Darcy looked up from the paper. "Enjoy your tea; then I'll get you started hemming another skirt. I just want to read the front section before I get busy."

Manda wandered around the room lost in thought, being careful not to spill. Maybe it wouldn't be a bad thing if she did go to Chicago with Darcy and her husband. If she liked this small city so much, she might love a big one. Anyway, it would be almost a year before Henry got out of prison, if at all. And she could tell she was going to like working for her sister.

She finished her tea and went to get Darcy's cup. She could wash them in the sink in the back room.

Darcy was still bent over the newspaper. "Do you know what train Lilly was taking?" she said without looking up.

"Sure, it was Republic's Old Number Twelve. Why?"

Darcy thrust the paper at her. She could see the big, black headline streaming across the top of the first page: *Train Wreck at Four Corners Kills 6. Many Injured.*

Manda felt her stomach drop. "This doesn't mean Lilly Gray."

Darcy turned to the last page of the front section and folded it for Manda. Near the bottom of a column, Old Number Twelve leaped out at her. Her mind raced. This was Friday. The wreck happened late Wednesday. It had to be Lilly's train.

"I have to go home," Manda said.

With key in hand, Darcy was already at the door. "Let's go back to the drugstore. They'll have a train schedule."

Manda forgot about her own predicament as fear for Lilly consumed her. "You should pray. God listens to you."

Darcy turned the sign in the window. "I already am. You do the same."

# 30

COPPER WAS NUMB in mind and body as the train rolled on toward Jackson. She didn't know how the sheriff managed to get the conductor to make an exception for them, and she didn't care. She supposed everyone who had anything to do with the dreadful accident was making exceptions and bending rules. Her only focus was on getting home and finding Lilly, and to do that with half a mind left, she had to keep herself in check.

John had caught on and had stopped trying to talk to her. She knew he was in his own torment of fear for Lilly, but she couldn't help him. She couldn't help anybody. Keeping her face turned to the window, she watched a brewing storm as miles passed by. A mantle of self-reproach as heavy as the leaden clouds settled on her shoulders. She toyed with guilt as if her how-could-I? litany might change the past. It seemed a lifetime ago that she had blithely turned her back on her family, her precious children, and gone off to minister to the Mortons. How could she have been so cavalier?

The *click-click-click* of the wheels on the track lulled her as heavy raindrops spattered against the window. John leaned across her, watching as lightning flashed a warning in the strangely green sky and the tops of trees twisted in a fierce wind.

With a fearsome screech the train stopped short. The force flung Copper forward. Bracing himself, John shot one arm in front of her, barely managing to keep her from slamming into another seat.

"Something's up," he said.

"Is that the train?" she asked, straining to be heard above the howling sound.

"No. It's the wind." He leaned over her. "Look out the window."

Just across a field they could see a twirling black mass of debris. As delicately as flowers plucked from a garden, the suction from the wind tweaked a post-and-rail fence from the ground and then deposited each piece, as neat as you please, along the fence line. Suddenly a barn burst apart, sending boards and roofing skyward. As if compelled, they stared as the mammoth twister dipped and lifted in an obscene dance of destruction.

"Wow," John kept saying. "Wow."

As abruptly as it had formed, the storm cloud dissipated into many impotent arms. Through the window, they watched men from the train sprinting across the field toward a white wood-sided house with half a roof.

John rose and started up the aisle.

Copper felt under the seat for her doctor's bag. "Wait for me. I'm coming with you."

The woman of the house and her three small children were unhurt. Her husband, she told them, had gone to check on an elderly neighbor whom they knew would be frightened by the coming storm.

"I wish you'd check on my cow," the lady said. "I'm scared to look."

Everyone from the train looked at the pile of splintered black boards and twisted tin roofing that had been the barn.

"Stay here," John said, and Copper did. The last thing she wanted to see was the family's cow at the bottom of that heap. Instead she waited on the porch with the farmwife and the three children.

The woman's eyes sparkled with tears. "I'll sure miss my Bossy. She was a good milker."

Copper murmured words of condolence as they watched the men heave rubbish to the side. Then the mood turned. They heard laughter and saw men slapping each other on the back. John turned toward the porch and motioned them over.

They hurried to what minutes ago had been the barn. Copper couldn't believe her eyes. The Guernsey stood in front of a feed box, chewing her cud, as placid as the day is long.

"Praise the good Lord. He saved her." The lady smiled through her tears. "We can fix the barn and the roof, but I couldn't replace my Bossy."

As if in acknowledgment, a rainbow arched across the sky. Copper could have fallen to her knees. The Lord was good. He was in control. Whatever they faced, He would see them through.

The men worked until the woman's husband came home, bringing the elderly neighbor with him.

*"Love thy neighbour as thyself,"* the man's deed reminded her. Though she was just as frightened and just as heartsick, she was no longer in the depths of despair.

After they walked back to the train, John saw her to her seat, then went back out to help clear the fallen tree that had brought the train to a screaming halt. It was late and dusk was falling. It felt like they would never get home. She rested her head on the seat back. All she could do was wait. Wait and pray.

They sat on the tracks for hours and didn't make it to Jackson until way after midnight. The station was deserted when they arrived. Nobody knew they were coming, so nobody waited with a ride. The livery wouldn't be open this late. They'd either have to walk the few miles home or wait until morning.

"Let's walk," she said. "I can't stand another minute of sitting."

They went past the telegraph agent's office, which was

located inside the train station. The door was open, and they could see the dispatcher's fingers tapping out Morse code on a set of brass keys. He squinted in the smoke from a cigarette. A half-empty mug of what looked like coffee was within easy reach. While typing with one hand, he put up the other as if to say, "Wait."

Finished with the message, he pushed a green eyeshade off his face. His hair stuck up behind it like a bad cowlick. A faint red line creased his forehead. "Say, ain't you the folks that went to the train wreck?" he asked, stubbing out his smoke in an overflowing ashtray.

"Yes," John said. "We're on our way home to Troublesome Creek."

Still sitting, he walked his chair to the doorway. "Ain't anybody coming to carry you home?"

"No, we didn't know we were coming tonight ourselves."

"Ain't you the ones had a girl on that train? What happened there?"

Copper tugged on John's sleeve. She didn't think she could bear to hear the story spoken to a stranger. "Let's go. We've a long walk yet."

"You can take my horse. He's the only one in the lot out back. The saddle's on the fence."

"That's mighty kind of you," John said.

"Glad to be of help. Leave me directions, and I'll borrow the stationmaster's nag and come fetch mine after my shift ends."

John fished a silver dollar from his pocket.

The man threw his hands up. "No, I ain't doing this for

pay. Your daughter's the talk of the town. Everybody's real concerned."

Despite her weariness, Copper was touched by the dispatcher's words. "Thank you," she said as John went to get the horse. "It's good to know people care."

He coughed dryly and lit another smoke. The chair creaked when he leaned back. "Some people say us that telegraph news over the wire're no better'n dogs sniffing after spoiled meat. But what I've learned is that folks care about other folks—that's why they read the news. And they always want to hear the rest of the story."

"I never thought about it that way, but it's true. You can tell people our daughter wasn't on the train after all. We're going home to find her."

"Tell you what," he said as a message jiggling across the wire caught his attention, "I won't send anything out until I know the end."

A coal-oil lamp in the kitchen window welcomed them home. Copper was thankful the children were asleep.

Remy hobbled into the room. She was fully clothed as if she had been waiting for them. "Ary news?"

Copper pulled a chair out from the table and sat down wearily. "We don't know where she is. I hoped against hope that she'd be here when we got home."

"I'm sorry, Purty. I was praying you'd bring her with you. I can't figure what could have happened."

Copper took off her gloves and unpinned her hat. "How are we going to stand this? How could we just lose her?"

Remy filled the kettle with water and set it on a hot burner.

"Have you not slept at all tonight?" Copper asked.

"I cain't get me no rest with Lilly out there somewheres all alone."

Copper rubbed her eyes. "Is Cara still here helping with the children?"

"Yup, I give her and Dimmert yore bed. He's kept everything up, and she's real good with the young'uns. Everybody's been good. We ain't cooked nothing save breakfast since you left."

"Looks like the storm followed us home," John said when he came in. Striking lightning cracked beyond the open door.

Remy put a bowl of brown beans and a triangle of corn bread on the table for him. For Copper she offered a smaller piece of the bread and a cup of sassafras with honey stirred in.

"I'll eat if you will," Copper said.

Remy fixed another plate and sat at the table with them.

John ate like he was starved, then served himself another bowl. "Are you hearing anything?" he asked Remy.

"There ain't hardly been time," Remy said. "Dimmert went scouting down by the creek once Brother Jasper left. We was thinking she might . . ."

Copper forced a sip of tea. She put a dab of honey on her corn bread and one on Remy's. "Remember when Lilly was little and got lost? We hunted the place over for her. Dimm and I walked up and down the creek and . . ."

"I'd almost forgot," Remy said. "I found her and set her back on the bank. She was splashing around having a good old time."

"She'd been chasing that cat Old Tom. God gave her back then, and He will again," Copper said.

Thunder boomed and shook the house. Rain pounded on the roof.

"It's been doing this off and on since yesterday noon," Remy said, licking honey off her fingers.

John pushed his plate away. "I'm going out."

"I wish you wouldn't." Copper followed him to the door. Rain whooshed in. "You won't find anything in this."

He took his old, brown oilcloth slicker from a peg and put it on. "I've got to do something," he said, brushing her cheek with his fingertips. "You keep the faith. Something good will come from this. You'll see."

She watched the rain swallow him up as soon as he stepped off the porch. *Please, Lord, let him be right.*

# 31

LILLY HAD NEVER been so bored. There was nothing to do. Nothing. Now that she knew she wouldn't be locked up much longer, she didn't even have her fear to entertain herself with. If it would just stop raining so the Stills could get in their buckboard and head out, her problems would be solved.

Besides, she had eaten all the cake and the pies. The dog had finished the biscuits. There was nothing left in the wicker hamper but a twist of salt and a cucumber. She didn't know why her mama had packed a cucumber. Lilly would have to be starving to eat one. And she was determined to not touch the food Mr. Still brought. Yuck. The packets made Steady happy, though.

She'd spent most of the stormy morning perched under the window, watching the sodden yard for signs of activity. Occasionally one of the boys—she guessed they were Tern's little brothers—would run out the door and splash around in a mud puddle until the grandmother called him back in. She always hollered the same thing, "You'll catch your death out there." The boys seemed to mind her pretty well.

Sometime during the night, Mr. Still had closed and barred the door again. She understood that he didn't want her to escape until he and his family made their getaway. He wasn't as completely evil as she'd first thought, but he was plenty mean. Anybody who would drown a puppy was mean in her book. And, she thought, by the way his mother treated him, he wasn't very smart. Dumb and mean was not a good combination. She sure didn't want to set him off again. The best thing for her to do was stay patient and quiet—very quiet.

Lying on her back on the pallet with Steady and the puppy beside her, she held her Bible at arm's length and read all the Bible stories she could think of: David and Goliath, Moses in the bulrushes, Esther and the reversal of fortune, and her favorite, the story of Daniel and of Shadrach, Meshach, Abednego, and the fiery furnace.

"Listen to what Daniel has to say to Melzar," she said to Steady. "'Prove thy servants, I beseech thee, ten days; and let them give us pulse to eat, and water to drink.' What do you suppose *pulse* means? I never noticed that before. They didn't like meat. I can tell that—but *pulse*? I thought that was like a heartbeat. But this has something to do with food. I suppose Daniel and the rest would more than likely eat cucumbers. I wish I had my dictionary so I could look it up."

Lilly put the Bible back on the box and picked up one of the musty newspapers. She had worked her way through the stack and had learned some fascinating things. She turned to her stomach and spread the paper on the pallet. Resting on her elbows, she began reading an article on the smallpox vaccination. On her upper arm was an ugly round mark from the vaccine she been given when they visited her grandmam in Philadelphia. Mama called it her badge of courage.

The date printed on the paper was October 1882. That was a long time ago. No wonder the paper nearly came apart when she separated the pages. The article explained how a simple milkmaid had given a doctor the idea for the smallpox vaccine. "Oh, listen to this," she said. "It's a funny poem."

*"Where are you going, my pretty milkmaid?"*
*"To see Doctor Jenner," the milkmaid said,*
*"I have such a cough, and it bothers me so*
*I promised Jack Robin for sure that I'd go*
*For a draught from the doctor today."*
*And she nodded her head with so saucy a smile,*
*That no one would think, who was looking the while,*
*That she needed the doctor, his pills or his plaster,*

*I doubt she could swear that she did, if you asked her;*
*That sunny bright morning in May.*

Lilly got so caught up in the poem that her voice trailed off. Steady whined and licked her arm. "Oh, sorry," she said. "You're wondering what happened. Well, Jack Robin—he's her boyfriend—sent the milkmaid to the doctor because he's afraid she will get the awful smallpox like some other folks in their village." Crooking her arm, she patted Steady's head. "You don't have to worry. Dogs don't get people disease. Here, I'll read the rest."

*Dr. Jenner looked grave, when she mentioned the matter;*
*He thought it too bad for so careless a chatter;*
*But saucy young Nancy had nothing to dread,*
*"But few of the milkmaids would get it," she said.*
*"For their hands had been sore from the cows,*
*And although it was horrid to milk when the beast*
*Had her bag all broken out, it was certain, at least,*
*To keep the smallpox from the house."*

*I hope Doctor Jenner that morning in May,*
*When he finished her pills and then sent her away,*
*Remembered enough of the lass and the stuff*
*Not to give her a dose for a cow;*
*For his mind went far off*
*From the girl and the cough;*
*But what does it matter, just now?*

336

*For her few simple words, while she waited,*
*Oh! Think with how much they were freighted,*
*When Jenner's quick mind they awakened, to find*
*How science could conquer the foe.*
*And gave every nation that blessed VACCINATION*
*That takes out the sting from the blow.*

"That is so funny. I can't wait to share it with Kate." If she could breathe better, she would have laughed, but while she was reading the poem, Steady had settled down in the small of her back. "You're squashing me." She rolled to her side and let the dog slide onto the floor.

The beagle stood and stretched a mile before circling back down.

"You're not much for conversation, are you?" Lilly scratched the spot between Steady's eyes. "I guess you're as bored as me."

The thatched roof muffled the sound of the rain. It might be July, but the room was chill. Lilly pulled one of the jackets up over her shoulders and spread it out to cover the puppy. All the little thing did was sleep and eat. She hoped it was healthy, but she'd sure be glad when she could take it for Mama to see.

She yawned and blinked and turned introspective while the storm raged on. The poem had been funny, but it also made her think about what she wanted to be. One time in school she had done a report on a famous woman. The woman's name was Elizabeth Blackwell. Her family came to America from England. Elizabeth decided to be a doctor

337

when a friend of hers, who was gravely ill, said she would get better treatment if she had been a man. Well, that got Elizabeth's dander up and Lilly's too.

During her research, Lilly had learned that Elizabeth decided to do something to make life better for women and so she went to medical school. Before she did her report, Lilly hadn't known that women could be doctors.

Rain dripped from a hole in the ceiling with a beat as even as seconds ticking from a clock. Lilly watched it fall and plop, fall and plop until she was nearly hypnotized. She blinked her eyes to break the spell.

She'd always thought she would be something like a teacher when she grew up or maybe work in a bank like the one Aunt Alice took her to when they went to the city. It was fun to see how quickly the teller's fingers slicked through stacks of paper money. She could do that, for she was very good with numbers.

What would it be like being a grown-up and being in charge of yourself? She wouldn't want to be a milkmaid, even though she liked cows—and she didn't want a boyfriend, even a nice one like Jack Robin. She would like to be like Dr. Jenner or Dr. Blackwell. Her mama helped people, but she wanted to do more so people wouldn't get sick in the first place, people like Adie Still. Maybe she could be a doctor like her father had been. Aunt Alice would like that. It was something to think about. She yawned again. Rain sure made you sleepy.

JAN WATSON

When Lilly awoke, she climbed to the lookout window. The rain had tapered off into a fine mist. The buckboard had been moved in front of the flat-rock stoop. She saw Tern talking to his father. Mr. Still went to the door and hollered for Mrs. Still. She came out with a stack of pots and a teakettle. These she set on the lowered tailgate. Tern jumped up on it and moved them closer to the front of the bed.

Mr. Still acted agitated, flinging his arms around and barking orders. He seemed to be trying to hurry his mother along. She turned her back and went inside. He and Tern followed. Soon everyone came out carrying something: bundles of linen, chairs, dishes, crocks, a broom, a cradle with the baby in it—all were piled in the back of the buckboard. Two boys struggled with a blanket chest. Feather ticks, bolsters, and a disassembled bed followed. Last, the old lady went back into the house and came out carrying a bright yellow bird in a cage. She said something to one of the boys, and he rooted around in the pile of stuff until he found a pillowcase. The lady covered the cage with the case before putting it on the seat between herself and Mr. Still.

Mr. Still closed the tailgate, took his seat, and flicked the reins. The buckboard started rolling. The littler boys held on to the sides, and Tern sat holding the baby.

The noise of the Still family and the squeaky-wheeled buckboard faded away as the gloaming of the day settled across the yard and crept unbidden into her hidey-hole. Lightning bugs lifted from the sparse grass and plentiful weeds. Their teensy lanterns flashed messages of longing.

From somewhere in the forest, a gentle mourning dove cooed its plaintive notes. Lilly thought she had never heard a more lonesome sound.

She felt as empty as the yard when the buckboard disappeared. Now she really was alone.

She climbed down and looked about the strange round room that had been her home since Wednesday. It had offered her many small comforts, but she couldn't wait to leave it. She packed her Bible and her brush and comb, her ruined watch and fob, the linen cloths she used for decoration, and the newspaper dated October 1882. Everything else she'd leave behind.

Steady barked and jumped against her. Running back to her baby, she lifted him by the neck, dragging him halfway across the floor before she let the little thing go and barked again.

"I'm not going to leave you," Lilly said.

But the dog would not stop her disconcerted howling.

"Steady! Stop! I've got work to do." Lilly positioned the boxes and the boards like she had done before.

The beagle jumped against one box and knocked the board down.

"What is wrong with you? Don't you see it's getting dark? We have to hurry and get out of here while we can still see."

Whining, the dog went back to the pup.

Lilly shook her head in frustration. She got her valise, and wrapping the puppy in one of the old jackets, she put it inside and set the valise by the door. Steady seemed to understand. She stopped barking.

With the fulcrum in place, Lilly was able to slide the bar on the outside of the door up and over the fixtures securing it in place. It made a satisfying thump when it hit the ground. She moved the boxes and boards out of the way and went to open the door. She would carry the puppy down the ladder first and leave him in the valise while she came back for Steady. Or should she take Steady first? Would the dog try to jump out the door if she thought Lilly was leaving with her puppy?

She crouched beside her dog and looked her in the eyes. "You trust me, right? I'll be back for you."

Steady licked her cheek in agreement.

Lilly lifted the carryall full of squirming puppy and with a huge feeling of relief opened the door. She couldn't believe her eyes. That stupid, mean, evil Mr. Still had left the ladder down. It lay as useless as a broken promise on the ground below. She judged the height. If she jumped safely, she could put the ladder in place and come back for the dogs. If she jumped and hit the ladder or a rock, she would probably break something important. She might lie there for days before she was found. That would leave Steady and the pup alone up here with no one to care for them. While she stood there, it got darker and darker until she couldn't see the ladder anymore.

Sitting down, she bawled like a baby. She cried until she got the hiccups and she couldn't catch her breath. Carefully, so as not to plunge out the door into the black-hearted night, she stood and pulled it shut. "I'm sorry, Steady. We'll need to wait until first light. It's too dangerous right now." She took the puppy from the valise and carried him back to the pallet.

The beagle stayed by the door, waiting.

# 32

COPPER WAS DRINKING strong black coffee and studying Manda's cryptic note for the hundredth time when the children woke up. Much as she had been sure it would, the note hadn't shed any light.

Mazy ran right up to her, climbing the chair rungs and hugging her neck. "Mama, where you at?"

"I've been on a trip, Mazy-bug. Did you miss me?"

"I cry."

"You did? I'm sorry." Copper brushed wisps of hair from Mazy's eyes. "Go get a brush and I'll fix your hair."

Jack got right down to business while leaning against her knees. "What did you bring me? It better be good."

"I've been on a train. I brought you a blue bandanna like the engineers wear."

Jack took the bandanna and studied it. He looked skeptical. "This looks like a handkerchief."

Copper felt tears welling up. The tart sweetness of her children was almost too much to bear, like the first bite of a green apple or the smell of wild roses in bloom. "This is a special handkerchief. Let me show you." She tied the blue napkin around his neck. "Now you're a conductor on a train," she said before pulling it up to cover his nose and mouth. "Now you're Jesse James."

Jack cocked his fingers like a gun. "Stick 'em up."

She held her arms in a position of surrender. "Please, Mr. James. Please don't take my money."

"I won't," he said. "Robbers don't steal from their mamas."

Another gem to share with John—if they ever shared again. Ever since the train ride home, she'd felt herself slipping away from him. If all they found was Lilly's body, or if—heaven forbid—they never found her, Copper wasn't sure she'd ever care again. She felt an overwhelming need to be alone with her grief. But of course she didn't have that option. Her other children needed her, and she needed them.

Molly hung on Cara's dress tail while Cara stirred a pot of oatmeal. She cast shy looks Copper's way and sucked her thumb. Mazy brought the brush, and Copper fixed her hair and then Merky's. She tied a bright red ribbon around each sweet head so the girls would think she'd also brought them something.

Merky preened for Cara.

"Don't you look like a pretty redbird," Cara said. "Would you take Mazy out to the porch while I finish your breakfast?"

Cara lifted Molly to her hip and with a last stir of the oatmeal set the pot on the warming shelf. "Let's go see your mama."

Molly tucked her head in the curve of Cara's shoulder.

Cara flashed Copper a grin. "She's making you pay."

"What will I do with this red ribbon?" Copper asked.

"I'll take it," Cara said. "I'd like to look like a pretty red-bird like Merky and Mazy."

Molly's thumb popped out and her head popped up. "No, mine."

Cara deposited her in Copper's lap.

"Who's my baby girl?" Copper asked, wielding the brush.

"My a baby bird."

"Then I'm a mama bird." She nuzzled Molly's neck. It smelled like talcum powder.

Merky opened the screen door. "Come out, Molly. Come on, Jack. We're playing nest."

Cara filled four small bowls with oatmeal. She stirred in cream and a bit of brown sugar. "I'm feeding the birds on the porch. There won't be so much to clean up."

Copper smiled. No wonder the kids loved Cara.

She saw John coming across the yard. He and Dimmert had left early to continue the search while she was doing the milking. She didn't know if he'd slept at all last night. She had rested some on the cot in the sickroom. Her body was so relieved to be home that it had forced her into sleep.

She put some bacon in the skillet and took a pan of biscuits from the oven.

John burst in, and the screen door slammed behind him. "We found something."

With a fork, she turned the bacon over, even though it hadn't started to brown. Wiping her hands on her apron, she turned. "What?"

He held Lilly's hat in his hands. "Is this hers?"

Copper's breath caught in her throat. She was afraid she'd have another spell like the one she had at the train station. She nodded as she took the straw skimmer with the blue and brown bias trim from him. "Where did you find it?"

"Dimmert spotted it. We were riding on the road up past the churchyard. It was lying in a patch of weeds."

The bacon sizzled on the stove. "Was there anything else?"

"I don't know. Dimmert's still there. I'm going right back, but I thought seeing this would make you feel better."

"Better? Why would seeing this make me feel better?" She jerked the hat away from him. The crown was smashed flat. The ribbon trim was torn and dirty. Something had gnawed on the brim. Her voice rose in anguish. "This is not my daughter! You ran home with this when you could have stayed and looked for her."

"Copper, don't you see this is a good sign?" he placated while trying to take her in his arms.

The bacon smoked in the skillet. The screen door cracked open. Cara slipped in. Averting her eyes, she took the skillet off the burner. They could see her hustling the children off the porch. The girls had oatmeal faces, and Jack had his bandanna over his nose.

"Let's go to the creek and play," Cara said. "Won't that be fun?"

Copper tried to get ahold of her emotions.

"Sweetheart," John said, "I wish you wouldn't take on so."

She clutched the battered hat to her heart and wailed. Her cries seemed to come from her seared innermost being. Was this how it felt when you lost your mind?

John came up behind her and wrapped her in a bear hug. "Stop. Stop this."

It was as if he had punctured her. The feelings flowed out like water circling a drain, leaving her cold and empty. She struggled to keep from screaming.

He sat her down and stood over her with a glass of water. "You'll drink this now. Slow and easy."

She did as she was told.

John poured himself a cup of coffee and pulled a chair up in front of her. He put his hand on her knee. "Don't you see what this hat means? She's out there. If she lost her hat, it means she was walking up the road past the church for some reason. I think she missed the coach and was going to see if Kate and her mother missed it also—maybe she thought it didn't come. Maybe she thought the time was wrong, or maybe she thought they'd catch it later."

She didn't answer, but as she listened, a little spark of hope ignited.

"I know in my gut Lilly is all right. I don't know why she's missing, but she'll be back." He patted her knee, then rose and pushed in his chair. "Men are gathering at the church-yard to help. We'll find her. Don't you worry."

She felt like her bones had dissolved. But she went to the stove and split the biscuits, laying a blackened piece of bacon between each one. She tied them up in a cloth for John to take with him. It was better than nothing. "You and Dimmert need to eat."

She had some time for prayer before the children came back. And she badly needed it. She had once again allowed her fear to replace her faith. A bit of Scripture came to her: "O ye of little faith." She walked around her kitchen, touch-ing things and talking to the Lord. She felt as if she were in the shadow of His wings. It was a sure and steady comfort.

On a peg behind the door, where they kept outdoor jackets and indoor sweaters and aprons and bonnets, she found a length of Lilly's white ribbon. *Protect Lilly, Lord,* she prayed while running the grosgrain through her fingers. *I know she's Your child before she's mine, but I beg of You, please let me keep her for a while. And please let me mean it when I say, "Your will be done." I know I'm not much of an example to others right now, and I'm sorry.*

When she finished, she felt calmer and for the moment stronger. God understood her mother's heart. He would for-give her momentary lapses; she was sure of it. She'd often felt that a mother's fierce and all-forgiving love was the closest thing on earth to the heavenly Father's love.

She poured a glass of milk fresh from the cow and began to sip it slowly. Cupping her belly with one hand, she made a promise. "I'll start taking better care of you, my little one, my tiny, secret baby. I've been selfish and I know it, but I'm better now." She would have to tell John soon. He wouldn't be happy about being kept in the dark.

She stepped out on the porch and gathered the children's dishes. The remains of oatmeal had stuck like glue. She wondered if Remy had eaten before she went to the little house. Copper had insisted she go for a lie-down even if she felt she couldn't sleep. Remy looked so exhausted and she wasn't strong to start with.

Back in the kitchen she put the dishes to soak before scraping the last of the oatmeal from the pot and stirring in some cream. She'd leave it on the warming shelf, covered with a linen towel, for Remy.

For now she should walk down to the creek and relieve Cara, who probably needed to go home for a while. She had her own house to tend to. She'd just started across the yard when she saw a horse and buggy. The man from the telegraph office was bringing someone with him. She shaded her eyes. It was Manda.

She went out to meet the buggy and thanked the man.

"You're ever so welcome," he said. "Miss Whitt here said she read about the wreck in the paper. She traveled purt near all night. I hope you don't mind, but I told her about your daughter. Say, I hear there's a search party out looking. I'd be much obliged if you all would let me help."

Amazed at how fast news of all types traveled, Copper thanked him again for his help and for bringing Manda home. She told him where to leave the horse until he came back and showed him the stall where his own was stabled.

Manda hung around outside. She hadn't said a word, and she didn't come in the barn. She seemed unusually reticent.

Coming up from the creek, the children swarmed around Manda like busy bees. Cara had washed their faces and hands in the creek. Manda greeted them shyly with few words. Copper supposed she was too hurt about Lilly to know what to say.

As outspoken as ever, Jack looked up at her and said, "What happened to your face?"

Manda touched her cheek. "I fell against the rail the other morning while I was slopping the hog."

Copper and Cara exchanged looks.

"I was wondering, Copper. Would you mind if I take all the kids to my house for the rest of the day? We've been wanting to have a tea party."

Copper hugged her neck. "Thank you, dear friend," she whispered in Cara's ear.

Cara hugged her back. "You stay strong."

"You mean me too?" Jack asked. "I get to have a tea party?"

Cara herded the children like so many sheep toward the long path that led to her house. "Of course. I've heard Jesse James loved tea."

# 33

THE TEASING SOUNDS of children arguing woke Lilly
early in the morning. Before she opened her eyes, she thought
she was at home. She lay on the scratchy pallet for the longest
time pretending she heard Mama going to milk and Manda
opening the oven door. She sniffed, sure she could smell rich
coffee brewing and remembered her first cup the morning
she went along to the stable. She wondered how the cats were
and if they missed her.

She swallowed. Her throat was as prickly as the pallet of
woolen clothing, and she felt chilled. "I don't feel so good,"
she said, waiting for Mama's cool hand on her forehead. The

prickly didn't go away, however, and neither did the chill of her skin or the children's strident voices.

She heard the door screech on its hinges as it opened and closed, but she didn't open her eyes. She didn't want to play this game anymore. For the moment she wasn't sure if last evening was a dream, watching the Stills gather their things in the buckboard, or maybe this was the dream.

"I want to go home," she said.

The dog rattled her water dish on the floor.

Opening one eye, Lilly looked at the dish. Empty. Regardless of how she felt, she had to get up. She emptied yesterday's water jug into Steady's bowl, then went to the door to retrieve another and a small bag that held a few pieces of ham, some corn bread, and an apple. She carried them back to the bed and gave a piece of ham and a wedge of bread to Steady. This was becoming a routine.

"I sure would like a bath," she said. She washed her hands before eating half the apple. It didn't feel good going down, but it looked better than the salty ham or the dry bread. "I forgot to say grace." She bowed her head. "Thank You, Father, for my daily corn bread. Steady thanks You more than me. Amen."

She climbed on the boxes to look out. Forevermore, the Stills were back. There went her plans for escape. She counted heads and saw everyone but Mr. Still and Tern. The old lady sat on the stoop with the baby. The boys ran wild in the yard. She couldn't imagine what had happened.

Getting off the boxes, she went back to her bed and lay down. She was through with this day already.

———————

Midmorning, Copper sat across from Manda at the kitchen table.

Manda fidgeted with her bonnet but didn't take it off. "I don't understand why they're looking for Lilly here. I thought she was on the train."

"We did too." Copper took Manda's hand. "Did you see Lilly get on the coach? Mrs. Jasper said Lilly didn't."

Remy huffed in. She had a small bundle under her arm. She looked at Manda sharply before she poured a cup of coffee and pulled out a chair.

"Maybe Lilly got on the wrong coach."

"There's only one. You know that," Copper said.

Sweat beaded around Manda's hairline. "I swear I thought I saw her."

"What do you mean you thought you saw her? Didn't you wait with her like we planned?" Copper asked.

"I was meaning to. Really I was. Lilly was sitting right there on the porch. I told her to wait while I went to slop the hog. But I slipped in some greasy mud and hit my head on the top rail of the pigpen. It knocked me out, and when I woke up, Lilly was gone. I ran to the stop and saw the coach leave. Where else would Lilly be?"

"Why'd you leave out of here, girl?" Remy asked.

Manda chewed on the end of her bonnet strings and mumbled. "I wanted to see my sister."

"Take that there bonnet off," Remy said, "afore ye sweat to death."

She slid it off. The light was not kind to her bruised cheekbones, badly swollen eye, and puffy lip.

"Mighty funny way to knock yourself out," Remy said. "Looks like somebody backhanded ye. Fess up, girl."

"Are you calling me a liar?"

"If the shoe fits," Remy said.

Copper didn't like the turn this conversation was taking. What in the world was Remy getting at? "Manda, you're not being accused of anything. We just need to know the full truth. Anything you can think of to help us trace Lilly's steps that day. Even if you don't think it has anything to do with Lilly, it could make all the difference."

"Seems odder than a two-headed cat that you'd run off to your sister's with your face all busted up." Remy peered at Manda over the rim of her saucer as she slurped sweetened coffee.

Manda's gaze darted around the room like she was looking for an escape. "I didn't notice, really. It just seemed the perfect opportunity. Everyone was gone, and I thought I'd—"

"Yup. We've got it. You'd just run off to have a little sisterly visit with Darcy Mae."

Copper nudged Remy under the table. Forevermore, she

sounded like a lawman. *Ease up,* her foot against Remy's leg relayed.

"That's not a crime as far as I know," Manda said. "Miz Copper, I'm truly sorry about Lilly. That's why I come back, because I had to know how she is, but I'm not staying any longer than you need me to. I'll help out any way I can for the time being, though."

"Well, I appreciate that." Copper stood, tipped Manda's chin, and retracted her eyelid. "Tell me about this eye. Is it getting better or worse?"

"Worse. I can barely see out of it, and it's sore to touch."

"You should go lie down. I'll make a bread poultice to draw out the soreness."

Remy's chair creaked when she reached behind her for her crutch. "Poultice my eye," she said, withdrawing something from a pillowcase and shaking it out.

*What now?* Copper thought. *I'm too weary for this.*

Manda blanched. "Where'd you get that?"

"From under the corn-shuck mattress where you left it. Funny, it ain't got a drop of pig slop on it. But it's tore at the waist and there's a splatter of blood. Yourn, I reckon."

The blood rushed from Copper's head. The air in the room grew dense and dark. Something ugly was coming.

With a shout, Manda started banging her forehead against the table like she was trying to dislodge a bad memory.

Remy slipped her hand between the table and Manda's forehead. "Ye ain't going to feel any better until you tell us what happened that morning. Truth's the only poultice that will draw out whatever pizen's in you."

Manda jumped up from the chair. Remy hopped backward, dropping her crutch, nearly falling. Copper caught her and retrieved the crutch. She and Remy watched in horror as Manda tugged on her hair.

"It was that middling man," she screeched. "That middling-fiddling music man."

Copper grabbed her hands. "What are you talking about? What man?"

Manda sank to the floor. "He attacked me in the barn. He pushed me up against the feed box. He tore my dress and slapped me hard." Her voice was distant like she was telling a dream.

*Oh, Lord, please no.* "Manda," Copper pleaded, kneeling with that searing pain in her heart again. "Did this man hurt Lilly? Did he carry her off? Please tell me what you know."

Manda looked at Copper. "No, he didn't hurt Lilly. He never touched her."

Copper wasn't sure whether Manda was telling the truth. The girl was traumatized; that was easy to tell. With great gentleness she slipped her arms around Manda and rocked her like she would Lilly if she ever got the chance again. "How do you know? How do you know he didn't hurt Lilly?"

"Because Lilly was on the porch when I went in the barn with him, and she was already gone when I came out."

A great distress rose in Copper's chest. Of all the things she had supposed might have happened to her daughter, she'd never thought of this. "But don't you see? He could have come back or he might have lain in wait for her. When you ran to the crossroads, he could have taken her then."

"No, he couldn't," Manda said.

"How do you know?"

"Because I stabbed him," Manda said, emotionless. "I stabbed him with the pitchfork."

"Oh, my word. Did you . . . ? Is he . . . ?"

"No, but I wish he was dead." Manda's head nodded in a tremor she couldn't seem to stop. "I do. I wish I'd stabbed him through the heart."

"Shh, shh, shh," Copper soothed as she rocked. An ugly question had to be asked if she was to help Manda. "Honey," she whispered, "are you intact?"

Manda leaned her head against Copper's chest. "Everything's the same but my heart."

---

Nobody came to open the door to the shack. It was good the day was overcast and not too warm. Lilly couldn't stand herself any longer, so she poured half the remaining water in the washbasin and bathed with Colgate's tooth powder. She was squeaky clean. She wished she had a second dress, but as Aunt Remy said, "If wishes were horses, then peasants would ride," or something to that effect. She changed her underclothes and her hose. Her knees were much better. She was careful not to pull the scabs off. She surely didn't want scars on her knees to match the one on her arm.

Thinking of scars made her think of the milkmaid poem and her decision to someday become a doctor. She wasn't entirely sure how to go about that, but she was sure it took a lot of knowledge. Aunt Alice had all Daddy Simon's medical books in her library. She also had all Lilly's grandfather's medical books. Until right this minute, she had forgotten that her grandfather was also a doctor. Hmmm, maybe it was supposed to be. Maybe this was why God let her be cast into this awful place—so she could figure that out. One thing was a given: God always had His reasons. Just look at those three pulse-eating fellows who were tossed into the fiery furnace. If you thought about them, then this wasn't so bad. Plus, she saved Steady and her baby. Sort of saved them anyway. They weren't home free yet.

She'd made up her mind, though. The next time Mr. Still opened that door, she was leaving. If she had to push him off the ladder, she would. Enough was enough. Then, while he was lying flat out on the ground trying to figure out what had happened, she'd climb down with Steady and the pup at the same time. She figured she would hang the valise around her neck and carry Steady under her arm.

"Where there's a will, there's a way. That's another of Aunt Remy's sayings," she told the dog, who looked at her with worshipful eyes. "My throat feels better. I know you were worried. I wish I had a cup of sassafras tea with honey, though."

She might as well see what the Stills were doing. If she

could tell when Mr. Still was coming her way, she could be better prepared to knock him off the ladder.

Mr. Still was walking past the hideout. Tern followed, rolling a wagon wheel. "You go on ahead to where we broke down, Tern. You can start fixing the buckboard. We'll catch up."

Tern stood there with the wheel. As soon as his father walked away, he looked up at Lilly. He mouthed something, but Lilly couldn't understand. She shook her head. He mouthed it again. She scrunched up her face.

He turned his back on her. "Daddy, will you need me to come back for anything?"

"No. Now get on, boy. It's a right smart piece to where we're going."

Tern glanced over his shoulder. Lilly nodded. Tern had sent her a message. She watched while he rolled the wheel away.

Mr. Still went into the house for maybe half an hour. Lilly got a charley horse in her leg from sitting doubled up for so long. Finally they all came out. Mr. Still led the horse to the front of the house. Lilly rubbed the crick from her calf as she watched the old lady climb into the saddle from the mounting block. Mr. Still handed her the baby and put the next smallest boy on the horse behind her.

"You took your sweet time a-coming back," the old lady said.

"I had to walk all the way to Dimmert Whitt's place. He wasn't home or I'd've had to wait until nightfall. It was easy pickings. He makes wheels himself, you recollect."

"Let's get on out," the grandma said. "It's a-fixing to storm again."

"Yeah, we need to shake a leg. While Tern was out scouting, he saw a posse of men searching all around the church—even in the cemetery. They're bound to come this way sooner than later."

"Did ye leave plenty of water?"

"Sure. The gal will be fine. Don't worry."

"Put the ladder back up. Give her a fighting chance at least."

# 34

MANDA'S HYSTERIA SEEMED spent. It took both Copper and Remy to get her up off the floor. She was still crying but no longer hysterical.

Someone knocked on the screen door. Copper turned to see who it was. She could see Ma Hawkins and some other ladies from church standing back from the door respectfully. "Take Manda to the sickroom, Remy, before they notice her," she said.

Copper opened the door to a gaggle of women holding pots and pans of food as well as cakes and pies. It looked like they'd been cooking for hours.

"We don't aim to put you to no trouble," Ma Hawkins

said. "But the men will need to eat. Where's a good place to set up a table?"

Copper was touched. She had not even thought of dinner, though it was almost noon. "Thank you," she said, stepping out. "You all have been so good."

"Any news?"

"They found her hat." Copper choked on the words.

The women sighed and clucked like hens settling on nests. Copper saw real concern on their faces. Many of them had also suffered great heartache.

Ma Hawkins patted her shoulder. "Now that's a good sign. That means she's somewhere hereabouts."

"I'll just go find the sawhorses," Copper said.

"You'll do no such thing," Ma Hawkins said. "My boys came along. I took the liberty of sending them to the barn. I knowed John would have something in there to set up a table with."

As she spoke, two lanky boys came out of the barn carrying the sawhorses and lengths of wood.

"Someone will need to find John and tell the men," Copper said, suddenly anxious to tell John what Manda said.

"My old man's headed over to the church. He's going to ring the bell, so they'll be here soon enough. You've only got to do one thing for us."

"Whatever you need," Copper said.

"You've got to eat the plate we fix you." All the women nodded. Copper could see that was truly all they wanted.

It was against her nature, but Copper sat in a rocking

chair waiting for John while her friends and neighbors set a veritable feast on the sawhorse tables. It was such a thoughtful gesture and so helpful. The men needed a good meal.

If these women hadn't come, she would have saddled Chessie and gone off to find John. Manda was telling the truth now, she was sure of that, but what might her story mean to Lilly's disappearance? John would have a clear head about this. He would stay strong, and she so badly needed that strength right now.

The men—some on horseback and others on foot—started coming in a few at a time until there were at least sixteen of them gathering around the table. The ladies poured milk and tea and heaped plates full of food. The men sat on the ground under shade trees to eat.

John and Dimmert were last to come in. Copper had to keep herself from running across the yard to John.

John stopped first at the table. "Man, this looks good enough to eat," Copper heard him say.

Ma Hawkins began to ladle food onto a plate. "Do you want chicken or ham? or both?"

"You hold on to that for me," he said. "I'll be right back."

"Anything?" Copper asked as soon as John stepped on the porch, although she could tell by his face the answer was no. It hurt her to see him so defeated.

"No, but we're getting close. I can feel it in my bones." He dipped the long-handled dipper into the water bucket on the shelf and drank it down. "If this storm will just hold off."

Copper hadn't even noticed the dark clouds forming over the mountains. "Not again."

"I know," he said. "We'll need to eat quick."

"Come inside. I have to tell you something for your ears alone."

"Have you eaten anything?" he asked, closing the door behind them.

"I'm okay. Please don't go on about me." She could see a flash of hurt in his eyes. Why was she lashing out at him? "I'm sorry."

He brushed her cheek with a dry kiss. "It's okay."

"Listen." She told him everything Manda said, from the lies to the truth. She saw the same horror and revulsion she herself had felt as she recounted the story.

"I'll have to talk to her," he said.

"I don't know. She's very upset."

"I'm sure that's true, but it has to be done. I'll get Dimmert. Having her brother will make it easier for her. And he should hear this, as well as the sheriff."

"The sheriff?"

"Didn't you see him there at the table? He's been with us all morning. He's laid out a grid according to where we found the hat."

Copper blanched. She would never get used to hearing Lilly spoken about this way. "I don't know the best way for you to handle this, but Manda wasn't violated. The sheriff mustn't ask about that."

"You go prepare Manda. I'll be right back."

Copper brought Manda into the sitting room.

The girl was trembling. "Do I have to do this?"

"I'm afraid you do."

The men came in. The sheriff took over. He led Manda through the events of Wednesday. He was thorough but kind. John thought to ask about Lilly's hat. Manda remembered Lilly was wearing it when she was sitting on the porch.

Dimmert stayed with his sister when the other men left the room. He sat on the settee and put his arm around her shoulder. "It will be all right, Sis. You done the right thing by coming back."

"I was so stupid. How could I believe in that man?"

"You ain't stupid—just young. He's the one that's stupid. I'll tell you one thing—he won't be playing any music if I catch hold of him."

Copper was saddened to hear the threat of violence coming from such a sweet man. It seemed ironic how quickly one person's evil action led even good men to hostility.

"You don't need to worry about that," Manda said. "I took care of it myself."

Copper left them alone. Dimmert would help Manda more than anyone. John was waiting for her in the kitchen. She walked outside with him. They saw a few of the men gathered around the sheriff out by the barn.

"I want to see what they're saying."

He didn't try to stop her, but when they got to the barn, he slipped his arm around her waist. "We want to be in on anything you're planning, Sheriff," John said.

"I know the man Miss Whitt's referring to," the sheriff said. "He's been run out of every town hereabouts. He's a drifter and a petty thief. A ne'er-do-well. I expect he's skipped town, but we'll track him down—given time."

"Say," the dispatcher from the train station cut in, "I can put his description and that he's wanted out over the wire and tell you where to find him by sundown."

"Well, there you go," the sheriff replied. "You get on back to town. Get this thing sent out, and we'll see what happens. Meanwhile the rest of us need to return to the job at hand. If we don't find her this afternoon, we'll start on this side of the creek tomorrow."

"Sheriff, do you think this scoundrel had anything to do with Lilly's disappearance?" John asked.

"My best guess is no, but stranger things have happened. We'll find out when we bring him in. I can assure you of that."

Copper clung to the sheriff's words the rest of the day. "My best guess is no," he'd said. She chose to believe him. It was either that or . . . what? Live as a shell for the rest of her life while trying to be a mother to her other children? How did anyone deal with this? She didn't have any answers, but she could pray.

Dark clouds as big as boulders rolled across the sky, but the rain held off. Cara brought the children back before supper. There were plenty of leftovers to feed them. Someone had thoughtfully set aside half a dozen chicken legs. Jack was in heaven.

"Take some of this home for Dimmert," Copper said as Cara prepared to leave. "It'll just spoil sitting here."

It was way past dark when John came home. Copper hadn't noticed the night steal in until he lit a lamp.

"Why are you sitting in the dark?" he asked.

"I'm just waiting for Lilly."

Standing at the stove, John ate the plate of food Copper had left for him. "I'm beat. We need to go to bed."

"You go on. I have to watch."

John left the room and returned with a pile of blankets from their bed and a bolster pillow. He arranged them right in front of the screen door. "We can rest here."

"If I lie down, I'm afraid I'll go to sleep. I don't want to sleep. What if I miss her?"

"You're not making sense," he said. "When Lilly comes home, she'll see the lamp in the window and she'll wake you up."

"Let me be."

"Well, no," he said. "I won't let you be. You'll lie down here, and I'll sit on the porch. I couldn't sleep anyway."

Copper let him guide her to the makeshift bed. Her whole body cried out with grief and weariness. "Promise? You promise you won't close your eyes?"

"I'll do my best, sweetheart." He plumped the pillow behind her head and covered her with a light cotton quilt.

"John," she said, sitting up and wrapping her arms around his neck, "I'm sorry I'm being so cross with you. I'm so sorry."

Leaning over her, he kissed her gently. "You have nothing to be sorry for."

She lay back down and closed her eyes. A few minutes later she roused. She could see him sitting on the porch steps through the blurred screen of the door. "John?"

"Yes?"

"We're going to have another baby."

"I suspected as much."

She was not really surprised to hear that. She couldn't keep anything from him. "Are you glad? I need for you to be glad."

"Thoughts of a new baby are a welcome gift right now. We'll be all right, you know."

Copper laid her head back down. Her husband was watching. She could rest.

⁂

Lilly was afraid Tern wouldn't come back. Maybe he was lost or maybe his mean father had caught him sneaking away. Before it got dark, she had tried her lever against the barricaded door. It wouldn't budge. The wooden bar was stuck, probably swollen from yesterday's storm. She wasn't strong enough to lift it.

It was awful here now that the Stills were gone. A bat had swooped in through one of the narrow windows and scared her silly. It was good to be afraid of some things. Bats were definitely in that category.

She had been dozing for a while when she heard a pounding on the door. Steady roused and started barking.

"Lilly," she heard, "it's me, Tern. I've come to get you out."

Lilly was never so glad to hear anyone in her whole life.

He pounded again. "This thing's stuck. Hold on."

Finally the door was open.

"All right," he said. "Come out backward and I'll help you."

Steady poked her head around Lilly. Tern rubbed the dog's ears. "I'm glad to see my dog."

"She's my dog now."

"What I meant is, I'm glad she's with you," he said.

Obviously, it wasn't easy to carry a beagle down a wobbly ladder, but Tern did it and started back up for her.

"I can climb down without any help," Lilly said. "You stay down there."

He ignored her. "It's dark. You might lose your footing."

Lilly's legs were shaking. She was afraid and she was glad for his presence. She wrapped the puppy in a piece from her nightgown and put it in the valise. "Will you take the puppy down next?"

"Puppy?"

"He's in here," she said, handing him the bag. "Be careful. He's awful squirmy."

She was glad it was dark and that she couldn't see the room behind her very well. It was hard to believe she was finally getting out. When Tern was ready for her, she stepped out into the night and went down the ladder. The ground was solid under her feet, but she felt weak as a new kitten and disoriented. The moon played peekaboo with heavy clouds. She didn't know the way home.

"Come on," Tern said. "I'll walk you home."

Steady's tail whipped against the back of her legs, nearly knocking her off-balance. Tern went ahead, carrying the valise. Lilly followed him. Steady followed her. It was obvious who Steady wanted to be with. Maybe she should feel bad about that but she didn't.

An owl hooted. From far away his mate answered.

"I love that sound," Tern said. "I like being out in the night when it's peaceful."

A canopy of tall pine trees whispered secrets over their heads. A night creature hunting in the dark scrambled out of the way.

Lilly stumbled over a root. She grabbed Tern's arm and held on. "I don't know where we are."

"I'm taking you the short way home. I didn't think you'd want to go past the pond."

She shuddered. She didn't want to think about that. They walked on. Tern held back brambles and kindly helped her over rocks. After a while they came upon the back of a cabin.

"Know where you are now?" Tern asked in a low voice.

"It's the little house," Lilly whispered.

"I'm going to leave you here." He set the valise down and patted Steady's head. "You'll be okay now."

Lilly was suddenly shy. "I'm really sorry about your mama."

"Yeah, me too." Tern kicked at the ground with the toe of his boot. "I reckon I won't see you again. We'll be moving farther on come morning. We won't stop traveling for two or three days."

Surprising herself, Lilly kissed his cheek. It felt smooth and warm. Tears trembled in her eyes. "Thank you, Tern Still. I can tell you have a kind heart."

"Take care of yourself, Lilly Gray Corbett."

Lilly bent to unfasten the carryall. She pulled the puppy out and held him closely to her chest. When she looked up, Tern was walking away. She watched until he disappeared. The path was still dark, but now she knew where she was. She carried the pup around the little cabin, through the side yard, and up to the porch. She saw her daddy John sitting on the top step. He was leaning against the rail, snoring.

"Daddy," she said, touching his knee. "Daddy."

He startled awake. "Lilly?"

"I found us some dogs."

"Oh, praise the Lord." Daddy pulled her onto his lap.

"John?" Mama said from behind the screen door.

"Copper, come out here! Lilly's home!"

Mama let the screen door slam loud enough to wake the house. She sat down on the step beside them and started crying. "Thank You, Lord," she praised over and over, kissing Lilly's cheeks for punctuation. "Oh, my baby girl, where have you been?"

Lilly sighed. "It's a long story. I don't want to talk about it right now."

"You're tired, aren't you? The story can wait until morning.

Your daddy made us a bed right inside the door. We'll lie down there."

Lilly was already nodding off with her head on Daddy's shoulder. She felt so safe and happy. Mama held the door as he carried her in and put her down on the pallet. Mama lay down beside her and pulled her close. The bolster pillow felt like heaven beneath her head. Steady whined and scratched at the screen door.

"Can they come in, Daddy? They've gotten used to sleeping with me."

He cracked the door, and Steady carried the puppy over the threshold. She dropped him right by Lilly, then sat there watching. Lilly knew she was wondering what was going to happen to her. She patted the floor beside the pallet. "Lie down."

She was almost asleep, but her eyes jerked open. She thought she heard a ladder thumping against a doorframe and rusty hinges screeching. Mama's arms tightened around her.

"Don't leave, Daddy," she said.

"I'm right here, Lilly."

She raised her head. He was sitting in one kitchen chair and resting his feet on another. Steady exhaled noisily, like she'd been holding her breath for a long time. Lilly ran the dog's silky ears through her fingers and slept, as safe as safe could be.

# 35

AS SUMMER TURNED to fall, Copper felt her family was fairly back to normal. Lilly was taller and becoming a young lady. Mazy and Molly had adopted one of the barn cat's kittens— thankfully they agreed to share. Kate Jasper took the other three, but she let Lilly name them. They were probably the only cats in the history of time to be named Verily, Inasmuch, and Cipher. It was good to know Lilly's sense of humor was intact.

Jack was even more rambunctious, if that was possible. He slept by himself now, probably because the puppy he'd named Brownie slept at the foot of his bed. Steady rarely left Lilly's side.

Much to John's chagrin, the house had indeed become a

zoo. As well as the dogs and the cat, a canary had joined the household. Lilly carried the bird all the way home from Alice's. It sat beside her on the train, singing in its wire cage.

Copper couldn't imagine why she wanted the bird. It looked to her like it would only bring back bad memories.

"But it wasn't all bad," Lilly said when she was questioned. "I learned lots and lots from my stay at the Stills'."

Lilly had told the story of her ordeal in bits and pieces over several weeks. Copper was amazed at her daughter's fortitude. She and John and Lilly spent many evenings pondering the events, amazed at how God had worked everything for good. If Manda had not gone into the barn, she would have made sure that Lilly didn't run off that day. And if Lilly had not gone to the pond near the Stills' house, she would have been on the train when it wrecked. Copper still couldn't bear to think about that.

Manda was living with Darcy in Eddyville. It was for the best. Manda had asked for forgiveness, and of course it was granted. She was a good girl at heart but with much to learn.

The middling man, as Manda dubbed him, had been arrested in a nearby town for a string of petty thieveries. He was serving time. They were all relieved Manda didn't have to press charges to get him put away. Fair or not, it would have ruined her reputation.

Isa Still was another story. Some of the same men, John included, who had searched so diligently for Lilly tirelessly hunted him the rest of the summer. It worried Lilly, and she was relieved when they gave up the pursuit. "What will happen to all the little boys and the baby if Mr. Still goes to prison?" she'd asked. "I don't think the grandma can take care of everyone by herself."

Lilly told only her mother about the boy named Tern. He was her secret, hers alone, and Copper respected her wishes. But she hoped and prayed that Lilly would never see any member of that strange family again.

Alice had sent boxes and boxes of books to Lilly—most of which had belonged to Simon and to Lilly's grandfather. They'd turned the sickroom into a bedroom for the twins, and John had built beautiful bookshelves in Lilly's room.

After many discussions with John, Copper agreed that it wasn't a good idea to bring her patients into the house. They would add a couple of rooms to the little house so Remy could live there. The walk from her cabin to the Pelfreys' was becoming more difficult for Remy. Plus, she relished the idea of being caretaker of the small clinic. Copper would be only a stone's throw away, but her home belonged to her family.

At John's request, Copper was training a couple of neighbor women to assist her in deliveries. They were bright and caring young women, quite capable of providing aftercare. Copper would not be away from home for such long spells, except, of course, for special cases like Emerald Morton and Cara Whitt, who was joyfully expecting a baby in early spring. Copper expected good outcomes for both women.

While Copper and her children were visiting Alice Upchurch in late August, Copper had paid a visit to the doctor who had delivered Lilly. No twins this time. Copper had laughed at John's obvious relief.

It had not been an easy thing taking her children on a train to visit Alice. But it had been necessary. If Copper had learned one thing this traumatic summer, it was that Lilly did not belong exclusively to her. She was God's child loaned to earth to accomplish whatever He wanted for her.

Copper suspected He had great plans for Lilly Gray. It was time for Copper to step aside.

# About the Author

A RETIRED REGISTERED nurse of twenty-five years, Jan Watson specialized in the care of newborns and their mothers. She attends Tates Creek Christian Church and lives in Lexington, Kentucky. Jan has three grown sons and a daughter-in-law.

*Still House Pond* follows *Sweetwater Run* and the Troublesome Creek series, which includes *Troublesome Creek*, *Willow Springs*, and *Torrent Falls*. Her awards include the 2004 Christian Writers Guild Operation First Novel contest and second place in the 2006 Inspirational Readers Choice Contest sponsored by the Faith, Hope, and Love Chapter of the RWA. *Troublesome Creek* was also a nominee for the Kentucky Literary Awards in 2006. *Willow Springs* was selected for *Library Journal*'s Best Genre Fiction category in 2007.

Jan's hobbies are reading, antiquing, and taking long walks with her Jack Russell terrier, Maggie.

Jan invites you to visit her Web site at www.janwatson.net. You can contact her through e-mail at author@janwatson.net.

"This is a settle-in-and-savor type of a read . . . with unforgettable characters that lodge themselves in your heart. . . ."

Jerry B. Jenkins

CP0061

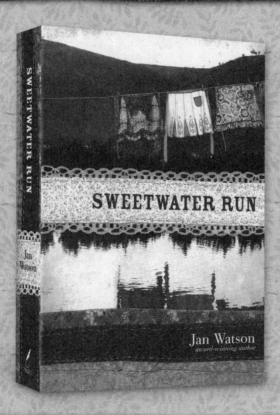

*have you visited*
# tyndalefiction.com
*lately?*

Only there can you find:

- ⤳ books hot off the press
- ⤳ first chapter excerpts
- ⤳ inside scoops on your favorite authors
- ⤳ author interviews
- ⤳ contests
- ⤳ fun facts
- ⤳ and much more!

Sign up for your **free** newsletter!

Visit us today at: **tyndalefiction.com**